THE FATHERS
OF ROARING CAMP . . .

The assemblage waiting outside Cherokee Sal's cabin numbered about a hundred men—one or two actual fugitives from justice, some criminal, all reckless. . . . The term "roughs" applied to them was a distinction rather than a definition. Perhaps in the minor details of fingers, toes, ears, etc., the camp may have been deficient, but these slight omissions did not detract from their aggregate force. The strongest man had but three fingers on his right hand; the best shot had but one eye.

Inside, Cherokee Sal was sinking fast.

These were the men who were to decide the fate of her unborn child . . .

PUT PLEASURE IN YOUR READING
Larger type makes the difference
This EASY EYE Edition is set in large, clear type—at least 30 percent larger than usual. It is printed on non-glare paper for better contrast and less eye-strain.

THE LUCK OF ROARING CAMP & OTHER STORIES

BRET HARTE

MAGNUM EASY EYE BOOKS
LANCER BOOKS · NEW YORK

A MAGNUM EASY EYE BOOK

THE LUCK OF ROARING CAMP
& OTHER STORIES

Special contents of this edition
copyright © 1968 by Lancer Books, Inc.
All rights reserved
Printed in the U.S.A.

RL 6-7; IL 6-10

Magnum Easy Eye Books are published by
LANCER BOOKS, INC. • 18 East 41st Street • New York, N.Y. 10017

CONTENTS

THE OUTCASTS OF
POKER FLAT

As Mr. John Oakhurst, gambler, stepped into the main street of Poker Flat on the morning of the 23d of November, 1850, he was conscious of a change in its moral atmosphere since the preceding night. Two or three men, conversing earnestly together, ceased as he approached, and exchanged significant glances. There was a Sabbath lull in the air, which, in a settlement unused to Sabbath influences, looked ominous.

Mr. Oakhurst's calm, handsome face betrayed small concern in these indications. Whether he was conscious of any predisposing cause was another question. "I reckon they're after somebody," he reflected; "likely it's me." He returned to his pocket the handkerchief with which he had been whipping away the red dust of Poker Flat from his neat boots, and quietly discharged his mind of any further conjecture.

In point of fact, Poker Flat was "after somebody." It had lately suffered the loss of several thousand dollars, two valuable horses, and a prominent citizen. It was experiencing a spasm of virtuous reaction, quite as lawless and ungovernable as any of the acts that had provoked it. A secret committee had determined to rid the town of all improper persons. This was done permanently in regard to two men who were then hanging from the boughs of a sycamore in the gulch, and temporarily in the banishment of certain other objectionable characters. I regret to say that some of these were ladies. It is but due to the sex, however, to state that their impropriety was professional, and it was only in such easily established standards of evil that Poker Flat ventured to sit in judgment.

Mr. Oakhurst was right in supposing that he was included in this category. A few of the committee had urged hanging him as a possible example and a sure method of reimbursing themselves from his pockets of the sums he had won from them. "It's agin justice," said Jim Wheeler, "to let this yer young man from Roaring Camp—an entire stranger—carry away our money." But a crude sentiment of equity residing in the breasts of those who had been fortunate enough to win from Mr. Oakhurst overruled this narrower local prejudice.

Mr. Oakhurst received his sentence with philosophic calmness, none the less coolly that he was aware of the hesitation of his judges. He was too much of a gambler not to accept fate. With him life was at best an uncertain game, and he recognized the usual percentage in favor of the dealer.

A body of armed men accompanied the deported wickedness of Poker Flat to the outskirts of the settlement. Besides Mr. Oakhurst, who was known to be a coolly desperate man, and for whose intimidation the armed escort was intended, the expatriated party consisted of a young woman familiarly known as "The Duchess"; another who had won the title of

"Mother Shipton"; and "Uncle Billy," a suspected sluice-robber and confirmed drunkard. The cavalcade provoked no comments from the spectators, nor was any word uttered by the escort. Only when the gulch which marked the uttermost limit of Poker Flat was reached, the leader spoke briefly and to the point. The exiles were forbidden to return at the peril of their lives.

As the escort disappeared, their pent-up feelings found vent in a few hysterical tears from the Duchess some bad language from Mother Shipton, and a Parthian volley of expletives from Uncle Billy. The philosophic Oakhurst alone remained silent. He listened calmly to Mother Shipton's desire to cut somebody's heart out, to the repeated statements of the Duchess that she would die in the road, and to the alarming oaths that seemed to be bumped out of Uncle Billy as he rode forward. With the easy good humor characteristic of his class, he insisted upon exchanging his own riding-horse, "Five-Spot," for the sorry mule which the Duchess rode. But even this act did not draw the party into any closer sympathy. The young woman readjusted her somewhat draggled plumes with a feeble, faded coquetry; Mother Shipton eyed the possessor of "Five-Spot" with malevolence, and Uncle Billy included the whole party in one sweeping anathema.

The road to Sandy Bar—a camp that, not having as yet experienced the regenerating influences of Poker Flat, consequently seemed to offer some invitation to the emigrants—lay over a steep mountain range. It was distant a day's severe travel. In that advanced season the party soon passed out of the moist, temperate regions of the foothills into the dry, cold, bracing air of the Sierras. The trail was narrow and difficult. At noon the Duchess, rolling out of her saddle upon the ground, declared her intention of going no farther, and the party halted.

The spot was singularly wild and impressive. A wooded amphitheatre, surrounded on three sides by precipitous cliffs of naked granite, sloped gently toward the crest of another precipice that overlooked the valley. It was, undoubtedly, the most suitable spot for a camp, had camping been advisable. But Mr. Oakhurst knew that scarcely half the journey to Sandy Bar was accomplished, and the party were not equipped or provisioned for delay. This fact he pointed out to his companions curtly, with a philosophic commentary on the folly of "throwing up their hand before the game was played out." But they were furnished with liquor, which in this emergency stood them in place of food, fuel, rest, and prescience. In spite of his remonstrances, it was not long before they were more or less under its influence. Uncle Billy passed rapidly from a bellicose state into one of stupor, the Duchess became maudlin, and Mother Shipton snored. Mr. Oakhurst alone remained erect, leaning against a rock, calmly surveying them.

Mr. Oakhurst did not drink. It interfered with a profession which required coolness, impassiveness, and presence of mind, and in his own language, he "couldn't afford it." As he gazed at his recumbent fellow exiles, the loneliness begotten of his pariah trade, his habits of life, his very vices, for the first time seriously oppressed him. He bestirred himself in dusting his black clothes, washing his hands and face, and other acts characteristic of his studiously neat habits, and for a moment forgot his annoyance. The thought of deserting his weaker and more pitiable companions never perhaps occurred to him. Yet he could not help feeling the want of that excitement which, singularly enough, was most conducive to that calm equanimity for which he was notorious. He looked at the gloomy walls that rose a thousand feet sheer above the circling pines around him, at the sky ominously clouded, at the valley below, already deepening into shadow; and doing so, suddenly he heard his own name called.

A horseman slowly ascended the trail. In the fresh, open face of the newcomer Mr. Oakhurst recognized Tom Simson, otherwise known as "The Innocent," of Sandy Bar. He had met him some months before over a "little game," and had, with perfect equanimity, won the entire fortune—amounting to some forty dollars—of that guileless youth. After the game was finished, Mr. Oakhurst drew the youthful speculator behind the door and thus addressed him: "Tommy, you're a good little man, but you can't gamble worth a cent. Don't try it over again." He then handed him his money back, pushed him gently from the room, and so made a devoted slave of Tom Simson.

There was a remembrance of this in his boyish and enthusiastic greeting of Mr. Oakhurst. He had started, he said, to go to Poker Flat to seek his fortune. "Alone?" No, not exactly alone; in fact (a giggle), he had run away with Piney Woods. Didn't Mr. Oakhurst remember Piney? She that used to wait on the table at the Temperance House? They had been engaged a long time, but old Jake Woods had objected, and so they had run away, and were going to Poker Flat to be married, and here they were. And they were tired out, and how lucky it was they had found a place to camp, and company. All this the Innocent delivered rapidly, while Piney, a stout, comely damsel of fifteen, emerged from behind the pine tree, where she had been blushing unseen, and rode to the side of her lover.

Mr. Oakhurst seldom troubled himself with sentiment, still less with propriety; but he had a vague idea that the situation was not fortunate. He retained, however, his presence of mind sufficiently to kick Uncle Billy, who was about to say something, and Uncle Billy was sober enough to recognize in Mr. Oakhurst's kick a superior power that would not bear trifling. He then endeavored to dissuade Tom Simson from delaying further, but in vain. He even pointed out the fact that there was no provision, nor means of making a camp. But, unluckily, the Innocent met this objection by assuring the party that he was provided with an extra mule loaded with provisions, and by the discovery of a rude attempt at a log house near the trail. "Piney can stay with Mrs. Oakhurst," said the Innocent, pointing to the Duchess, "and I can shift for myself."

Nothing but Mr. Oakhurst's admonishing foot saved Uncle Billy from bursting into a roar of laughter. As it was, he felt compelled to retire up the canyon until he could recover his gravity. There he confided the joke to the tall pine trees, with many slaps of his leg, contortions of his face, and the usual profanity. But when he returned to the party, he found them seated by a fire—for the air had grown strangely chill and the sky overcast—in apparently amicable conversation. Piney was actually talking in an impulsive girlish fashion to the Duchess, who was listening with an interest and animation she had not shown for many days. The Innocent was holding forth, apparently with equal effect, to Mr. Oakhurst and Mother Shipton, who was actually relaxing into amiability. "Is this yer a d—d picnic?" said Uncle Billy, with inward scorn, as he surveyed the sylvan group, the glancing firelight, and the tethered animals in the foreground. Suddenly an idea mingled with the alcoholic fumes that disturbed his brain. It was apparently of a jocular nature, for he felt impelled to slap his leg again and cram his fist into his mouth.

As the shadows crept slowly up the mountain, a slight breeze rocked the tops of the pine trees and moaned through their long and gloomy aisles. The ruined cabin, patched and covered with pine boughs, was set apart for the ladies. As the lovers parted, they unaffectedly exchanged a kiss, so honest and sincere that it might have been heard above the swaying pines. The frail Duchess and the malevolent Mother Shipton were probably too stunned to remark upon this last evidence of simplicity, and so turned without a word to the hut. The fire was replenished, the men lay down before the door, and in a few minutes were asleep.

Mr. Oakhurst was a light sleeper. Toward morning he awoke benumbed and cold. As he stirred the dying fire, the wind, which was now blowing strongly, brought to his cheek that which caused the blood to leave it—snow!

He started to his feet with the intention of awakening the sleepers, for there was no time to lose. But turning to where Uncle Billy had been lying, he found him gone. A suspicion leaped to his brain, and a curse to his lips. He ran to the spot where the mules had been tethered—they were no longer there. The tracks were already rapidly disappearing in the snow.

The momentary excitement brought Mr. Oakhurst back to the fire with his usual calm. He did not waken the sleepers. The Innocent slumbered peacefully, with a smile on his good-humored, freckled face; the virgin Piney slept beside her frailer sisters as sweetly as though attended by celestial guardians; and Mr. Oakhurst, drawing his blanket over his shoulders, stroked his mustaches and waited for the dawn. It came slowly in a whirling mist of snowflakes that dazzled and confused the eye. What could be seen of the landscape appeared magically changed. He looked over the valley, and summed up the present and future in two words, "Snowed in!"

A careful inventory of the provisions, which, fortunately for the party, had been stored within the hut, and so escaped the felonious fingers of Uncle Billy, disclosed the fact that with care and prudence they might last ten days longer. "That is," said Mr. Oakhurst *sotto voce* to the Innocent, "if you're willing to board us. If you ain't—and perhaps you'd better not— you can wait till Uncle Billy gets back with provisions." For some occult reason, Mr. Oakhurst could not bring himself to disclose Uncle Billy's rascality, and so offered the hypothesis that he had wandered from the camp and had accidentally stampeded the animals. He dropped a warning to the Duchess and Mother Shipton, who of course knew the facts of their associate's defection. "They'll find out the truth about us *all* when they find out anything," he added significantly, "and there's no good frightening them now."

Tom Simson not only put all his worldly store at the disposal of Mr. Oakhurst, but seemed to enjoy the prospect of their enforced seclusion. "We'll have a good camp for a week, and then the snow'll melt, and we'll all go back together." The cheerful gayety of the young man and Mr. Oakhurst's calm infected the others. The Innocent, with the aid of pine boughs, extemporized a thatch for the roofless cabin, and the Duchess directed Piney in the rearrangement of the interior with a taste and tact that opened the blue eyes of that provincial maiden to their fullest extent. "I reckon now you're used to fine things at Poker Flat," said Piney. The Duchess turned away sharply to conceal something that reddened her cheeks through their professional tint, and Mother Shipton requested Piney not to "chatter."

But when Mr. Oakhurst returned from a weary search for the trail, he heard the sound of happy laughter echoed from the rocks. He stopped in some alarm, and his thoughts first naturally reverted to the whiskey, which he had prudently cached. "And yet it don't somehow sound like whiskey," said the gambler. It was not until he caught sight of the blazing fire through the still blinding storm, and the group around it, that he settled to the conviction that it was "square fun."

Whether Mr. Oakhurst had cached his cards with the whiskey as something debarred the free access of the community, I cannot say. It was certain that, in Mother Shipton's words, he "didn't say 'cards' once" during that evening. Haply the time was beguiled by an accordion, produced somewhat ostentatiously by Tom Simson from his pack. Notwithstanding some difficulties attending the manipulation of this instrument, Piney Woods managed to pluck several reluctant melodies from its keys to an accompaniment by the Innocent on a pair of bone castanets. But the crowning festivity of the evening was reached in a rude campmeeting hymn, which the lovers, joining hands, sang with great earnestness and vociferation. I fear that a certain defiant tone and covenanter's swing to its chorus, rather than any devotional quality, caused it speedily to infect the others, who at last joined in the refrain:

"I'm proud to live in the service of the Lord,
    And I'm bound to die in His army."

The pines rocked, the storm eddied and whirled above the miserable group, and the flames of their altar leaped heavenward, as if in token of the vow.

At midnight the storm abated, the rolling clouds parted, and the stars glittered keenly above the sleeping camp. Mr. Oakhurst, whose professional habits had enabled him to live on the smallest possible amount of sleep, in dividing the watch with Tom Simson somehow managed to take upon himself the greater part of that duty. He excused himself to the Innocent by saying that he had "often been a week without sleep." "Doing what?" asked Tom. "Poker!" replied Oakhurst sententiously. "When a man gets a streak of luck—nigger-luck—he don't get tired. The luck gives in first. Luck," continued the gambler reflectively, "is a mighty queer thing. All you know about it for certain is that it's bound to change. And it's finding out when it's going to change that makes you. We've had a streak of bad luck since we left Poker Flat—you come along, and slap you get into it, too. If you can hold your cards right along you're all right. For," added the gambler, with cheerful irrelevance—

" 'I'm proud to live in the service of the Lord,
    And I'm bound to die in His army.' "

The third day came, and the sun, looking through the white-curtained valley, saw the outcasts divide their slowly decreasing store of provision for the morning meal. It was one of the peculiarities of that mountain climate that its rays diffused a kindly warmth over the wintry landscape, as if in regretful commiseration of the past. But it revealed drift on drift of snow piled high around the hut—a hopeless, uncharted, trackless sea of white lying below the rocky shores to which the castaways still clung. Through the marvelously clear air the smoke of the pastoral village of Poker Flat rose miles away. Mother Shipton saw it, and from a remote pinnacle of her rocky fastness hurled in that direction a final malediction. It was her last vituperative attempt, and perhaps for that reason was invested with a certain degree of sublimity. It did her good, she privately informed the Duchess. "Just you go out there and cuss, and see." She then set herself to the task of amusing "the child," as she and the Duchess were pleased to call Piney. Piney was no chicken, but it was a soothing and original theory of the pair thus to account for the fact that she didn't swear and wasn't improper.

When night crept up again through the gorges, the reedy notes of the accordion rose and fell in fitful spasms and long-drawn gasps by the flickering campfire. But music failed to fill entirely the aching void left by insufficient food, and a new diversion was proposed by Piney—storytelling. Neither Mr. Oakhurst nor his female companions caring to relate their personal experiences, this plan would have failed too, but for the Innocent. Some months before he had chanced upon a stray copy of Mr. Pope's ingenious translation of the Iliad. He now proposed to narrate the principal incidents of that poem—having thoroughly mastered the argument and fairly forgotten the words—in the current vernacular of Sandy Bar. And so for the rest of that night the Homeric demigods again walked the earth. Trojan bully and wily Greek wrestled in the winds, and the great pines in the canyon seemed to bow to the wrath of the son of Peleus. Mr. Oakhurst listened with quiet satisfaction. Most especially was he interested in the fate of "Ash-heels," as the Innocent persisted in denominating the "swift-footed Achilles."

So, with small food and much of Homer and the accordion, a week passed over the heads of the outcasts. The sun again forsook them, and again from leaden skies the snowflakes were sifted over the land. Day by day closer around them drew the snowy circle, until at last they looked from their prison over drifted walls of dazzling white that towered twenty feet above their heads. It became more and more difficult to replenish their fires, even from the fallen trees beside them, now half hidden in the drifts. And yet no one complained. The lovers turned from the dreary prospect and looked into each other's eyes, and were happy. Mr. Oakhurst settled himself coolly to the losing game before him. The Duchess, more cheerful than she had been, assumed the care of Piney. Only Mother Shipton—once the strongest of the party— seemed to sicken and fade. At midnight on the tenth day she called Oakhurst to her side. "I'm going," she said, in a voice of querulous weakness, "but don't say anything about it. Don't waken the kids. Take the bundle from under my head, and open it." Mr. Oakhurst did so. It contained Mother Shipton's rations for the last week, untouched. "Give 'em to the child," she said, pointing to the sleeping Piney. "You've starved yourself," said the gambler. "That's what they call it," said the woman querulously, as she lay down again, and turning her face to the wall, passed quietly away.

The accordion and the bones were put aside that day, and Homer was forgotten. When the body of Mother Shipton had been committed to the snow, Mr. Oakhurst took the Innocent aside, and showed him a pair of snowshoes, which he had fashioned from the old pack-saddle. "There's one chance in a hundred to save her yet," he said, pointing to Piney; "but it's there," he added, pointing toward Poker Flat. "If you can reach there in two days she's safe." "And you?" asked Tom Simson. "I'll stay here," was the curt reply.

The lovers parted with a long embrace. "You are not going, too?" said the Duchess, as she saw Mr. Oakhurst apparently waiting to accompany him. "As far as the canyon," he replied. He turned suddenly and kissed the Duchess, leaving her pallid face aflame, and her trembling limbs rigid with amazement.

Night came, but not Mr. Oakhurst. It brought the storm again and the whirling snow. Then the Duchess, feeding the fire, found that someone had quietly piled beside the hut enough fuel to last a few days longer. The tears rose to her eyes, but she hid them from Piney.

The women slept but little. In the morning, looking into each other's faces, they read their fate. Neither spoke, but Piney, accepting the position of the stronger, drew near and placed her arm around the Duchess's waist. They kept this attitude for the rest of the day. That night the storm reached its greatest fury, and rending asunder the protecting vines, invaded the very hut.

Toward morning they found themselves unable to feed the fire, which gradually died away. As the embers slowly blackened, the Duchess crept closer to Piney, and broke the silence of many hours: "Piney, can you pray?" "No, dear," said Piney simply. The Duchess, without knowing exactly why, felt relieved, and putting her head upon Piney's shoulder, spoke no more. And so reclining, the younger and purer pillowing the head of her soiled sister upon her virgin breast, they fell asleep.

The wind lulled as if it feared to waken them. Feathery drifts of snow, shaken from the long pine boughs, flew like white winged birds, and settled about them as they slept. The moon through the rifted clouds looked down upon what had been the camp. But all human stain, all trace of earthly travail, was hidden beneath the spotless mantle mercifully flung from above.

They slept all that day and the next, nor did they waken when voices and footsteps broke the silence of the camp. And when pitying fingers brushed the snow from their wan faces, you could scarcely have told from the equal peace that dwelt upon them which was she that had sinned. Even the law of Poker Flat recognized this, and turned away, leaving them still locked in each other's arms.

But at the head of the gulch, on one of the largest pine trees, they found the deuce of clubs pinned to the bark with a bowie knife. It bore the following, written in pencil in a firm hand:

✝

BENEATH THIS TREE

LIES THE BODY

OF

JOHN OAKHURST,

WHO STRUCK A STREAK OF BAD LUCK

ON THE 23D OF NOVEMBER, 1850,

AND

HANDED IN HIS CHECKS

ON THE 7TH DECEMBER, 1850.

↓

And pulseless and cold, with a derringer by his side and a bullet in his heart, though still calm as in life, beneath the snow lay he who was at once the strongest and yet the weakest of the outcasts of Poker Flat.

THE LUCK OF ROARING CAMP

There was commotion in Roaring Camp. It could not have been a fight, for in 1850 that was not novel enough to have called together the entire settlement. The ditches and claims were not only deserted, but "Tuttle's grocery" had contributed its gamblers, who, it will be remembered, calmly continued their game the day that French Pete and Kanaka Joe shot each other to death over the bar in the front room. The whole camp was collected before a rude cabin on the outer edge of the clearing. Conversation was carried on in a low tone, but the name of a woman was frequently repeated. It was a name familiar enough in the camp—"Cherokee Sal."

Perhaps the less said of her the better. She was a coarse and, it is to be feared, a very sinful woman. But at that time she was the only woman in Roaring Camp, and was just then lying in sore extremity, when she most needed the ministration of her own sex. Dissolute, abandoned, and irreclaimable, she was yet suffering a martyrdom hard enough to bear even when veiled by sympathizing womanhood, but now terrible in her loneliness. The primal curse had come to her in that original isolation which must have made the punishment of the first transgression so dreadful. It was, perhaps, part of the expiation of her sin that, at a moment when she most lacked her sex's intuitive tenderness and care, she met only the half-contemptuous faces of her masculine associates. Yet a few of the spectators were, I think, touched by her sufferings. Sandy Tipton thought it was "rough on Sal," and in the contemplation of her condition, for a moment rose superior to the fact that he had an ace and two bowers in his sleeve.

It will be seen also that the situation was novel. Deaths were by no means uncommon in Roaring Camp, but a birth was a new thing. People had been dismissed from the camp effectively, finally, and with no possibility of return; but this was the first time that anybody had been introduced *ab initio*. Hence the excitement.

"You go in there, Stumpy," said a prominent citizen known as "Kentuck," addressing one of the loungers. "Go in there, and see what you kin do. You've had experience in them things."

Perhaps there was a fitness in the selection. Stumpy, in other climes, had been the putative head of two families; in fact, it was owing to some legal informality in these proceedings that Roaring Camp—a city of refuge—was indebted to his company. The crowd approved the choice, and Stumpy was wise enough to bow to the majority. The door closed on the extempore surgeon and midwife, and Roaring Camp sat down outside, smoked its pipe, and awaited the issue.

The assemblage numbered about a hundred men. One or two of these were actual fugitives from justice, some were criminal, and all were reckless. Physically they exhibited no indication of their past lives and character. The greatest scamp had a Raphael face, with a profusion of blond hair; Oakhurst, a gambler, had the melancholy air and intellectual abstraction of a Hamlet; the coolest and most courageous man was scarcely over five feet in height, with a soft voice and an embarrassed, timid manner. The term "roughs" applied to them was a distinction rather than a definition. Perhaps in the minor details of fingers, toes, ears, etc., the camp may have been deficient, but these slight omissions did not detract from their aggregate force. The strongest man had but three fingers on his right hand; the best shot had but one eye.

Such was the physical aspect of the men that were dispersed around the cabin. The camp lay in a triangular valley between two hills and a river. The only outlet was a steep trail over the summit of a hill that faced the cabin, now illuminated by the rising moon. The suffering woman might have seen it from the rude bunk whereon she lay—seen it winding like a silver thread until it was lost in the stars above.

A fire of withered pine boughs added sociability to the gathering. By degrees the natural levity of Roaring Camp returned. Bets were freely offered and taken regarding the results. Three to five that "Sal would get through with it"; even that the child would survive; side bets as to the sex and complexion of the coming stranger. In the midst of an excited discussion an exclamation came from those nearest the door, and the camp stopped to listen. Above the swaying and moaning of the pines, the swift rush of the river, and the crackling of the fire rose a sharp, querulous cry—a cry unlike anything heard before in the camp. The pines stopped moaning, the river ceased to rush, and the fire to crackle. It seemed as if Nature had stopped to listen too.

The camp rose to its feet as one man! It was proposed to explode a barrel of gunpowder; but in consideration of the situation of the mother, better counsels prevailed, and only a few revolvers were discharged; for whether owing to the rude surgery of the camp, or some other reason, Cherokee Sal was sinking fast. Within an hour she had climbed, as it were, that rugged road that led to the stars, and so passed out of Roaring Camp, its sin and shame, forever. I do not think that the announcement disturbed them much, except in speculation as to the fate of the child. "Can he live now?" was asked of Stumpy. The answer was doubtful. The only other being of Cherokee Sal's sex and maternal condition in the settlement was an ass. There was some conjecture as to fitness, but the experiment was tried. It was less problematical than the ancient treatment of Romulus and Remus, and apparently as successful.

When these details were completed, which exhausted another hour, the door was opened, and the anxious crowd of men, who had already formed themselves into a queue, entered in single file. Beside the low bunk or shelf, on which the figure of the mother was starkly outlined below the blankets, stood a pine table. On this a candlebox was placed, and within it, swathed in staring red flannel, lay the last arrival at Roaring Camp. Beside the candlebox was placed a hat. Its use was soon indicated "Gentlemen," and Stumpy, with a singular mixture of authority and *ex officio* complacency—"gentlemen will please pass in at the front door, round the table, and out at the back door. Them as wishes to contribute anything toward the orphan will find a hat handy." The first man entered with his hat on; he uncovered, however, as he looked about him, and so unconsciously set an example to the next. In such communities good and bad actions are catching. As the procession filed in comments were audible—criticisms addressed perhaps rather to Stumpy in the character of showman: "Is that him?" "Mighty small specimen"; "Hasn't more'n got the color"; "Ain't bigger nor a derringer." The contributions were as characteristic: A silver tobacco box; a doubloon; a navy revolver, silver mounted; a gold specimen; a very beautifully embroidered lady's handkerchief (from Oakhurst the gambler); a diamond breastpin; a diamond ring (suggested by the pin, with the remark from the giver that he "saw that pin and went two diamonds better"); a slung shot; a Bible (contributor not detected); a golden spur; a silver teaspoon (the initials, I regret to say, were not the giver's); a pair of surgeon's shears; a lancet; a Bank of England note for £5; and about $200 in loose gold and silver coin. During these proceedings Stumpy maintained a silence as impassive as the dead on his left, a gravity as inscrutable as that of the newly born on his right. Only one incident occurred to break the monotony of the curious procession. As Kentuck bent over the candlebox half curiously, the child turned, and, in a spasm of pain, caught at his groping finger and held it fast for a moment. Kentuck looked foolish and embarrassed. Something like a blush tried to assert itself in his weather-beaten cheek. "The d—d little cuss!" he said, as he extricated his finger, with perhaps more tenderness and care than he might have been deemed capable of showing. He held that finger a little apart from its fellows as he went out, and examined it curiously. The examination provoked the same original remark in regard to the child. In fact, he seemed to enjoy repeating it. "He rastled with my finger," he remarked to Tipton, holding up the member, "the d—d little cuss!"

It was four o'clock before the camp sought repose. A light burnt in the cabin where the watchers sat, for Stumpy did not go to bed that night. Nor did Kentuck. He drank quite freely, and related with great gusto his experience, invariably ending with his characteristic condemnation of the newcomer. It seemed to relieve him of any unjust implication of sentiment, and Kentuck had the weaknesses of the nobler sex. When everybody else had gone to bed, he walked down to the river and whistled reflectingly. Then he walked up the gulch past the cabin, still whistling with demonstrative unconcern. At a large redwood tree he paused and retraced his steps, and again passed the cabin. Halfway down to the river's bank he again paused, and then returned and knocked at the door. It was opened by Stumpy. "How goes it?" said Kentuck, looking past Stumpy toward the candlebox. "All serene!" replied Stumpy. "Anything up?" "Nothing." There was a pause—an embarrassing one—Stumpy still holding the door. Then Kentuck had recourse to his finger, which he held up to Stumpy. "Rastled with it—the d—d little cuss," he said, and retired.

The next day Cherokee Sal had such rude sepulture as Roaring Camp afforded. After her body had been committed to the hillside, there was a formal meeting of the camp to discuss what should be done with her infant. A resolution to adopt it was unanimous and enthusiastic. But an animated discussion in regard to the manner and feasibility of providing for its wants at once sprang up. It was remarkable that the argument partook of none of those fierce personalities with which discussions were usually conducted at Roaring Camp. Tipton proposed that they should send the child to Red Dog—a distance of forty miles —where female attention could be procured. But the unlucky suggestion met with fierce and unanimous opposition. It was evident that no plan which entailed parting from their new acquisition would for a moment be entertained. "Besides," said Tom Ryder, "them fellows at Red Dog would swap it, and ring in somebody else on us." A disbelief in the honesty of other camps prevailed at Roaring Camp, as in other places.

The introduction of a female nurse in the camp also met with objection. It was argued that no decent woman could be prevailed to accept Roaring Camp as her home, and the speaker urged that "they didn't want any more of the other kind." This unkind allusion to the defunct mother, harsh as it may seem, was the first spasm of propriety—the first symptom of the camp's regeneration. Stumpy advanced nothing. Perhaps he felt a certain delicacy in interfering with the selection of a possible successor in office. But when questioned, he averred stoutly that he and "Jinny" —the mammal before alluded to—could manage to rear the child. There was something original, independent, and heroic about the plan that pleased the camp. Stumpy was retained. Certain articles were sent for to Sacramento. "Mind," said the treasurer, as he pressed a bag of gold dust into the expressman's hand, "the best that can be got—lace, you know, and filigree work and frills—d—n the cost!"

Strange to say, the child thrived. Perhaps the invigorating climate of the mountain camp was compensation for material deficiencies. Nature took the foundling to her broader breast. In that rare atmosphere of the Sierra foothills—that air pungent with balsamic odor, that ethereal cordial at once bracing and exhilarating—he may have found food and nourishment, or a subtle chemistry that transmuted ass's milk to lime and phosphorus. Stumpy inclined to the belief that it was the latter and good nursing. "Me and that ass," he would say, "has been father and mother to him! Don't you," he would add, apostrophizing the helpless bundle before him, "never to go back on us."

By the time he was a month old the necessity of giving him a name became apparent. He had generally been known as "the Kid," "Stumpy's Boy," "The Coyote" (an allusion to his vocal powers), and even by Kentuck's endearing diminutive of "The d—d little cuss." But these were felt to be vague and unsatisfactory, and were at last dismissed under another influence. Gamblers and adventurers are generally superstitious, and Oakhurst one day declared that the baby had brought "the luck" to Roaring Camp. It was certain that of late they had been successful. "Luck" was the name agreed upon, with the prefix of Tommy for greater convenience. No allusion was made to the mother, and the father was unknown. "It's better," said the philosophical Oakhurst, "to take a fresh deal all round. Call him Luck, and start him fair." A day was accordingly set apart for the christening. What was meant by this ceremony the reader may imagine who has already gathered some idea of the reckless irreverence of Roaring Camp. The master of ceremonies was one "Boston," a noted wag, and the occasion seemed to promise the greatest facetiousness. This ingenious satirist had spent two days in preparing a burlesque of the Church service, with pointed local allusions. The choir was properly trained, and Sandy Tipton was to stand godfather. But after the procession had marched to the grove with music and banners, and the child had been deposited before a mock altar, Stumpy stepped before the expectant crowd. "It ain't my style to spoil fun, boys," said the little man, stoutly eying the faces around him, "but it strikes me that this thing ain't exactly on the squar. It's playing it pretty low down on this yer baby to ring in fun on him that he ain't goin' to understand. And ef there's goin' to be any godfathers round, I'd like to see who's got any better rights than me." A silence followed Stumpy's speech. To the credit of all humorists be it said that the first man to acknowledge its justice was the satirist thus stopped of his fun. "But," said Stumpy, quickly following up his advantage, "we're here for a christening, and we'll have it. I proclaim you Thomas Luck, according to the laws of the United States and the State of California, so help me God." It was the first time that the name of the Deity had been otherwise uttered than profanely in the camp. The form of christening was perhaps even more ludicrous than the satirist had conceived; but strangely enough, nobody saw it and nobody laughed. "Tommy" was christened as seriously as he would have been under a Christian roof, and cried and was comforted in as orthodox fashion.

And so the work of regeneration began in Roaring Camp. Almost imperceptibly a change came over the settlement. The cabin assigned to "Tommy Luck"—or "The Luck," as he was more frequently called—first showed signs of improvement. It was kept scrupulously clean and whitewashed. Then it was boarded, clothed, and papered. The rosewood cradle, packed eighty miles by mule, had, in Stumpy's way of putting it, "sorter killed the rest of the furniture." So the rehabilitation of the camp became a necessity. The men who were in the habit of lounging in at Stumpy's to see "how 'The Luck' got on" seemed to appreciate the change, and in self-defense the rival establishment of "Tuttle's grocery" bestirred itself and imported a carpet and mirrors. The reflections of the latter on the appearance of Roaring Camp tended to produce stricter habits of personal cleanliness. Again Stumpy imposed a kind of quarantine upon those who aspired to the honor and privilege of holding The Luck. It was a cruel mortification to Kentuck—who, in the carelessness of a large nature and the habits of frontier life, had begun to regard all garments as a second cuticle, which, like a snake's, only sloughed off through decay—to be debarred this privilege from certain prudential reasons. Yet such was the subtle influence of innovation that he thereafter appeared regularly every afternoon in a clean shirt and face still shining from his ablutions. Nor were moral and social sanitary laws neglected. "Tommy," who was supposed to spend his whole existence in a persistent attempt to repose, must not be disturbed by noise. The shouting and yelling, which had gained the camp its infelicitous title, were not permitted within hearing distance of Stumpy's. The men conversed in whispers or smoked with Indian gravity. Profanity was tacitly given up in these sacred precincts, and throughout the camp a popular form of expletive, known as "D—n the luck!" and "Curse the luck!" was abandoned, as having a new personal bearing. Vocal music was not interdicted, being supposed to have a soothing, tranquilizing quality; and one song, sung by "Man-o'-War Jack," an English sailor from her Majesty's Australian colonies, was quite popular as a lullaby. It was a lugubrious recital of the exploits of "the Arethusa, Seventy-four," in a muffled minor, ending with a prolonged dying fall at the burden of each verse, "On b-oo-o-ard of the Arethusa." It was a fine sight to see Jack holding The Luck, rocking from side to side as if with the motion of a ship, and crooning forth this naval ditty. Either through the peculiar rocking of Jack or the length of his song—it contained ninety stanzas, and was continued with conscientious deliberation to the bitter end—the lullaby generally had the desired effect. At such times the men would lie at full length under the trees in the soft summer twilight, smoking their pipes and drinking in the melodious utterances. An indistinct idea that this was pastoral happiness pervaded the camp. "This 'ere kind o' think," said the Cockney Simmons, meditatively reclining on his elbow, "is 'evingly." It reminded him of Greenwich.

On the long summer days The Luck was usually

carried to the gulch from whence the golden store of
Roaring Camp was taken. There, on a blanket spread
over pine boughs, he would lie while the men were
working in the ditches below. Latterly there was a
rude attempt to decorate this bower with flowers and
sweet-smelling shrubs, and generally some one would
bring him a cluster of wild honeysuckles, azaleas, or
the painted blossoms of Las Mariposas. The men had
suddenly awakened to the fact that there were beauty
and significance in these trifles, which they had so
long trodden carelessly beneath their feet. A flake of
glittering mica, a fragment of variegated quartz, a
bright pebble from the bed of the creek, became beautiful to eyes thus cleared and strengthened, and were
invariably put aside for The Luck. It was wonderful
how many treasures the woods and hillsides yielded
that "would do for Tommy." Surrounded by play-
things such as never child out of fairyland had before, it is to be hoped that Tommy was content. He
appeared to be serenely happy, albeit there was an in-
fantine gravity about him, a contemplative light in
his round gray eyes, that sometimes worried Stumpy.
He was always tractable and quiet, and it is recorded
that once, having crept beyond his "corral"—a hedge
of tessellated pine boughs, which surrounded his bed
—he dropped over the bank on his head in the soft
earth, and remained with his mottled legs in the air
in that position for at least five minutes with unflinch-
ing gravity. He was extricated without a murmur. I
hesitate to record the many other instances of his sa-
gacity, which rest, unfortunately, upon the statements
of prejudiced friends. Some of them were not without a tinge of superstition. "I crep' up the bank just

now," said Kentuck one day, in a breathless state of excitement, "and dern my skin if he wasn't a-talking to a jay bird as was a-sittin' on his lap. There they was, just as free and sociable as anything you please, a-jawin' at each other just like two cherrybums." Howbeit, whether creeping over the pine boughs or lying lazily on his back blinking at the leaves above him, to him the birds sang, the squirrels chattered, and the flowers bloomed. Nature was his nurse and play-fellow. For him she would let slip between the leaves golden shafts of sunlight that fell just within his grasp; she would send wandering breezes to visit him with the balm of bay and resinous gum; to him the tall red-woods nodded familiarly and sleepily, the bumblebees buzzed, and the rooks cawed a slumbrous accompaniment.

Such was the golden summer of Roaring Camp. They were "flush times," and the luck was with them. The claims had yielded enormously. The camp was jealous of its privileges and looked suspiciously on strangers. No encouragement was given to immigration, and, to make their seclusion more perfect, the land on either side of the mountain wall that surrounded the camp they duly preempted. This, and a reputation for singular proficiency with the revolver, kept the reserve of Roaring Camp inviolate. The expressman—their only connecting link with the surrounding world—sometimes told wonderful stories of the camp. He would say, "They've a street up there in 'Roaring' that would lay over any street in Red Dog. They've got vines and flowers round their houses, and they wash themselves twice a day. But they're mighty rough on strangers, and they worship an Ingin baby."

With the prosperity of the camp came a desire for further improvement. It was proposed to build a hotel in the following spring, and to invite one or two decent families to reside there for the sake of The Luck, who might perhaps profit by female companionship. The sacrifice that this concession to the sex cost these men, who were fiercely skeptical in regard to its general virtue and usefulness, can only be accounted for by their affection for Tommy. A few still held out. But the resolve could not be carried into effect for three months, and the minority meekly yielded in the hope that something might turn up to prevent it. And it did.

The winter of 1851 will long be remembered in the foothills. The snow lay deep on the Sierras, and every mountain creek became a river, and every river a lake. Each gorge and gulch was transformed into a tumultuous watercourse that descended the hillsides, tearing down giant trees and scattering its drift and debris along the plain. Red Dog had been twice under water, and Roaring Camp had been forewarned. "Water put the gold into them gulches," said Stumpy. "It's been here once and will be here again!" And that night the North Fork suddenly leaped over its banks and swept up the triangular valley of Roaring Camp.

In the confusion of rushing water, crashing trees, and crackling timber, and the darkness which seemed to flow with the water and blot out the fair valley, but little could be done to collect the scattered camp. When the morning broke, the cabin of Stumpy, nearest the river-bank, was gone. Higher up the gulch they found the body of its unlucky owner; but the pride, the hope, the joy, The Luck, of Roaring Camp had disappeared. They were returning with sad hearts when a shout from the bank recalled them.

It was a relief-boat from down the river. They had picked up, they said, a man and an infant, nearly exhausted, about two miles below. Did anybody know them, and did they belong here?

It needed but a glance to show them Kentuck lying there, cruelly crushed and bruised, but still holding The Luck of Roaring Camp in his arms. As they bent over the strangely assorted pair, they saw that the child was cold and pulseless. "He is dead," said one. Kentuck opened his eyes. "Dead?" he repeated feebly. "Yes, my man, and you are dying too." A smile lit the eyes of the expiring Kentuck. "Dying!" he repeated; "he's a-taking me with him. Tell the boys I've got The Luck with me now"; and the strong man, clinging to the frail babe as a drowning man is said to cling to a straw, drifted away into the shadowy river that flows forever to the unknown sea.

TENNESSEE'S PARTNER

I do not think that we ever knew his real name. Our ignorance of it certainly never gave us any social inconvenience, for at Sandy Bar in 1854 most men were christened anew. Sometimes these appellatives were derived from some distinctiveness of dress, as in the case of "Dungaree Jack"; or from some peculiarity of habit, as shown in "Saleratus Bill," so called from an undue proportion of that chemical in his daily bread; or from some unlucky slip, as exhibited in "The Iron Pirate," a mild, inoffensive man, who earned that baleful title by his unfortunate mispronunciation of the term "iron pyrites." Perhaps this may have been the beginning of a rude heraldry; but I am constrained to think that it was because a man's real name in that day rested solely upon his own unsupported statement. "Call yourself Clifford, do you?" said Boston, addressing a timid newcomer with infinite scorn; "Hell is full of such Cliffords!" He then introduced the unfortunate man, whose name happened to be really Clifford, as "Jaybird Charley,"—an unhallowed inspiration of the moment that clung to him ever after.

37

But to return to Tennessee's Partner, whom we never knew by any other than this relative title. That he had ever existed as a separate and distinct individuality we only learned later. It seems that in 1853 he left Poker Flat to go to San Francisco, ostensibly to procure a wife. He never got any farther than Stockton. At that place he was attracted by a young person who waited upon the table at the hotel where he took his meals. One morning he said something to her which caused her to smile not unkindly, to somewhat coquettishly break a plate of toast over his upturned, serious, simple face, and to retreat to the kitchen. He followed her, and emerged a few moments later, covered with more toast and victory. That day week they were married by a justice of the peace, and returned to Poker Flat. I am aware that something more might be made of this episode, but I prefer to tell it as it was current at Sandy Bar—in the gulches and barrooms—where all sentiment was modified by a strong sense of humor.

Of their married felicity but little is known, perhaps for the reason that Tennessee, then living with his partner, one day took occasion to say something to the bride on his own account, at which, it is said, she smiled not unkindly and chastely retreated—this time as far as Marysville, where Tennessee followed her, and where they went to housekeeping without the aid of a justice of the peace. Tennessee's Partner took the loss of his wife simply and seriously, as was his fashion. But to everybody's surprise, when Tennessee one day returned from Marysville, without his partner's wife—she having smiled and retreated with somebody else—Tennessee's Partner was the first man to shake his hand and greet him with affection. The boys who had gathered in the canyon to see the shooting were naturally indignant. Their indignation might have found vent in sarcasm but for a certain look in Tennessee's Partner's eye that indicated a lack of humorous appreciation. In fact, he was a grave man, with a steady application to practical detail which was unpleasant in a difficulty.

Meanwhile a popular feeling against Tennessee had grown up on the Bar. He was known to be a gambler; he was suspected to be a thief. In these suspicions Tennessee's Partner was equally compromised; his continued intimacy with Tennessee after the affair above quoted could only be accounted for on the hypothesis of a copartnership of crime. At last Tennessee's guilt became flagrant. One day he overtook a stranger on his way to Red Dog. The stranger afterward related that Tennessee beguiled the time with interesting anecdote and reminiscence, but illogically concluded the interview in the following words: "And now, young man, I'll trouble you for your knife, your pistols, and your money. You see your weppings might get you into trouble at Red Dog, and your money's temptation to the evilly disposed. I think you said your address was San Francisco. I shall endeavor to call." It may be stated here that Tennessee had a fine flow of humor, which no business preoccupation could wholly subdue.

This exploit was his last. Red Dog and Sandy Bar made common cause against the highwayman. Tennessee was hunted in very much the same fashion as his prototype, the grizzly. As the toils closed around him, he made a desperate dash through the Bar, emptying his revolver at the crowd before the Arcade Saloon, and so on up Grizzly Canyon; but at its farther extremity he was stopped by a small man on a gray horse. The men looked at each other a moment in silence. Both were fearless, both self-possessed and independent, and both types of a civilization that in the seventeenth century would have been called heroic, but in the nineteenth simply "reckless."

"What have you got there?—I call," said Tennessee quietly.

"Two bowers and an ace," said the stranger as quietly, showing two revolvers and a bowie knife.

"That takes me," returned Tennessee; and with this gambler's epigram, he threw away his useless pistol and rode back with his captor.

It was a warm night. The cool breeze which usually sprang up with the going down of the sun behind the chaparral-crested mountain was that evening withheld from Sandy Bar. The little canyon was stifling with heated resinous odors, and the decaying driftwood on the Bar sent forth faint sickening exhalations. The feverishness of day and its fierce passions still filled the camp. Lights moved restlessly along the bank of the river, striking no answering reflection from its tawny current. Against the blackness of the pines the windows of the old loft above the express office stood out staringly bright; and through their curtainless panes the loungers below could see the forms of those who were even then deciding the fate of Tennessee. And above all this, etched on the dark firmament, rose the Sierra, remote and passionless, crowned with remoter passionless stars.

The trial of Tennessee was conducted as fairly as

was consistent with a judge and jury who felt themselves to some extent obliged to justify, in their verdict, the previous irregularities of arrest and indictment. The law of Sandy Bar was implacable, but not vengeful. The excitement and personal feeling of the chase were over; with Tennessee safe in their hands, they were ready to listen patiently to any defense, which they were already satisfied was insufficient. There being no doubt in their own minds, they were willing to give the prisoner the benefit of any that might exist. Secure in the hypothesis that he ought to be hanged on general principles, they indulged him with more latitude of defense than his reckless hardihood seemed to ask. The Judge appeared to be more anxious than the prisoner, who, otherwise unconcerned, evidently took a grim pleasure in the responsibility he had created. "I don't take any hand in this yer game," had been his invariable but good-humored reply to all questions. The Judge—who was also his captor—for a moment vaguely regretted that he had not shot him "on sight" that morning, but presently dismissed this human weakness as unworthy of the judicial mind. Nevertheless, when there was a tap at the door, and it was said that Tennessee's Partner was there on behalf of the prisoner, he was admitted at once without question. Perhaps the younger members of the jury, to whom the proceedings were becoming irksomely thoughtful, hailed him as a relief.

For he was not, certainly, an imposing figure. Short and stout, with a square face, sunburned into a preternatural redness, clad in a loose duck "jumper" and trousers streaked and splashed with red soil, his aspect under any circumstances would have been quaint, and was now even ridiculous. As he stooped to deposit at his feet a heavy carpetbag he was carrying, it became obvious, from partially developed legends and inscriptions, that the material with which his trousers had been patched had been originally intended for a less ambitious covering. Yet he advanced with great gravity, and after shaking the hand of each person in the room with labored cordiality, he wiped his serious perplexed face on a red bandana handkerchief, a shade lighter than his complexion, laid his powerful hand upon the table to steady himself, and thus addressed the Judge:

"I was passin' by," he began, by way of apology, "and I thought I'd just step in and see how things was gittin' on with Tennessee thar—my pardner. It's a hot night. I disremember any sich weather before on the Bar."

He paused a moment, but nobody volunteering any other meteorological recollection, he again had recourse to his pocket handkerchief, and for some moments mopped his face diligently.

"Have you anything to say on behalf of the prisoner?" said the Judge finally.

"Thet's it," said Tennessee's Partner, in a tone of relief. "I come yar as Tennessee's pardner—knowing him nigh on four year, off and on, wet and dry, in luck and out o' luck. His ways ain't aller my ways, but thar ain't any p'ints in that young man, thar ain't any liveliness as he's been up to, as I don't know. And you sez to me, sez you—confidential-like, and between man and man—sez you, 'Do you know anything in his behalf?' and I sez to you, sez I—confidential-like, as between man and man—'What should a man know of his pardner?' "

"Is this all you have to say?" asked the Judge impatiently, feeling, perhaps, that a dangerous sympathy of humor was beginning to humanize the court.

"Thet's so," continued Tennessee's Partner. "It ain't for me to say anything agin' him. And now, what's the case? Here's Tennessee wants money, wants it bad, and doesn't like to ask it of his old pardner. Well, what does Tennessee do? He lays for a stranger, and he fetches that stranger; and you lays for *him*, and you fetches *him;* and the honors is easy. And I put it to you, bein' a fa'r-minded man, and to you, gentlemen all, as fa'r-minded men, ef this isn't so."

"Prisoner," said the Judge, interrupting, "have you any questions to ask this man?"

"No! no!" continued Tennessee's Partner hastily. "I play this yer hand alone. To come down to the bedrock, it's just this: Tennessee thar has played it pretty rough and expensivelike on a stranger, and on this yer camp. And now, what's the fair thing? Some would say more, some would say less. Here's seventeen hundred dollars in coarse gold and a watch—it's about all my pile—and call it square!" And before a hand could be raised to prevent him, he had emptied the contents of the carpetbag upon the table.

For a moment his life was in jeopardy. One or two men sprang to their feet, several hands groped for hidden weapons, and a suggestion to "throw him from the window" was only overridden by a gesture from the Judge. Tennessee laughed. And apparently oblivious of the excitement, Tennessee's Partner improved the opportunity to mop his face again with his handkerchief.

When order was restored, and the man was made to understand by the use of forcible figures and rhetoric that Tennessee's offense could not be condoned by money, his face took a more serious and sanguinary hue, and those who were nearest to him noticed that his rough hand trembled slightly on the table. He hesitated a moment as he slowly returned the gold to the carpetbag, as if he had not yet entirely caught the elevated sense of justice which swayed the tribunal, and was perplexed with the belief that he had not offered enough. Then he turned to the Judge, and saying, "This yer is a lone hand, played alone, and without my pardner," he bowed to the jury and was about to withdraw, when the Judge called him back:

"If you have anything to say to Tennessee, you had better say it now."

For the first time that evening the eyes of the prisoner and his strange advocate met. Tennessee smiled, showed his white teeth, and saying, "Euchred, old man!" held out his hand. Tennessee's Partner took it in his own, and saying, "I just dropped in as I was passin' to see how things was gettin' on," let the hand passively fall, and adding that "it was a warm night," again mopped his face with his handkerchief, and without another word withdrew.

The two men never again met each other alive. For the unparalleled insult of a bribe offered to Judge Lynch—who, whether bigoted, weak, or narrow, was at least incorruptible—firmly fixed in the mind of that mythical personage any wavering determination of Tennessee's fate; and at the break of day he was marched, closely guarded, to meet it at the top of Marley's Hill.

How he met it, how cool he was, how he refused to say anything, how perfect were the arrangements of the committee, were all duly reported, with the addition of a warning moral and example to all future evil-doers, in the *Red Dog Clarion* by its editor, who was present, and to whose vigorous English I cheerfully refer the reader. But the beauty of that midsummer morning, the blessed amity of earth and air and sky, the awakened life of the free woods and hills, the joyous renewal and promise of Nature, and above all, the infinite serenity that thrilled through each, was not reported, as not being a part of the social lesson. And yet, when the weak and foolish deed was done, and a life, with its possibilities and responsibilities, had passed out of the misshapen thing that dangled between earth and sky, the birds sang, the flowers bloomed, the sun shone, as cheerily as before; and possibly the *Red Dog Clarion* was right.

Tennessee's Partner was not in the group that surrounded the ominous tree. But as they turned to disperse, attention was drawn to the sinular appearance of a motionless donkey cart halted at the side of the road. As they approached, they at once recognized the venerable Jenny and the two-wheeled cart as the property of Tennessee's Partner, used by him in carrying dirt from his claim; and a few paces distant the owner of the equipage himself, sitting under a buckeye tree, wiping the perspiration from his glowing face. In answer to an inquiry, he said he had come for the body of the "diseased," "if it was all the same to the committee." He didn't wish to "hurry anything"; he could "wait." He was not working that day; and when the gentlemen were done with the "diseased," he would take him. "Ef thar is any present," he added, in his simple, serious way, "as would care to jine in the fun'l, they kin come." Perhaps it was from a sense of humor, which I have already intimated was a feature of Sandy Bar—perhaps it was from something even better than that, but two thirds of the loungers accepted the invitation at once.

It was noon when the body of Tennessee was delivered into the hands of his partner. As the cart drew up to the fatal tree, we noticed that it contained a rough oblong box—apparently made from a section of sluicing—and half filled with bark and the tassels of pine. The cart was further decorated with slips of willow and made fragrant with buckeye blossoms. When the body was deposited in the box, Tennessee's Partner drew over it a piece of tarred canvas, and gravely mounting the narrow seat in front, with his feet upon the shafts, urged the little donkey forward. The equipage moved slowly on, at that decorous pace which was habitual with Jenny even under less solemn circumstances. The men—half curiously, half jestingly, but all good-humoredly—strolled along beside the cart, some in advance, some a little in the rear of the homely catafalque. But whether from the narrowing of the road or some present sense of decorum, as the cart passed on, the company fell to the rear in couples, keeping step, and otherwise assuming the external show of a formal procession. Jack Folinsbee, who had at the outset played a funeral march in dumb show upon an imaginary trombone, desisted from a lack of sympathy and appreciation—not having, per-

haps, your true humorist's capacity to be content
with the enjoyment of his own fun.

The way led through Grizzly Canyon, by this
time clothed in funeral drapery and shadows. The red-
woods, burying their moccasined feet in the red soil,
stood in Indian file along the track, trailing an uncouth
benediction from their bending boughs upon the passing bier. A hare, surprised into helpless inactivity, sat
upright and pulsating in the ferns by the roadside as
the cortege went by. Squirrels hastened to gain a secure outlook from higher boughs; and the blue jays,
spreading their wings, fluttered before them like out-
riders, until the outskirts of Sandy Bar were reached,
and the solitary cabin of Tennessee's Partner.

Viewed under more favorable circumstances, it
would not have been a cheerful place. The unpic-
turesque site, the rude and unlovely outlines, the unsavory details, which distinguish the nest-building of
the California miner, were all here with the dreari-
ness of decay superadded. A few paces from the cabin
there was a rough enclosure, which, in the brief days
of Tennessee's Partner's matrimonial felicity, had
been used as a garden, but was now overgrown with
fern. As we approached it, we were surprised to find
that what we had taken for a recent attempt at cultivation was the broken soil about an open grave.

The cart was halted before the enclosure, and re-
jecting the offers of assistance with the same air of
simple self-reliance he had displayed throughout,
Tennessee's Partner lifted the rough coffin on his back,
and deposited it unaided within the shallow grave.
He then nailed down the board which served as a lid,
and mounting the little mound of earth beside it, took

off his hat and slowly mopped his face with his handkerchief. This the crowd felt was a preliminary
to speech, and they disposed themselves variously on
stumps and boulders, and sat expectant.

"When a man," began Tennessee's Partner slowly,
"has been running free all day, what's the natural
thing for him to do? Why, to come home. And if he
ain't in a condition to go home, what can his best
friend do? Why, bring him home. And here's Tennessee has been running free, and we brings him home
from his wandering." He paused and picked up a fragment of quartz, rubbed it thoughtfully on his sleeve,
and went on: "It ain't the first time that I've packed
him on my back, as you see'd me now. It ain't the first
time that I brought him to this yer cabin when
he couldn't help himself; it ain't the first time that I
and Jinny have waited for him on yon hill, and picked
him up and so fetched him home, when he couldn't
speak and didn't know me. And now that it's the last
time, why"—he paused and rubbed the quartz gently
on his sleeve—"you see it's sort of rough on his
pardener. And now, gentlemen," he added abruptly,
picking up his long-handled shovel, "the fun'l's over;
and my thanks, and Tennessee's thanks, to you for
your trouble."

Resisting any proffers of assistance, he began to fill
in the grave, turning his back upon the crowd, that
after a few moments' hesitation gradually withdrew.
As they crossed the little ridge that hid Sandy Bar
from view, some, looking back, thought they could see
Tennessee's Partner, his work done, sitting upon the
grave, his shovel between his knees, and his face
buried in his red bandana handkerchief. But it was

argued by others that you couldn't tell his face from his handkerchief at that distance, and this point remained undecided.

In the reaction that followed the feverish excitement of that day, Tennessee's Partner was not forgotten. A secret investigation had cleared him of any complicity in Tennessee's guilt, and left only a suspicion of his general sanity. Sandy Bar made a point of calling on him, and proffering various uncouth but well-meant kindnesses. But from that day his rude health and great strength seemed visibly to decline; and when the rainy season fairly set in, and the tiny grass blades were beginning to peep from the rocky mound above Tennessee's grave, he took to his bed.

One night, when the pines beside the cabin were swaying in the storm and trailing their slender fingers over the roof, and the roar and rush of the swollen river were heard below, Tennessee's Partner lifted his head from the pillow, saying, "It is time to go for Tennessee; I must put Jinny in the cart"; and would have risen from his bed but for the restraint of his attendant. Struggling, he still pursued his singular fancy: "There, now, steady, Jinny, steady, old girl. How dark it is! Look out for the ruts, and look out for him, too, old gal. Sometimes, you know, when he's blind drunk, he drops down right in the trail. Keep on straight up to the pine on the top of the hill. Thar! I told you so!—thar he is—coming this way, too—all by himself, sober, and his face a-shining. Tennessee! Pardner!"

And so they met.

THE IDYL OF
RED GULCH

Sandy was very drunk. He was lying under an azalea bush, in pretty much the same attitude in which he had fallen some hours before. How long he had been lying there he could not tell, and didn't care; how long he should lie there was a matter equally indefinite and unconsidered. A tranquil philosophy, born of his physical condition, suffused and saturated his moral being.

The spectacle of a drunken man, and of this drunken man in particular, was not, I grieve to say, of sufficient novelty in Red Gulch to attract attention. Earlier in the day some local satirist had erected a temporary tombstone at Sandy's head, bearing the inscription, "Effects of McCorkle's whiskey—kills at forty rods," with a hand pointing to McCorkle's saloon. But this, I imagine, was, like most local satire, personal; and was a reflection upon the unfairness of the process rather than a commentary upon the impropriety of the result. With this facetious exception, Sandy had been undisturbed. A wandering mule, released from his pack, had cropped the scant herbage beside him, and sniffed curiously at the prostrate man; a vagabond dog, with that deep sympathy which the species have for drunken men, had licked his dusty boots and curled himself up at his feet, and lay there, blinking one eye in the sunlight, with a simulation of dissipation that was ingenious and doglike in its implied flattery of the unconscious man beside him.

Meanwhile the shadows of the pine trees had slowly swung around until they crossed the road, and their trunks barred the open meadow with gigantic parallels of black and yellow. Little puffs of red dust, lifted by the plunging hoofs of passing teams, dispersed in a grimy shower upon the recumbent man. The sun sank lower and lower, and still Sandy stirred not. And then the repose of this philosopher was disturbed, as other philosophers have been, by the intrusion of an unphilosophical sex.

"Miss Mary," as she was known to the little flock that she had just dismissed from the log schoolhouse beyond the pines, was taking her afternoon walk. Observing an unusually fine cluster of blossoms on the azalea bush opposite, she crossed the road to pluck it, picking her way through the red dust, not without certain fierce little shivers of disgust and some feline circumlocution. And then she came suddenly upon Sandy!

Of course she uttered the little staccato cry of her sex. But when she had paid that tribute to her physical weakness she became overbold and halted for a moment—at least six feet from this prostrate monster—with her white skirts gathered in her hand, ready for flight. But neither sound nor motion came from the bush. With one little foot she then overturned the satirical headboard, and muttered "Beasts!"—

an epithet which probably, at that moment, conveniently classified in her mind the entire male population of Red Gulch. For Miss Mary, being possessed of certain rigid notions of her own, had not, perhaps, properly appreciated the demonstrative gallantry for which the Californian has been so justly celebrated by his brother Californians, and had, as a newcomer, perhaps fairly earned the reputation of being "stuck up."

As she stood there she noticed, also, that the slant sunbeams were heating Sandy's head to what she judged to be an unhealthy temperature, and that his hat was lying uselessly at his side. To pick it up and to place it over his face was a work requiring some courage, particularly as his eyes were open. Yet she did it and made good her retreat. But she was somewhat concerned, on looking back, to see that the hat was removed, and that Sandy was sitting up and saying something.

The truth was that in the calm depths of Sandy's mind he was satisfied that the rays of the sun were beneficial and healthful; that from childhood he had objected to lying down in a hat; that no people but condemned fools, past redemption, ever wore hats; and that his right to dispense with them when he pleased was inalienable. This was the statement of his inner consciousness. Unfortunately, its outward expression was vague, being limited to a repetition of the following formula: "Su'shine all ri'! Wasser maar, eh? Wass up, su'shine?"

Miss Mary stopped, and taking fresh courage from her vantage of distance, asked him if there was anything that he wanted.

"Wass up? Wasser maar?" continued Sandy, in a very high key.

"Get up, you horrid man!" said Miss Mary, now thoroughly incensed; "get up and go home."

Sandy staggered to his feet. He was six feet high, and Miss Mary trembled. He started forward a few paces and then stopped.

"Wass I go home for?" he suddenly asked, with great gravity.

"Go and take a bath," replied Miss Mary, eying his grimy person with great disfavor.

To her infinite dismay, Sandy suddenly pulled off his coat and vest, threw them on the ground, kicked off his boots, and plunging wildly forward, darted headlong over the hill in the direction of the river.

"Goodness heavens! the man will be drowned!" said Miss Mary; and then, with feminine inconsistency, she ran back to the schoolhouse and locked herself in.

That night, while seated at supper with her hostess, the blacksmith's wife, it came to Miss Mary to ask, demurely, if her husband ever got drunk. "Abner," responded Mrs. Stidger reflectively—"let's see! Abner hasn't been tight since last 'lection." Miss Mary would have liked to ask if he preferred lying in the sun on these occasions, and if a cold bath would have hurt him; but this would have involved an explanation, which she did not then care to give. So she contented herself with opening her gray eyes widely at the red-cheeked Mrs. Stidger—a fine specimen of Southwestern efflorescence—and then dismissed the subject altogether. The next day she wrote to her dearest friend in Boston: "I think I find the intoxicated portion of this community the least objectionable. I refer, my dear, to the men, of course. I do not know anything that could make the women tolerable."

In less than a week Miss Mary had forgotten this episode, except that her afternoon walks took thereafter, almost unconsciously, another direction. She noticed, however, that every morning a fresh cluster of azalea blossoms appeared among the flowers on her desk. This was not strange, as her little flock were aware of her fondness for flowers, and invariably kept her desk bright with anemones, syringas, and lupines; but on questioning them, they one and all professed ignorance of the azaleas. A few days later, Master Johnny Stidger, whose desk was nearest to the window, was suddenly taken with spasms of apparently gratuitous laughter that threatened the discipline of the school. All that Miss Mary could get from him was that someone had been "looking in the winder." Irate and indignant, she sallied from her hive to do battle with the intruder. As she turned the corner of the schoolhouse she came plump upon the quondam drunkard, now perfectly sober, and inexpressibly sheepish and guilty-looking.

These facts Miss Mary was not slow to take a feminine advantage of, in her present humor. But it was somewhat confusing to observe, also, that the beast, despite some faint signs of past dissipation, was amiable-looking—in fact, a kind of blond Samson, whose corn-colored silken beard apparently had never yet known the touch of barber's razor or Delilah's shears. So that the cutting speech which quivered on her ready tongue died upon her lips, and she contented herself with receiving his stammering apology with supercilious eyelids and the gathered skirts of uncontamination. When she re-entered the school-room, her eyes fell upon the azaleas with a new sense of revelation; and then she laughed, and the little people all laughed, and they were all unconsciously very happy.

It was a hot day, and not long after this, that two short-legged boys came to grief on the threshold of the school with a pail of water, which they had laboriously brought from the spring, and that Miss Mary compassionately seized the pail and started for the spring herself. At the foot of the hill a shadow crossed her path, and a blue-shirted arm dexterously but gently relieved her of her burden. Miss Mary was both embarrassed and angry. "If you carried more of that for yourself," she said spitefully to the blue arm, without deigning to raise her lashes to its owner, "you'd do better." In the submissive silence that followed she regretted the speech, and thanked him so sweetly at the door that he stumbled. Which caused the children to laugh again—a laugh in which Miss Mary joined, until the color came faintly into her pale cheek. The next day a barrel was mysteriously placed beside the door, and as mysteriously filled with fresh spring-water every morning.

Nor was this superior young person without other quiet attentions. "Profane Bill," driver of the Slumgullion Stage, widely known in the newspapers for his "gallantry" in invariably offering the box seat to the fair sex, had excepted Miss Mary from this attention, on the ground that he had a habit of "cussin' on up-grades," and gave her half the coach to herself. Jack Hamlin, a gambler, having once silently ridden with her in the same coach, afterward threw a decanter at the head of a confederate for mentioning her name in a barroom. The over-dressed mother of a pupil whose paternity was doubtful had often lingered near this astute vestal's temple, never daring to enter its sacred precincts, but content to worship the priestess from afar.

With such unconscious intervals the monotonous procession of blue skies, glittering sunshine, brief twilights, and starlit nights passed over Red Gulch. Miss Mary grew fond of walking in the sedate and proper woods. Perhaps she believed, with Mrs. Stidger, that the balsamic odors of the firs "did her chest good," for certainly her slight cough was less frequent and her step was firmer; perhaps she had learned the unending lesson which the patient pines are never weary of repeating to heedful or listless ears. And so one day she planned a picnic on Buckeye Hill, and took the children with her. Away from the dusty road, the straggling shanties, the yellow ditches, the clamor of restless engines, the cheap finery of shop windows, the deeper glitter of paint and colored glass, and the thin veneering which barbarism takes upon itself in such localities, what infinite relief was theirs! The last heap of ragged rock and clay passed, the last unsightly chasm crossed—how the waiting woods opened their long files to receive them! How the children—perhaps because they had not yet grown quite away from the breast of the bounteous Mother—threw themselves face downward on her brown bosom with uncouth caresses, filling the air with their laughter; and how Miss Mary herself—felinely fastidious and intrenched as she was in the purity of spotless skirts, collar, and cuffs—forgot all, and ran like a crested quail at the head of her brood, until, romping, laughing, and panting, with a loosened braid of brown hair, a hat hanging by a knotted ribbon from her throat, she came suddenly and violently, in the heart of the forest, upon the luckless Sandy!

The explanations, apologies, and not overwise conversation that ensued need not be indicated here. It would seem, however, that Miss Mary had already established some acquaintance with this ex-drunkard. Enough that he was soon accepted as one of the party; that the children, with that quick intelligence which Providence gives the helpless, recognized a friend, and played with his blond beard and long silken mustache, and took other liberties—as the helpless are apt to do. And when he had built a fire against a tree, and had shown them other mysteries of woodcraft, their admiration knew no bounds. At the close of two such foolish, idle, happy hours he found himself lying at the feet of the schoolmistress, gazing dreamily in her face as she sat upon the sloping hillside weaving wreaths of laurel and syringa, in very much the same attitude as he had lain when first they met. Nor was the similitude greatly forced. The weakness of an easy, sensuous nature, that had found a dreamy exaltation in liquor, it is to be feared was now finding an equal intoxication in love.

I think that Sandy was dimly conscious of this himself. I know that he longed to be doing something—slaying a grizzly, scalping a savage, or sacrificing himself in some way for the sake of this sallow-faced, gray-eyed schoolmistress. As I should like to present him in an heroic attitude, I stay my hand with great difficulty at this moment, being only withheld from introducing such an episode by a strong conviction that it does not usually occur at such times. And I trust that my fairest reader, who remembers that in a real crisis it is always some uninteresting stranger or unromantic policeman, and not Adolphus, who rescues, will forgive the omission.

So they sat there undisturbed—the woodpeckers chattering overhead and the voices of the children coming pleasantly from the hollow below. What they said matters little. What they thought—which might have been interesting—did not transpire. The woodpeckers only learned how Miss Mary was an orphan; how she left her uncle's house to come to California for the sake of health and independence; how Sandy was an orphan too; how he came to California for excitement; how he had lived a wild life, and how he was trying to reform; and other details, which from a woodpecker's viewpoint undoubtedly must have seemed stupid and a waste of time. But even in such trifles was the afternoon spent; and when the children were again gathered, and Sandy, with a delicacy which the schoolmistress well understood, took leave of them quietly at the outskirts of the settlement, it had seemed the shortest day of her weary life.

As the long, dry summer withered to its roots, the school term of Red Gulch—to use a local euphuism —"dried up" also. In another day Miss Mary would be free, and for a season, at least, Red Gulch would know her no more. She was seated alone in the schoolhouse, her cheek resting on her hand, her eyes half closed in one of those daydreams in which Miss Mary, I fear, to the danger of school discipline, was lately in the habit of indulging. Her lap was full of mosses, ferns, and other woodland memories. She was so preoccupied with these and her own thoughts that a gentle tapping at the door passed unheard, or translated itself into the remembrance of far-off woodpeckers. When at last it asserted itself more distinctly, she started up with a flushed cheek and opened the door. On the threshold stood a woman, the self-assertion and audacity of whose dress were in singular contrast to her timid, irresolute bearing.

Miss Mary recognized at a glance the dubious mother of her anonymous pupil. Perhaps she was disappointed, perhaps she was only fastidious; but as she coldly invited her to enter, she half unconsciously settled her white cuffs and collar, and gathered closer her own chaste skirts. It was, perhaps, for this reason that the embarrassed stranger, after a moment's hesitation, left her gorgeous parasol open and sticking in the dust beside the door, and then sat down at the farther end of a long bench. Her voice was husky as she began—

"I heerd tell that you were goin' down to the Bay tomorrow, and I couldn't let you go until I came to thank you for your kindness to my Tommy."

Tommy, Miss Mary said, was a good boy, and deserved more than the poor attention she could give him.

"Thank you, miss; thank ye!" cried the stranger, brightening even through the color which Red Gulch knew facetiously as her "war paint," and striving, in her embarrassment, to drag the long bench nearer the schoolmistress. "I thank you, miss, for that; and if I am his mother, there ain't a sweeter, dearer, better boy lives than him. And if I ain't much as says it, thar ain't a sweeter, dearer, angeler teacher lives than he's got."

Miss Mary, sitting primly behind her desk, with a ruler over her shoulder, opened her gray eyes widely at this, but said nothing.

"It ain't for you to be complimented by the like of me, I know," she went on hurriedly. "It ain't for me to be comin' here, in broad day, to do it, either; but I come to ask a favor—not for me, miss—not for me, but for the darling boy."

Encouraged by a look in the young school-mistress's eye, and putting her lilac-gloved hands together, the fingers downward, between her knees, she went on, in a low voice:

"You see, miss, there's no one the boy has any claim on but me, and I ain't the proper person to bring him up. I thought some last year of sending him away to Frisco to school, but when they talked of bringing a schoolma'am here, I waited till I saw you, and then I knew it was all right, and I could keep my boy a little longer. And, oh! miss, he loves you so much; and if you could hear him talk about you in his pretty way, and if he could ask you what I ask you now, you couldn't refuse him.

"It is natural," she went on rapidly, in a voice that trembled strangely between pride and humility—"it's natural that he should take to you, miss, for his father, when I first knew him, was a gentleman—and the boy must forget me, sooner or later—and so I ain't a-goin' to cry about that. For I come to ask you to take my Tommy—God bless him for the bestest, sweetest boy that lives—to—to—take him with you."

She had risen and caught the young girl's hand in her own, and had fallen on her knees beside her.

"I've money plenty, and it's all yours and his. Put him in some good school, where you can go and see him, and help him to—to—to forget his mother. Do with him what you like. The worst you can do will be kindness to what he will learn with me. Only take him out of this wicked life, this cruel place, this home of shame and sorrow. You will! I know you will—won't you? You will—you must not, you cannot say no! You will make him as pure, as gentle as yourself; and when he has grown up, you will tell him his father's name —the name that hasn't passed my lips for years—the name of Alexander Morton, whom they call here Sandy! Miss Mary!—do not take your hand away! Miss Mary, speak to me! You will take my boy? Do not put your face from me. I know it ought not to look on such as me. Miss Mary!—my God, be merciful!— she is leaving me!"

Miss Mary had risen, and in the gathering twilight, had felt her way to the open window. She stood there, leaning against the casement, her eyes fixed on the last rosy tints that were fading from the western sky. There was still some of its light on her pure young forehead, on her white collar, on her clasped white hands, but all fading slowly away. The suppliant had dragged herself, still on her knees, beside her.

"I know it takes time to consider. I will wait here all night; but I cannot go until you speak. Do not deny me now. You will!—I see it in your sweet face— such a face as I have seen in my dreams. I see it in your eyes, Miss Mary!—you will take my boy!"

The last red beam crept higher, suffused Miss

Mary's eyes with something of its glory, flickered, and faded, and went out. The sun had set on Red Gulch. In the twilight and silence Miss Mary's voice sounded pleasantly.

"I will take the boy. Send him to me tonight."

The happy mother raised the hem of Miss Mary's skirts to her lips. She would have buried her hot face in its virgin folds, but she dared not. She rose to her feet.

"Does—this man—know of your intention?" asked Miss Mary suddenly.

"No, nor cares. He has never even seen the child to know it."

"Go to him at once—tonight—now! Tell him what you have done. Tell him I have taken his child, and tell him—he must never see—see—the child again. Wherever it may be, he must not come; wherever I may take it, he must not follow! There, go now, please —I'm weary, and—have much yet to do!"

They walked together to the door. On the threshold the woman turned.

"Good night!"

She would have fallen at Miss Mary's feet. But at the same moment the young girl reached out her arms, caught the sinful woman to her own pure breast for one brief moment, and then closed and locked the door.

It was with a sudden sense of great responsibility that Profane Bill took the reins of the Slumgullion stage the next morning, for the schoolmistress was one of his passengers. As he entered the highroad, in obedience to a pleasant voice from the "inside," he suddenly reined up his horses and respectfully waited, as

Tommy hopped out at the command of Miss Mary.

"Not that bush, Tommy—the next."

Tommy whipped out his new pocketknife, and cutting a branch from a tall azalea bush, returned with it to Miss Mary.

"All right now?"

"All right!"

And the stage-door closed on the Idyl of Red Gulch.

BROWN OF CALAVERAS

A subdued tone of conversation, and the absence of cigar smoke and boot heels at the windows of the Wingdam stagecoach, made it evident that one of the inside passengers was a woman. A disposition on the part of loungers at the stations to congregate before the window, and some concern in regard to the appearance of coats, hats, and collars, further indicated that she was lovely. All of which Mr. Jack Hamlin, on the box-seat, noted with the smile of cynical philosophy. Not that he depreciated the sex, but that he recognized therein a deceitful element, the pursuit of which sometimes drew mankind away from the equally uncertain blandishments of poker—of which it may be remarked that Mr. Hamlin was a professional exponent.

So that when he placed his narrow boot on the wheel and leaped down he did not even glance at the window from which a green veil was fluttering, but lounged up and down with that listless and grave indifference of his class, which was, perhaps, the next thing to good breeding. With his closely buttoned figure and self-contained air he was a marked contrast to the other passengers, with their feverish restlessness and boisterous emotion; and even Bill Masters, a graduate of Harvard, with his slovenly dress, his overflowing vitality, his intense appreciation of lawlessness and barbarism, and his mouth filled with crackers and cheese, I fear cut but an unromantic figure beside this lonely calculator of chances, with his pale Greek face and Homeric gravity.

The driver called "All aboard!" and Mr. Hamlin returned to the coach. His foot was upon the wheel, and his face raised to the level of the open window, when, at the same moment, what appeared to him to be the finest eyes in the world suddenly met his. He quietly dropped down again, addressed a few words to one of the inside passengers, effected an exchange of seats, and as quietly took his place inside. Mr. Hamlin never allowed his philosophy to interfere with decisive and prompt action.

I fear that this irruption of Jack cast some restraint upon the other passengers, particularly those who were making themselves most agreeable to the lady. One of them leaned forward, and apparently conveyed to her information regarding Mr. Hamlin's profession in a single epithet. Whether Mr. Hamlin heard it, or whether he recognized in the informant a distinguished jurist, from whom, but a few evenings before, he had won several thousand dollars, I cannot say. His colorless face betrayed no sign; his black eyes, quietly observant, glanced indifferently past the legal gentleman, and rested on the much more pleasing features of his neighbor. An Indian stocism—said to be an inheritance from his maternal ancestor—stood him in good service, until the rolling wheels rattled upon the river gravel at Scott's Ferry, and the stage drew up at the International Hotel for dinner. The legal gentleman and a member of Congress leaped out, and stood ready to assist the descending goddess, while Colonel Starbottle of Siskiyou took charge of her parasol and shawl. In this multiplicity of attention there was a momentary confusion and delay. Jack Hamlin quietly opened the *opposite* door of the coach, took the lady's hand, with that decision and positiveness which a hesitating and undecided sex know how to admire, and in an instant had dexterously and gracefully swung her to the ground and again lifted her to the platform. An audible chuckle on the box, I fear, came from that other cynic, Yuba Bill, the driver. "Look keerfully arter that baggage, Kernel," said the expressman, with affected concern, as he looked after Colonel Starbottle, gloomily bringing up the rear of the triumphant procession to the waiting room.

Mr. Hamlin did not stay for dinner. His horse was already saddled and awaiting him. He dashed over the ford, up the gravelly hill, and out into the dusty perspective of the Wingdam road, like one leaving an unpleasant fancy behind him. The inmates of dusty cabins by the roadside shaded their eyes with their hands and looked after him, recognizing the man by his horse, and speculating what "was up with Comanche Jack." Yet much of this interest centered in the horse, in a community where the time made by "French Pete's" mare in his run from the Sheriff of Calaveras eclipsed all concern in the ultimate fate of that worthy.

The sweating flanks of his gray at length recalled him to himself. He checked his speed, and turning into a byroad sometimes used as a cutoff, trotted leisurely along, the reins hanging listlessly from his fingers. As he rode on, the character of the landscape changed and became more pastoral. Openings in groves of pine and sycamore disclosed some rude attempts at cultivation—a flowering vine trailed over the porch of one cabin, and a woman rocked her cradled babe under the roses of another. A little farther on, Mr. Hamlin came upon some barelegged children wading in the willowy creek, and so wrought upon them with a badinage peculiar to himself that they were emboldened to climb up his horse's legs and over his saddle, until he was fain to develop an exaggerated ferocity of demeanor, and to escape, leaving behind some kisses and coin. And then, advancing deeper into the woods, where all signs of habitation failed, he began to sing, uplifting a tenor so singularly sweet, and shaded by a pathos so subdued and tender, that I wot the robins and linnets stopped to listen. Mr. Hamlin's voice was not cultivated; the subject of his song was some sentimental lunacy, borrowed from the negro minstrels; but there thrilled through all some occult quality of tone and expression that was unspeakably touching. Indeed, it was a wonderful sight to see this sentimental blackleg, with a pack of cards in his pocket and a revolver at his back, sending his voice before him through the dim woods with a plaint about his "Nelly's grave," in a way that overflowed the eyes of the listener. A sparrow hawk, fresh from his sixth victim, possibly recognizing in Mr. Hamlin a kindred spirit, stared at him in surprise, and was fain to confess the superiority of man. With a superior predatory capacity *he* couldn't sing.

But Mr. Hamlin presently found himself again on the highroad and at his former pace. Ditches and banks of gravel, denuded hillsides, stumps, and decayed trunks of trees, took the place of woodland and ravine, and indicated his approach to civilization. Then a church steeple came in sight, and he knew that he had reached home. In a few moments he was clattering down the single narrow street that lost itself in a chaotic ruin of races, ditches, and tailings at the foot of the hill, and dismounted before the gilded windows of the Magnolia saloon. Passing through the long barroom, he pushed open a green baize door, entered a dark passage, opened another door with a passkey, and found himself in a dimly lighted room, whose furniture, though elegant and costly for the locality, showed signs of abuse. The inlaid center table was overlaid with stained disks that were not contemplated in the original design, the embroidered armchairs were discolored, and the green velvet lounge, on which Mr. Hamlin threw himself, was soiled at the foot with the red soil of Wingdam.

Mr. Hamlin did not sing in his cage. He lay still, looking at a highly colored painting above him, representing a young creature of opulent charms. It occurred to him then, for the first time, that he had never seen exactly that kind of a woman, and that, if he should, he would not probably fall in love with her. Perhaps he was thinking of another style of beauty. But just then someone knocked at the door. Without rising, he pulled a cord that apparently shot back a bolt, for the door swung open, and a man entered.

The newcomer was broad-shouldered and robust —a vigor not borne out in the face, which, though handsome, was singularly weak and disfigured by dissipation. He appeared to be, also, under the influence of liquor, for he started on seeing Mr. Hamlin, and said, "I thought Kate was here"; stammered, and seemed confused and embarrassed.

Mr. Hamlin smiled the smile which he had before worn on the Wingdam coach, and sat up, quite refreshed and ready for business.

"You didn't come up on the stage," continued the newcomer, "did you?"

"No," replied Hamlin; "I left it at Scott's Ferry. It isn't due for half an hour yet. But how's luck, Brown?"

"D—d bad," said Brown, his face suddenly assuming an expression of weak despair. "I'm cleaned out again, Jack," he continued, in a whining tone, that formed a pitiable contrast to his bulky figure; "can't you help me with a hundred till tomorrow's cleanup? You see I've got to send money home to the old woman, and—you've won twenty times that amount from me."

The conclusion was, perhaps, not entirely logical, but Jack overlooked it, and handed the sum to his visitor. "The old-woman business is about played out, Brown," he added, by way of commentary; "why don't you say you want to buck ag'in' faro? You know you ain't married!"

"Fact, sir," said Brown, with a sudden gravity, as if the mere contact of the gold with the palm of the hand had imparted some dignity to his frame. "I've got a wife—a d—d good one, too, if I do say it—in the States. It's three years since I've seen her, and a year since I've writ to her. When things is about straight, and we get down to the lead, I'm going to send for her."

"And Kate?" queried Mr. Hamlin, with his previous smile.

Mr. Brown of Calaveras essayed an archness of glance to cover his confusion, which his weak face and whiskey-muddled intellect but poorly carried out, and said—

"D—n it, Jack, a man must have a little liberty, you know. But come, what do you say to a little game? Give us a show to double this hundred."

Jack Hamlin looked curiously at his fatuous friend. Perhaps he knew that the man was predestined to lose the money, and preferred that it should flow back into his own coffers rather than any other. He nodded his head, and drew his chair toward the table. At the same moment there came a rap upon the door.

Mr. Hamlin shot back the bolt and the door opened. But, for the first time in his life, he staggered to his feet utterly unnerved and abashed, and for the first time in his life the hot blood crimsoned his color-less cheeks to his forehead. For before him stood the lady he had lifted from the Wingdam coach, whom Brown, dropping his cards with a hysterical laugh, greeted as—

"My old woman, by thunder!"

They say that Mrs. Brown burst into tears and re-proaches of her husband. I saw her in 1857 at Marys-ville, and disbelieve the story. And the *Wingdam Chronicle* of the next week, under the head of "Touching Reunion," said: "One of those beautiful and touching incidents peculiar to California life occurred last week in our city. The wife of one of Wingdam's eminent pioneers, tired of the effete civilization of the East and its inhospitable climate, resolved to join her noble husband upon these golden shores. Without informing him of her intention, she undertook the long journey, and arrived last week. The joy of the husband may be easier imagined than described. The meeting is said to have been indescribably affecting. We trust her example may be followed."

Whether owing to Mrs. Brown's influence, or to some more successful speculations, Mr. Brown's financial fortune from that day steadily improved. He bought out his partners in the "Nip and Tuck" lead, with money which was said to have been won at poker a week or two after his wife's arrival, but which rumor, adopting Mrs. Brown's theory that Brown had forsworn the gaming table, declared to have been furnished by Mr. Jack Hamlin. He built and furnished the Wingdam House, which pretty Mrs. Brown's great popularity kept overflowing with guests. He was elected to the Assembly, and gave largess to churches. A street in Wingdam was named in his honor.

Yet it was noted that in proportion as he waxed wealthy and fortunate, he grew pale, thin, and anxious. As his wife's popularity increased, he became fretful and impatient. The most uxorious of husbands, he was absurdly jealous. If he did not interfere with his wife's social liberty, it was because it was maliciously whispered that his first and only attempt was met by an outburst from Mrs. Brown that terrified him into silence. Much of this kind of gossip came from those of her own sex whom she had supplanted in the chivalrous attentions of Wingdam, which, like most popular chivalry, was devoted to an admiration of power, whether of masculine force or feminine beauty. It should be remembered, too, in her extenuation, that since her arrival she had been the unconscious priestess of a mythological worship, perhaps not more ennobling to her womanhood than that which distinguished an older Greek democracy. I think that Brown was dimly conscious of this. But his only confidant was Jack Hamlin, whose infelix reputation naturally precluded any open intimacy with the family, and whose visits were infrequent.

It was midsummer and a moonlit night, and Mrs. Brown, very rosy, large-eyed, and pretty, sat upon the piazza, enjoying the fresh incense of the mountain breeze, and, it is to be freared, another incense which was not so fresh nor quite as innocent. Beside her sat Colonel Starbottle and Judge Boompointer, and a later addition to her court in the shape of a foreign tourist. She was in good spirits.

"What do you see down the road?" inquired the gallant Colonel, who had been conscious for the last few minutes that Mrs. Brown's attention was diverted.

"Dust," said Mrs. Brown, with a sigh. "Only Sister Anne's 'flock of sheep.' "

The Colonel, whose literary recollections did not extend farther back than last week's paper, took a more practical view. "It ain't sheep," he continued; "it's a horseman. Judge, ain't that Jack Hamlin's gray?"

But the Judge didn't know; and as Mrs. Brown suggested the air was growing too cold for further investigations, they retired to the parlor.

Mr. Brown was in the stable, where he generally retired after dinner. Perhaps it was to show his contempt for his wife's companions; perhaps, like other weak natures, he found pleasure in the exercise of absolute power over inferior animals. He had a certain gratification in the training of a chestnut mare, whom he could beat or caress as pleased him, which he couldn't do with Mrs. Brown. It was here that he recognized a certain gray horse which had just come in, and looking a little farther on, found his rider. Brown's greeting was cordial and hearty; Mr. Hamlin's somewhat restrained. But, at Brown's urgent request, he followed him up the back stairs to a narrow corridor, and thence to a small room looking out upon the stable yard. It was plainly furnished with a bed, a table, a few chairs, and a rack for guns and whips.

"This yer's my home, Jack," said Brown with a sigh, as he threw himself upon the bed and motioned his companion to a chair. "Her room's t' other end of the hall. It's more'n six months since we've lived together, or met, except at meals. It's mighty rough papers on the head of the house, ain't it?" he said with a forced laugh. "But I'm glad to see you, Jack, d—d glad," and he reached from the bed, and again shook the unresponsive hand of Jack Hamlin.

"I brought ye up here, for I didn't want to talk in the stable; though, for the matter of that, it's all round town. Don't strike a light. We can talk here in the moonshine. Put up your feet on that winder and sit here beside me. Thar's whiskey in that jug."

Mr. Hamlin did not avail himself of the information. Brown of Calaveras turned his face to the wall, and continued—

"If I didn't love the woman, Jack, I wouldn't mind. But it's loving her, and seeing her day arter day goin' on at this rate, and no one to put down the brake; that's what gits me! But I'm glad to see ye, Jack, d—d glad."

In the darkness he groped about until he had found and wrung his companion's hand again. He would have detained it, but Jack slipped it into the buttoned breast of his coat, and asked listlessly, "How long has this been going on?"

"Ever since she came here; ever since the day she walked into the Magnolia. I was a fool then; Jack, I'm a fool now; but I didn't know how much I loved her till then. And she hasn't been the same woman since.

"But that ain't all, Jack; and it's what I wanted to see you about, and I'm glad you've come. It ain't that she doesn't love me any more; it ain't that she fools with every chap that comes along; for perhaps I staked her love and lost it, as I did everything else at the Magnolia; and perhaps foolin' is nateral to some women, and thar ain't no great harm done, 'cept to the fools. But, Jack, I think—I think she loves somebody else. Don't move, Jack! don't move; if your pistol hurts ye, take it off.

'It's been more'n six months now that she's seemed unhappy and lonesome, and kinder nervous and scared-like. And sometimes I've ketched her lookin' at me sort of timid and pitying. And she writes to somebody. And for the last week she's been gathering her own things—trinkets, and furbelows, and jew'lry —and, Jack, I think she's goin' off. I could stand all but that. To have her steal away like a thief!" He put his face downward to the pillow, and for a few moments there was no sound but the ticking of a clock on the mantel. Mr. Hamlin lit a cigar, and moved to the open window. The moon no longer shone into the room, and the bed and its occupant were in shadow. "What shall I do, Jack?" said the voice from the darkness.

The answer came promptly and clearly from the window side, "Spot the man, and kill him on sight."

"But, Jack"—

"He's took the risk!"

"But will that bring *her* back?"

Jack did not reply, but moved from the window towards the door.

"Don't go yet, Jack; light the candle and sit by the table. It's a comfort to see ye, if nothin' else."

Jack hesitated and then complied. He drew a pack of cards from his pocket and shuffled them, glancing at the bed. But Brown's face was turned to the wall. When Mr. Hamlin had shuffled the cards, he cut them, and dealt one card on the opposite side of the table towards the bed, and another on his side of the table for himself. The first was a deuce; his own card a king. He then shuffled and cut again. This time "dummy" had a queen and himself a four-spot. Jack brightened up for the third deal. It brought his adversary a deuce and himself a king again. "Two out of three," said Jack audibly.

"What's that, Jack?" said Brown.

"Nothing."

Then Jack tried his hand with dice; but he always threw sixes and his imaginary opponent aces. The force of habit is sometimes confusing.

Meanwhile some magnetic influence in Mr. Hamlin's presence, or the anodyne of liquor, or both, brought surcease of sorrow, and Brown slept. Mr. Hamlin moved his chair to the window and looked out on the town of Wingdam, now sleeping peacefully, its harsh outlines softened and subdued, its glaring colors mellowed and sobered in the moonlight that flowed over all. In the hush he could hear the gurgling of water in the ditches and the sighing of the pines beyond the hill. Then he looked up at the firmament, and as he did so a star shot across the twinkling field. Presently another, and then another. The phenomenon suggested to Mr. Hamlin a fresh augury. If in another fifteen minutes another star should fall— He sat there, watch in hand, for twice that time, but the phenomenon was not repeated.

The clock struck two, and Brown still slept. Mr. Hamlin approached the table and took from his pocket a letter, which he read by the flickering candlelight. It contained only a single line, written in pencil, in a woman's hand—

"Be at the corral with the buggy at three."

The sleeper moved uneasily and then awoke. "Are you there, Jack?"

"Yes."

"Don't go yet. I dreamed just now, Jack—dreamed of old times. I thought that Sue and me was being married agin, and that the parson, Jack, was—who do you think?—you!"

The gambler laughed, and seated himself on the bed, the paper still in his hand.

"It's a good sign, ain't it?" queried Brown.

"I reckon! Say, old man, hadn't you better get up?"

The "old man," thus affectionately appealed to, rose, with the assistance of Hamlin's outstretched hand.

"Smoke?"

Brown mechanically took the proffered cigar.

"Light?"

Jack had twisted the letter into a spiral, lit it, and held it for his companion. He continued to hold it until it was consumed, and dropped the fragment— a fiery star—from the open window. He watched it as it fell, and then returned to his friend.

"Old man," he said, placing his hands upon Brown's shoulders, "in ten minutes I'll be on the road, and gone like that spark. We won't see each other agin; but, before I go, take a fool's advice: sell out all you've got, take your wife with you, and quit the country. It ain't no place for you nor her. Tell her she must go; make her go if she won't. Don't whine because you can't be a saint and she ain't an angel. Be a man, and treat her like a woman. Don't be a d—d fool. Good-by."

He tore himself from Brown's grasp and leaped down the stairs like a deer. At the stable door he collared the half-sleeping hostler, and backed him against the wall. "Saddle my horse in two minutes, or I'll"— The ellipsis was frightfully suggestive.

"The missis said you was to have the buggy," stammered the man.

"D—n the buggy!"

The horse was saddled as fast as the nervous hands of the astounded hostler could manipulate buckle and strap.

"Is anything up, Mr. Hamlin?" said the man, who, like all his class, admired the *élan* of his fiery patron, and was really concerned in his welfare.

"Stand aside!"

The man fell back. With an oath, a bound, and clatter, Jack was into the road. In another moment, to the man's half-awakened eyes, he was but a moving cloud of dust in the distance, towards which a star just loosed from its brethren was trailing a stream of fire.

But early that morning the dwellers by the Wingdam turnpike, miles away, heard a voice, pure as a skylark's, singing afield. They who were asleep turned over on their rude couches to dream of youth, and love, and olden days. Hard-faced men and anxious gold-seekers, already at work, ceased their labors and leaned upon their picks to listen to a romantic vagabond ambling away against the rosy sunrise.

SALOMY JANE'S KISS

Only one shot had been fired. It had gone wide of its mark,—the ringleader of the Vigilantes,—and had left Red Pete, who had fired it, covered by their rifles and at their mercy. For his hand had been cramped by hard riding, and his eye distracted by their sudden onset, and so the inevitable end had come. He submitted sullenly to his captors; his companion fugitive and horse-thief gave up the protracted struggle with a feeling not unlike relief. Even the hot and revengeful victors were content. They had taken their men alive. At any time during the long chase they could have brought them down by a rifle-shot, but it would have been unsportsmanlike, and have ended in a free fight, instead of an example. And, for the matter of that, their doom was already sealed. Their end, by a rope and a tree, although not sanctified by law, would have at least the deliberation of justice. It was the tribute paid by the Vigilantes to that order which they had themselves disregarded in the pursuit and capture. Yet this strange logic of the frontier sufficed them, and gave a certain dignity to the climax.

"Ef you've got anything to say to your folks, say it *now,* and say it quick," said the ringleader.

Red Pete glanced around him. He had been run to earth at his own cabin in the clearing, whence a few relations and friends, mostly women and children, non-combatants, had outflowed, gazing vacantly at the twenty Vigilantes who surrounded them. All were accustomed to scenes of violence, blood-feud, chase, and hardship; it was only the suddenness of the onset and its quick result that had surprised them. They looked on with dazed curiosity and some disappointment; there had been no fight to speak of—no spectacle! A boy, nephew of Red Pete, got upon the rain-barrel to view the proceedings more comfortably; a tall, handsome, lazy Kentucky girl, a visiting neighbor, leaned against the doorpost, chewing gum. Only a yellow hound was actively perplexed. He could not make out if a hunt were just over or beginning, and ran eagerly backwards and forwards, leaping alternately upon the captives and the captors.

The ringleader repeated his challenge. Red Pete gave a reckless laugh and looked at his wife.

At which Mrs. Red Pete came forward. It seemed that she had much to say, incoherently, furiously, vindictively, to the ringleader. His soul would roast in hell for that day's work! He called himself a man, skunkin' in the open and afraid to show himself except with a crowd of other "Kiyi's" around a house of women and children. Heaping insult upon insult, inveighing against his low blood, his ancestors, his dubious origin, she at last flung out a wild taunt of his invalid wife, the insult of a woman to a woman, until his white face grew rigid, and only that Western-

American fetich of the sanctity of sex kept his twitching fingers from the lock of his rifle. Even her husband noticed it, and with a half-authoritative "Let up on that, old gal," and a pat of his freed left hand on her back, took his last parting. The ringleader, still white under the lash of the woman's tongue, turned abruptly to the second captive. "And if *you've* got anybody to say 'good-by' to, now's your chance."

The man looked up. Nobody stirred or spoke. He was a stranger there, being a chance confederate picked up by Red Pete, and known to no one. Still young, but an outlaw from his abandoned boyhood, of which father and mother were only a forgotten dream, he loved horses and stole them, fully accepting the frontier penalty of life for the interference with that animal on which a man's life so often depended. But he understood the good points of a horse, as was shown by the one he bestrode—until a few days before the property of Judge Boompointer. This was his sole distinction.

The unexpected question stirred him for a moment out of the attitude of reckless indifference, for attitude it was, and a part of his profession. But it may have touched him that at that moment he was less than his companion and his virago wife. However, he only shook his head. As he did so his eye casually fell on the handsome girl by the doorpost, who was looking at him. The ringleader, too, may have been touched by his complete loneliness, for *he* hesitated. At the same moment he saw that the girl was looking at his friendless captive.

A grotesque idea struck him.

"Salomy Jane, ye might do worse than come yere

and say 'good-by' to a dying man, and him a stranger," he said.

There seemed to be a subtle stroke of poetry and irony in this that equally struck the apathetic crowd. It was well known that Salomy Jane Clay thought no small potatoes of herself, and always held off the local swain with a lazy, nymph-like scorn. Nevertheless, she slowly disengaged herself from the doorpost, and, to everybody's astonishment, lounged with languid grace and outstretched hand towards the prisoner. The color came into the gray, reckless mask which the doomed man wore as her right hand grasped his left, just loosed by his captors. Then she paused; her shy, fawn-like eyes grew bold, and fixed themselves upon him. She took the chewing-gum from her mouth, wiped her red lips with the back of her hand, by a sudden lithe spring placed her foot on his stirrup, and, bounding to the saddle, threw her arms about his neck and pressed a kiss upon his lips.

They remained thus for a hushed moment—the man on the threshold of death, the young woman in the fullness of youth and beauty—linked together. Then the crowd laughed; in the audacious effrontery of the girl's act the ultimate fate of the two men was forgotten. She slipped languidly to the ground; *she* was the focus of all eyes,—she only! The ringleader saw it and his opportunity. He shouted: "Time's up! Forward!" urged his horse beside his captives, and the next moment the whole cavalcade was sweeping over the clearing into the darkening woods.

Their destination was Sawyer's Crossing, the headquarters of the committee, where the council was still sitting, and where both culprits were to expiate the

offense of which that council had already found them
guilty. They rode in great and breathless haste,—a
haste in which, strangely enough, even the captives
seemed to join. That haste possibly prevented them
from noticing the singular change which had taken
place in the second captive since the episode of the
kiss. His high color remained, as if it had burned
through his mask of indifference; his eyes were quick,
alert, and keen, his mouth half open as if the girl's
kiss still lingered there. And that haste had made them
careless, for the horse of the man who led him slipped
in a gopher-hole, rolled over, unseated his rider, and
even dragged the bound and helpless second captive
from Judge Boompointer's favorite mare. In an instant they were all on their feet again, but in that supreme moment the second captive felt the cords which
bound his arms had slipped to his wrists. By keeping
his elbows to his sides, and obliging the others to
help him mount, it escaped their notice. By riding
close to his captors, and keeping in the crush of the
throng, he further concealed the accident, slowly working his hands downwards out of his bonds.

Their way lay through a sylvan wilderness, mid-leg
deep in ferns, whose tall fronds brushed their horses'
sides in their furious gallop and concealed the flapping
of the captive's loosened cords. The peaceful vista,
more suggestive of the offerings of nymph and shep-
herd than of human sacrifice, was in a strange contrast to this whirlwind rush of stern, armed men. The
westering sun pierced the subdued light and the
tremor of leaves with yellow lances; birds started into
song on blue and dove-like wings, and on either side
of the trail of this vengeful storm could be heard the

murmur of hidden and tranquil waters. In a few moments they would be on the open ridge, whence sloped the common turnpike to "Sawyer's," a mile away. It was the custom of returning cavalcades to take this hill at headlong speed, with shouts and cries that heralded their coming. They withheld the latter that day, as inconsistent with their dignity; but, emerging from the wood, swept silently like an avalanche down the slope. They were well under way, looking only to their horses, when the second captive slipped his right arm from the bonds and succeeded in grasping the reins that lay trailing on the horse's neck. A sudden vaquero jerk, which the well-trained animal understood, threw him on his haunches with his forelegs firmly planted on the slope. The rest of the cavalcade swept on; the man who was leading the captive's horse by the riata, thinking only of another accident, dropped the line to save himself from being dragged backwards from his horse. The captive wheeled, and the next moment was galloping furiously up the slope.

It was the work of a moment; a trained horse and an experienced hand. The cavalcade had covered nearly fifty yards before they could pull up; the freed captive had covered half that distance uphill. The road was so narrow that only two shots could be fired, and these broke dust two yards ahead of the fugitive. They had not dared to fire low; the horse was the more valuable animal. The fugitive knew this in his extremity also, and would have gladly taken a shot in his own leg to spare that of his horse. Five men were detached to recapture or kill him. The latter seemed inevitable. But he had calculated his chances; before they could reload he had reached the woods again;

winding in and out between the pillared tree trunks, he offered no mark. They knew his horse was superior to their own; at the end of two hours they returned, for he had disappeared without track or trail. The end was briefly told in the "Sierra Record:"—

"Red Pete, the notorious horse-thief, who had so long eluded justice, was captured and hung by the Sawyer's Crossing Vigilantes last week; his confederate, unfortunately, escaped on a valuable horse belonging to Judge Boompointer. The judge had refused one thousand dollars for the horse only a week before. As the thief, who is still at large, would find it difficult to dispose of so valuable an animal without detection, the chances are against either of them turning up again."

Salomy Jane watched the cavalcade until it had disappeared. Then she became aware that her brief popularity had passed. Mrs. Red Pete, in stormy hysterics, had included her in a sweeping denunciation of the whole universe, possibly for simulating an emotion in which she herself was deficient. The other women hated her for her momentary exaltation above them; only the children still admired her as one who had undoubtedly "canoodled" with a man "a-going to be hung"—a daring flight beyond their wildest ambition. Salomy Jane accepted the change with charming unconcern. She put on her yellow nankeen sunbonnet, —a hideous affair that would have ruined any other woman, but which only enhanced the piquancy of her fresh brunette skin,—tied the strings, letting the blueblack braids escape below its frilled curtain behind, jumped on her mustang with a casual display of agile

ankles in shapely white stockings, whistled to the
hound, and waving her hand with a "So long,
sonny!" to the lately bereft but admiring nephew,
flapped and fluttered away in her short brown holland
gown.

Her father's house was four miles distant. Contrasted with the cabin she had just quitted, it was a
superior dwelling, with a long "lean-to" at the rear,
which brought the eaves almost to the ground and
made it look like a low triangle. It had a long barn
and cattle sheds, for Madison Clay was a "great"
stock-raiser and the owner of a "quarter section." It
had a sitting-room and a parlor organ, whose transpor-
tation thither had been a marvel of "packing." These
things were supposed to give Salomy Jane an undue
importance, but the girl's reserve and inaccessibility
to local advances were rather the result of a cool, lazy
temperament and the preoccupation of a large, protecting admiration for her father, for some years a
widower. For Mr. Madison Clay's life had been threatened in one or two feuds,—it was said, not without
cause,—and it is possible that the pathetic spectacle
of her father doing his visiting with a shotgun may
have touched her closely and somewhat prejudiced
her against the neighboring masculinity. The thought
that cattle, horses, and "quarter section" would one
day be hers did not disturb her calm. As for Mr. Clay,
he accepted her as housewifely, though somewhat
"interfering," and, being one of "his own womankind,"
therefore not without some degree of merit.

"Wot's this yer I'm hearin' of your doin's over at
Red Pete's? Honeyfoglin' with a horse-thief, eh?" said
Mr. Clay two days later at breakfast.

"I reckon you heard about the straight thing, then," said Salomy Jane unconcernedly, without looking round.

"What do you kalkilate Rube will say to it? What are you goin' to tell *him?*" said Mr. Clay sarcastically.

"Rube," or Reuben Waters, was a swain supposed to be favored particularly by Mr. Clay. Salomy Jane looked up.

"I'll tell him that when *he's* on his way to be hung, I'll kiss him,—not till then," said the young lady brightly.

This delightful witticism suited the paternal humor, and Mr. Clay smiled; but, nevertheless, he frowned a moment afterwards.

"But this yer hoss-thief got away arter all, and that's a hoss of a different color," he said grimly.

Salomy Jane put down her knife and fork. This was certainly a new and different phase of the situation. She had never thought of it before, and, strangely enough, for the first time she became interested in the man. "Got away?" she repeated. "Did they let him off?"

"Not much," said her father briefly. "Slipped his cords, and going down the grade pulled up short, just like a vaquero agin a lassoed bull, almost draggin' the man leadin' him off his hoss, and he skyuted up the grade. For that matter, on that hoss o' Judge Boompointer's he mout have dragged the whole posse of 'em down on their knees ef he liked! Sarved 'em right, too. Instead of stringin' him up afore the door, or shootin' him on sight, they must allow to take him down afore the hull committee 'for an example.' 'Example' be blowed! Ther' 's example enough when some stranger comes unbeknownst slap onter a man hanged to a tree and plugged full of holes. *That's* an example, and *he* knows what it means. Wot more do ye want? But then those Vigilantes is allus clingin' and hangin' onter some mere scrap o' the law they're pretendin' to despise. It makes me sick! Why, when Jake Myers shot your ole Aunt Viney's second husband, and I laid in wait for Jake afterwards in the Butternut Hollow, did *I* tie him to his hoss and fetch him down to your Aunt Viney's cabin 'for an example' before I plugged him? No!" in deep disgust. "No! Why, I just meandered through the woods, careless-like, till he comes out, and I just rode up to him, and I said"—

But Salomy Jane had heard her father's story before. Even one's dearest relatives are apt to become tiresome in narration. "I know, Dad," she interrupted; "but this yer man,—this hoss-thief,—did *he* get clean away without gettin' hurt at all?"

"He did, and unless he's fool enough to sell the hoss, he kin keep away, too. So ye see, ye can't ladle out purp stuff about a 'dyin' stranger' to Rube. He won't swaller it."

"All the same, Dad," returned the girl cheerfully, "I reckon to say it, and say *more;* I'll tell him that ef *he* manages to get away too, I'll marry him—there! But ye don't ketch Rube takin' any such risks in gettin' ketched, or in gettin' away arter!"

Madison Clay smiled grimly, pushed back his chair, rose, dropped a perfunctory kiss on his daughter's hair, and, taking his shotgun from the corner, departed on a peaceful Samaritan mission to a cow who had dropped a calf in the far pasture. Inclined as he was to Reuben's wooing from his eligibility as to property, he was conscious that he was sadly deficient in certain qualities inherent in the Clay family. It certainly would be a kind of *mésalliance*.

Left to herself, Salomy Jane stared a long while at the coffeepot, and then called the two squaws who assisted her in her household duties, to clear away the things while she went up to her own room to make her bed. Here she was confronted with a possible prospect of that proverbial bed she might be making in her willfulness, and on which she must lie, in the photograph of a somewhat serious young man of refined features—Reuben Waters—stuck in her window-frame. Salomy Jane smiled over her last witticism regarding him and enjoyed it, like your true humorist, and then, catching sight of her own handsome face in the little mirror, smiled again. But wasn't it funny about that horse-thief getting off after all? Good Lordy! Fancy Reuben hearing he was alive and going round with that kiss of hers set on his lips! She laughed again, a little more abstractedly. And he had returned it like a man, holding her tight and almost breathless, and he going to be hung the next minute! Salomy Jane had been kissed at other times, by force, chance, or stratagem. In a certain ingenuous forfeit game of the locality, known as "I'm apinin'," many had "pined" for a "sweet kiss" from Salomy Jane, which she had yielded in a sense of honor and fair play. She had never been kissed like this before—she would never again; and yet the man was alive! And behold, she could see in the mirror that she was blushing!

She should hardly know him again. A young man with very bright eyes, a flushed and sunburnt cheek, a kind of fixed look in the face, and no beard; no, none that she could feel. Yet he was not at all like Reuben, not a bit. She took Reuben's picture from the window, and laid it on her workbox. And to think she did not even know this young man's name! That was queer. To be kissed by a man whom she might never know! Of course he knew hers. She wondered if he remembered it and her. But of course he was so glad to get off with his life that he never thought of anything else. Yet she did not give more than four or five minutes to these speculations, and, like a sensible girl, thought of something else. Once again, however, in opening the closet, she found the brown holland gown she had worn on the day before; thought it very unbecoming, and regretted that she had not worn her best gown on her visit to Red Pete's cottage. On such an occasion she really might have been more impressive.

When her father came home that night she asked him the news. No, they had *not* captured the second horse-thief, who was still at large. Judge Boompointer talked of invoking the aid of the despised law. It remained, then, to see whether the horse-thief was fool enough to try to get rid of the animal. Red Pete's body had been delivered to his widow. Perhaps it would only be neighborly for Salomy Jane to ride over to the funeral. But Salomy Jane did not take to the suggestion kindly, nor yet did she explain to her father that, as the other man was still living, she did not care to undergo a second disciplining at the widow's hands. Nevertheless, she contrasted her situation with that of the widow with a new and singular satisfaction. It might have been Red Pete who had escaped. But he had not the grit of the nameless one. She had already settled his heroic quality.

"Ye ain't harkenin' to me, Salomy."

Salomy Jane started.

"Here I'm askin' ye if ye've see that hound Phil Larrabee sneaking by yer to-day?"

Salomy Jane had not. But she became interested and self-reproachful, for she knew that Phil Larrabee was one of her father's enemies. "He wouldn't dare to go by here unless he knew you were out," she said quickly.

"That's what gets me," he said, scratching his grizzled head. "I've been kind o' thinkin' o' him all day, and one of them Chinamen said he saw him at Sawyer's Crossing. He was a kind of friend o' Pete's wife. That's why I thought yer might find out ef he'd been there." Salomy Jane grew more self-reproachful at her father's self-interest in her "neighborliness." "But that ain't all," continued Mr. Clay. "Thar was tracks over the far pasture that warn't mine. I followed them, and they went round and round the house two or three times, ez ef they mout hev bin prowlin', and then I lost 'em in the woods again. It's just like that sneakin' hound Larrabee to hev bin lyin' in wait for me and afraid to meet a man fair and square in the open."

"You just lie low, dad, for a day or two more, and let me do a little prowlin'," said the girl, with sympathetic indignation in her dark eyes. "Ef it's that skunk, I'll spot him soon enough and let you know whar he's hiding."

"You'll just stay where ye are, Salomy," said her father decisively. "This ain't no woman's work—

though I ain't sayin' you haven't got more head for it than some men I know."

Nevertheless, that night, after her father had gone to bed, Salomy Jane sat by the open window of the sitting-room in an apparent attitude of languid contemplation, but alert and intent of eye and ear. It was a fine moonlit night. Two pines near the door, solitary pickets of the serried ranks of distant forest, cast long shadows like paths to the cottage, and sighed their spiced breath in the windows. For there was no frivolity of vine or flower round Salomy Jane's bower. The clearing was too recent, the life too practical, for vanities like these. But the moon added a vague elusiveness to everything, softened the rigid outlines of the sheds, gave shadows to the lidless windows, and touched with merciful indirectness the hideous débris of refuse gravel and the gaunt scars of burnt vegetation before the door. Even Salomy Jane was affected by it, and exhaled something between a sigh and a yawn with the breath of the pines. Then she suddenly sat upright.

Her quick ear had caught a faint "click, click," in the direction of the wood; her quicker instinct and rustic training enabled her to determine that it was the ring of a horse's shoe on flinty ground; her knowledge of the locality told her it came from the spot where the trail passed over an outcrop of flint, scarcely a quarter of a mile from where she sat, and within the clearing. It was no errant "stock," for the foot was *shod* with iron; it was a mounted trespasser by night, and boded no good to a man like Clay.

She rose, threw her shawl over her head, more for disguise than shelter, and passed out of the door. A sudden impulse made her seize her father's shotgun from the corner where it stood,—not that she feared any danger to herself, but that it was an excuse. She made directly for the wood, keeping in the shadow of the pines as long as she could. At the fringe she halted; whoever was there must pass her before reaching the house.

Then there seemed to be a suspense of all nature. Everything was deadly still—even the moonbeams appeared no longer tremulous; soon there was a rustle as of some stealthy animal among the ferns, and then a dismounted man stepped into the moonlight. It was the horse-thief—the man she had kissed!

For a wild moment a strange fancy seized her usually sane intellect and stirred her temperate blood. The news they had told her was *not* true; he had been hung, and this was his ghost! He looked as white and spirit-like in the moonlight, dressed in the same clothes, as when she saw him last. He had evidently seen her approaching, and moved quickly to meet her. But in his haste he stumbled slightly; she reflected suddenly that ghosts did not stumble, and a feel of relief came over her. And it was no assassin of her father that had been prowling around—only this unhappy fugitive. A momentary color came into her cheek; her coolness and hardihood returned; it was with a tinge of sauciness in her voice that she said:—

"I reckoned you were a ghost."

"I mout have been," he said, looking at her fixedly; "but I reckon I'd have come back here all the same."

"It's a little riskier comin' back alive," she said, with a levity that died on her lips, for a singular nervousness, half fear and half expectation, was beginning to take the place of her relief of a moment ago. "Then it was *you* who was prowlin' round and makin' tracks in the far pasture?"

"Yes; I came straight here when I got away."

She felt his eyes were burning her, but did not dare to raise her own. "Why," she began, hesitated, and ended vaguely. "*How* did you get here?"

"You helped me!"

"I?"

"Yes. That kiss you gave me put life into me— gave me strength to get away. I swore to myself I'd come back and thank you, alive or dead."

Every word he said she could have anticipated, so plain the situation seemed to her now. And every word he said she knew was the truth. Yet her cool common sense struggled against it.

"What's the use of your escaping, ef you're comin' back here to be ketched again?" she said pertly.

He drew a little nearer to her, but seemed to her the more awkward as she resumed her self-possession. His voice, too, was broken, as if by exhaustion, as he said, catching his breath at intervals:—

"I'll tell you. You did more for me than you think. You made another man o' me. I never had a man, woman, or child do to me what you did. I never had a friend—only a pal like Red Pete, who picked me up 'on shares.' I want to quit this yer—what I'm doin'. I want to begin by doin' the square thing to you"— He stopped, breathed hard, and then said brokenly, "My hoss is over thar, staked out. I want to give him to you. Judge Boompointer will give you a thousand dollars for him. I ain't lyin'; it's God's truth! I saw it on the handbill agin a tree. Take him, and I'll get away afoot. Take him. It's the only thing I can do for you, and I know it don't half pay for what you did. Take it; your father can get a reward for you, if you can't."

Such were the ethics of this strange locality that neither the man who made the offer nor the girl to whom it was made was struck by anything that seemed illogical or indelicate, or at all inconsistent with justice or the horse-thief's real conversion. Salomy Jane nevertheless dissented, from another and weaker reason.

"I don't want your hoss, though I reckon dad might; but you're just starvin'. I'll get suthin'." She turned towards the house.

"Say you'll take the hoss first," he said, grasping her hand. At the touch she felt herself coloring and struggled, expecting perhaps another kiss. But he dropped her hand. She turned again with a saucy gesture, said, "Hol' on; I'll come right back," and slipped away, the mere shadow of a coy and flying nymph in the moonlight, until she reached the house.

Here she not only procured food and whiskey, but added a long dust-coat and hat of her father's to her burden. They would serve as a disguise for him and hide that heroic figure, which she thought everybody must now know as she did. Then she rejoined him breathlessly. But he put the food and whiskey aside.

"Listen," he said; "I've turned the hoss into your corral. You'll find him there in the morning, and no one will know but that he got lost and joined the other horses."

Then she burst out. "But you—*you*—what will become of you? You'll be ketched!"

"I'll manage to get away," he said in a low voice, "ef—ef"—

"Ef what?" she said tremblingly.

"Ef you'll put the heart in me again,—as you did!" he gasped.

She tried to laugh—to move away. She could do neither. Suddenly he caught her in his arms, with a long kiss, which she returned again and again. Then they stood embraced as they had embraced two days before, but no longer the same. For the cool, lazy Salomy Jane had been transformed into another woman —a passionate, clinging savage. Perhaps something of her father's blood had surged within her at that supreme moment. The man stood erect and determined.

"Wot's your name?" she whispered quickly. It was a woman's quickest way of defining her feelings.

"Dart."

"Yer first name?"

"Jack."

"Let me go now, Jack. Lie low in the woods till to-morrow sunup. I'll come again."

He released her. Yet she lingered a moment. "Put on those things," she said, with a sudden happy flash of eyes and teeth, "and lie close till I come." And then she sped away home.

But midway up the distance she felt her feet going slower, and something at her heartstrings seemed to be pulling her back. She stopped, turned, and glanced to where he had been standing. Had she seen him then, she might have returned. But he had disappeared. She gave her first sigh, and then ran quickly again. It must be nearly ten o'clock! It was not very long to morning!

She was within a few steps of her own door, when the sleeping woods and silent air appeared to suddenly awake with a sharp "crack!"

She stopped, paralyzed. Another "crack!" followed, that echoed over to the far corral. She recalled herself instantly and dashed off wildly to the woods again.

As she ran she thought of one thing only. He had been "dogged" by one of his old pursuers and attacked. But there were two shots, and he was unarmed. Suddenly she remembered that she had left her father's gun standing against the tree where they were talking. Thank God! she may again have saved him. She ran to the tree; the gun was gone. She ran hither and thither, dreading at every step to fall upon his lifeless body. A new thought struck her; she ran to the corral. The horse was not there! He must have been able to regain it, and escaped, *after* the shots had been fired. She drew a long breath of relief, but it was caught up in an apprehension of alarm. Her father, awakened from his sleep by the shots, was hurriedly approaching her.

"What's up now, Salomy Jane?" he demanded excitedly.

"Nothin'," said the girl, with an effort. "Nothin', at least, that *I* can find." She was usually truthful because fearless, and a lie stuck in her throat; but she was no longer fearless, thinking of *him.* "I wasn't abed; so I ran out as soon as I heard the shots fired," she answered in return to his curious gaze.

"And you've hid my gun somewhere where it can't be found," he said reproachfully. "Ef it was that sneak Larrabee, and he fired them shots to lure me out, he might have potted me, without a show, a dozen times in the last five minutes."

She had not thought since of her father's enemy! It

might indeed have been he who had attacked Jack. But she made a quick point of the suggestion. "Run in, Dad, run in and find the gun; you've got no show out here without it." She seized him by the shoulders from behind, shielding him from the woods, and hurried him, half expostulating, half struggling, to the house.

But there no gun was to be found. It was strange; it must have been mislaid in some corner! Was he sure he had not left it in the barn? But no matter now. The danger was over; the Larrabee trick had failed; he must go to bed now, and in the morning they would make a search together. At the same time she had inwardly resolved to rise before him and make another search of the wood, and perhaps—fearful joy as she recalled her promise!—find Jack alive and well, awaiting her!

Salomy Jane slept little that night, nor did her father. But towards morning he fell into a tired man's slumber until the sun was well up the horizon. Far different was it with his daughter: she lay with her face to the window, her head half lifted to catch every sound, from the creaking of the sun-warped shingles above her head to the far-off moan of the rising wind in the pine-trees. Sometimes she fell into a breathless, half-ecstatic trance, living over every moment of the stolen interview; feeling the fugitive's arm still around her, his kisses on her lips; hearing his whispered voice in her ears—the birth of her new life! This was followed again by a period of agonizing dread—that he might even then be lying, his life ebbing away, in the woods, with her name on his lips, and she resting here inactive, until she half started from her bed to go to his succor. And this went on until a pale opal glow

came into the sky, followed by a still paler pink on
the summit of the white Sierras, when she rose and
hurriedly began to dress. Still so sanguine was her
hope of meeting him, that she lingered yet a moment
to select the brown holland skirt and yellow sunbonnet
she had worn when she first saw him. And she had
only seen him twice! Only *twice!* It would be cruel,
too cruel, not to see him again!

She crept softly down the stairs, listening to the long-
drawn breathing of her father in his bedroom, and
then, by the light of a guttering candle, scrawled a
note to him, begging him not to trust himself out of the
house until she returned from her search, and leaving
the note open on the table, swiftly ran out into the
growing day.

Three hours afterwards Mr. Madison Clay awoke to
the sound of loud knocking. At first this forced itself
upon his consciousness as his daughter's regular morning summons, and was responded to by a grunt of
recognition and a nestling closer in the blankets. Then
he awoke with a start and a muttered oath, remember-
ing the events of last night, and his intention to get
up early, and rolled out of bed. Becoming aware by
this time that the knocking was at the outer door, and
hearing the shout of a familiar voice, he hastily pulled
on his boots, his jean trousers, and fastening a single suspender over his shoulder as he clattered downstairs, stood in the lower room. The door was open,
and waiting upon the threshold was his kinsman, an
old ally in many a blood-feud—Breckenridge Clay!

"You *are* a cool one, Mad!" said the latter in half-
admiring indignation.

"What's up?" said the bewildered Madison.

"*You* ought to be, and scootin' out o' this," said Breckenridge grimly. "It's all very well to 'know nothin';' but here Phil Larrabee's friends hev just picked him up, drilled through with slugs and deader nor a crow, and now they're lettin' loose Larrabee's two half-brothers on you. And you must go like a derned fool and leave these yer things behind you in the bresh," he went on querulously, lifting Madison Clay's dust-coat, hat, and shotgun from his horse, which stood saddled at the door. "Luckily I picked them up in the woods comin' here. Ye ain't got more than time to get over the state line and among your folks thar afore they'll be down on you. Hustle, old man! What are you gawkin' and starin' at?"

Madison Clay had stared amazed and bewildered —horror-stricken. The incidents of the past night for the first time flashed upon him clearly—hopelessly! The shots; his finding Salomy Jane alone in the woods; her confusion and anxiety to rid herself of him; the disappearance of the shutgun; and now this new discovery of the taking of his hat and coat for a disguise! *She* had killed Phil Larrabee in that disguise, after provoking his first harmless shot! She, his own child, Salomy Jane, had disgraced herself by a man's crime; had disgraced him by usurping his right, and taking a mean advantage, by deceit, of a foe!

"Gimme that gun," he said hoarsely.

Breckenridge handed him the gun in wonder and slowly gathering suspicion. Madison examined nipple and muzzle; one barrel had been discharged. It was true! The gun dropped from his hand.

"Look here, old man," said Breckenridge, with a darkening face, "there's bin no foul play here. Thar's bin no hiring of men, no deputy to do this job. *You* did it fair and square—yourself?"

"Yes, by God!" burst out Madison Clay, in a hoarse voice. "Who says I didn't?"

Reassured, yet believing that Madison Clay had nerved himself for the act by an over-draught of whiskey, which had affected his memory, Breckenridge said curtly, "Then wake up and 'lite' out, ef ye want me to stand by you."

"Go to the corral and pick me out a hoss," said Madison slowly, yet not without a certain dignity of manner. "I've suthin' to say to Salomy Jane afore I go." He was holding her scribbled note, which he had just discovered, in his shaking hand.

Struck by his kinsman's manner, and knowing the dependent relations of father and daughter, Breckenridge nodded and hurried away. Left to himself, Madison Clay ran his fingers through his hair, and straightened out the paper on which Salomy Jane had scrawled her note, turned it over, and wrote on the back:—

You might have told me you did it, and not leave your ole father to find it out how you disgraced yourself with him, too, by a low-down, underhanded, woman's trick! I've said I done it, and took the blame myself, and all the sneakiness of it that folks suspect. If I get away alive—and I don't care much which—you needn't foller. The house and stock are yours; but you ain't any longer the daughter of your disgraced father,
MADISON CLAY.

He had scarcely finished the note when, with a

clatter of hoofs and a led horse, Breckenridge reappeared at the door elate and triumphant. "You're in nigger luck, Mad! I found that stole hoss of Judge Boompointer's had got away and strayed among your stock in the corral. Take him and you're safe; he can't be outrun this side of the state line."

"I ain't no hoss-thief," said Madison grimly.

"Nobody sez ye are, but you'd be wuss—a fool— ef you didn't take him. I'm testimony that you found him among your hosses; I'll tell Judge Boompointer you've got him, and ye kin send him back when you're safe. The judge will be mighty glad to get him back, and call it quits. So ef you've writ to Salomy Jane, come."

Madison Clay no longer hesitated. Salomy Jane might return at any moment,—it would be part of her "fool womanishness,"—and he was in no mood to see her before a third party. He laid the note on the table, gave a hurried glance around the house, which he grimly believed he was leaving forever, and, striding to the door, leaped on the stolen horse, and swept away with his kinsman.

But that note lay for a week undisturbed on the table in full view of the open door. The house was invaded by leaves, pine cones, birds, and squirrels during the hot, silent, empty days, and at night by shy, stealthy creatures, but never again, day or night, by any of the Clay family. It was known in the district that Clay had flown across the state line, his daughter was believed to have joined him the next day, and the house was supposed to be locked up. It lay off the main road, and few passed that way. The starving cattle in the corral at last broke bounds and spread over the woods. And one night a stronger blast than usual swept through the house and carried the note from the table to the floor, where, whirled into a crack in the flooring, it slowly rotted.

But though the sting of her father's reproach was spared her, Salomy Jane had no need of the letter to know what had happened. For as she entered the woods in the dim light of that morning, she saw the figure of Dart gliding from the shadow of a pine towards her. The unaffected cry of joy that rose from her lips died there as she caught sight of his face in the open light.

"You are hurt," she said, clutching his arm passionately.

"No," he said. "But I wouldn't mind that if"—

"You're thinkin' I was afeard to come back last night when I heard the shootin', but I *did* come," she went on feverishly. "I ran back here when I heard the two shots, but you were gone. I went to the corral, but your hoss wasn't there, and I thought you'd got away."

"I *did* get away," said Dart gloomily. "I killed the man, thinkin' he was huntin' *me,* and forgettin' I was disguised. He thought I was your father."

"Yes," said the girl joyfully, "he was after dad, and *you*—you killed him." She again caught his hand admiringly.

But he did not respond. Possibly there were points of honor which this horse-thief felt vaguely with her father. "Listen," he said grimly. "Others think it was your father killed him. When *I* did it—for he fired at me first—I ran to the corral again and took my hoss, thinkin' I might be follered. I made a clear circuit of the house, and when I found he was the only one, and no one was follerin', I come back here and took off my disguise. Then I heard his friends find him in the wood, and I know they suspected your father. And then another man come through the woods while I was hidin' and found the clothes and took them away." He stopped and stared at her gloomily.

But all this was unintelligible to the girl. "Dad would have got the better of him ef you hadn't," she said eagerly, "so what's the difference?"

"All the same," he said gloomily, "I must take his place."

She did not understand, but turned her head to her master. "Then you'll go back with me and tell him *all?*" she said obediently.

"Yes," he said.

She put her hand in his, and they crept out of the wood together. She foresaw a thousand difficulties, but, chiefest of all, that he did not love as she did. *She* would not have taken these risks against their happiness.

But alas for ethics and heroism. As they were issuing from the wood they heard the sound of galloping hoofs, and had barely time to hide themselves before Madison Clay, on the stolen horse of Judge Boompointer, swept past them with his kinsman.

Salomy Jane turned to her lover.

And here I might, as a moral romancer, pause, leaving the guilty, passionate girl eloped with her disreputable lover, destined to lifelong shame and misery, misunderstood to the last by a criminal, fastidious parent. But I am confronted by certain facts, on which this romance is based. A month later a handbill was posted on one of the sentinel pines, announcing that the property would be sold by auction to the highest bidder by Mrs. John Dart, daughter of Madison Clay, Esq., and it was sold accordingly. Still later—by ten years—the chronicler of these pages visited a certain "stock" or "breeding farm," in the "Blue Grass Country," famous for the popular racers it has produced. He was told that the owner was the "best judge of horseflesh in the country." "Small wonder," added his informant, "for they say as a young man out in California he was a horse-thief, and only saved himself by eloping with some rich farmer's daughter. But he's a straight-out and respectable man now, whose word about horses can't be bought; and as for his wife, *she's* a beauty! To see her at the 'Springs,' rigged out in the latest fashion, you'd never think she had ever lived out of New York or wasn't the wife of one of its millionaires."

THE POET OF SIERRA FLAT

As the enterprising editor of the "Sierra Flat
Record" stood at his case setting type for his next
week's paper, he could not help hearing the woodpeckers who were busy on the roof above his head. It
occurred to him that possibly the birds had not yet
learned to recognize in the rude structure any improvement on Nature, and this idea pleased him so much
that he incorporated it in the editorial article which
he was then doubly composing. For the editor was
also printer of the "Record"; and although that remarkable journal was reputed to exert a power felt
through all Calaveras and a great part of Tuolumne
County, strict economy was one of the conditions of
its beneficent existence.

Thus preoccupied, he was startled by the sudden irruption of a small roll of manuscript, which was
thrown through the open door and fell at his feet. He
walked quickly to the threshold and looked down the
tangled trail which led to the highroad. But there was
nothing to suggest the presence of his mysterious contributor. A hare limped slowly away, a green-and-
gold lizard paused upon a pine stump, the woodpeck-

ers ceased their work. So complete had been his sylvan seclusion, that he found it difficult to connect any human agency with the act; rather the hare seemed to have an inexpressibly guilty look, the woodpeckers to maintain a significant silence, and the lizard to be conscience-stricken into stone.

An examination of the manuscript, however, corrected this injustice to defenseless Nature. It was evidently of human origin,—being verse, and of exceeding bad quality. The editor laid it aside. As he did so he thought he saw a face at the window. Sallying out in some indignation, he penetrated the surrounding thicket in every direction, but his search was as fruitless as before. The poet, if it were he, was gone.

A few days after this the editorial seclusion was invaded by voices of alternate expostulation and entreaty. Stepping to the door, the editor was amazed at beholding Mr. Morgan McCorkle, a well-known citizen of Angel's and a subscriber to the "Record," in the act of urging, partly by force and partly by argument, an awkward young man toward the building. When he had finally effected his object, and, as it were, safely landed his prize in a chair, Mr. McCorkle took off his hat, carefully wiped the narrow isthmus of forehead which divided his black brows from his stubby hair, and, with an explanatory wave of his hand toward his reluctant companion, said, "A borned poet, and the cussedest fool you ever seed!"

Accepting the editor's smile as a recognition of the introduction, Mr. McCorkle panted and went on: "Didn't want to come! 'Mister Editor don't want to see me, Morg,' sez he. 'Milt,' sez I, 'he do; a borned poet like you and a gifted genius like he oughter come

together sociable!' And I fetched him. Ah, will yer?"
The born poet had, after exhibiting signs of great distress, started to run. But Mr. McCorkle was down upon him instantly, seizing him by his long linen coat, and settled him back in his chair. " 'T ain't no use stampeding. Yer ye are and yer ye stays. For yer a borned poet,—ef ye are as shy as a jackass rabbit. Look it 'im now!"

He certainly was not an attractive picture. There was hardly a notable feature in his weak face, except his eyes, which were moist and shy, and not unlike the animal to which Mr. McCorkle had compared him. It was the face that the editor had seen at the window.

"Knowed him for fower year,—since he war a boy," continued Mr. McCorkle in a loud whisper. "Allers the same, bless you! Can jerk a rhyme as easy as turnin' jack. Never had any eddication; lived out in Missooray all his life. But he's chock full o' poetry. On'y this mornin' sez I to him,—he camps along o' me,—'Milt!' sez I, 'are breakfast ready?' and he up and answers back quite peart and chipper, 'The breakfast it is ready, and the birds is singing free, and it's risin' in the dawnin' light is happiness to me!' When a man," said Mr. McCorkle, dropping his voice with deep solemnity, "gets off things like them, without any call to do it, and handlin' flapjacks over a cookstove at the same time,—that man's a borned poet."

There was an awkward pause. Mr. McCorkle beamed patronizingly on his protégé. The born poet looked as if he were meditating another flight,—not a metaphorical one. The editor asked if he could do anything for them.

"In course you can," responded Mr. McCorkle, "that's jest it. Milt, where's that poetry?"

The editor's countenance fell as the poet produced from his pocket a roll of manuscript. He, however, took it mechanically and glanced over it. It was evidently a duplicate of the former mysterious contribution.

The editor then spoke briefly but earnestly. I regret that I cannot recall his exact words, but it appeared that never before, in the history of the "Record," had the pressure been so great upon its columns. Matters of paramount importance, deeply affecting the material progress of Sierra, questions touching the absolute integrity of Calaveras and Tuolumne as social communities, were even now waiting expression. Weeks, nay, months, must elapse before that pressure would be removed, and the "Record" could grapple with any but the sternest of topics. Again, the editor had noticed with pain the absolute decline of poetry in the foothills of the Sierras. Even the works of Byron and Moore attracted no attention in Dutch Flat, and a prejudice seemed to exist against Tennyson in Grass Valley. But the editor was not without hope for the future. In the course of four or five years, when the country was settled—

"What would be the cost to print this yer?" interrupted Mr. McCorkle quietly.

"About fifty dollars, as an advertisement," responded the editor with cheerful alacrity.

Mr. McCorkle placed the sum in the editor's hand. "Yer see thet's what I sez to Milt. 'Milt,' sez I, 'pay as you go, for you are a borned poet. Hevin' no call to write, but doin' it free and spontaneous like, in course you pays. Thet's why Mr. Editor never printed your poetry.' "

"What name shall I put to it?" asked the editor.

"Milton."

It was the first word that the born poet had spoken during the interview, and his voice was so very sweet and musical that the editor looked at him curiously, and wondered if he had a sister.

"Milton! Is that all?"

"Thet's his furst name," exclaimed Mr. McCorkle.

The editor here suggested that as there had been another poet of that name—

"Milt might be took for him! Thet's bad," reflected Mr. McCorkle with simple gravity. "Well, put down his full name,—Milton Chubbuck."

The editor made a note of the fact. "I'll set it up now," he said. This was also a hint that the interview was ended. The poet and patron, arm in arm, drew towards the door. "In next week's paper," said the editor smilingly, in answer to the child-like look of inquiry in the eyes of the poet, and in another moment they were gone.

The editor was as good as his word. He straightway betook himself to his case, and, unrolling the manuscript, began his task. The woodpeckers on the roof recommenced theirs, and in a few moments the former sylvan seclusion was restored. There was no sound in the barren, barn-like room but the birds above, and below the click of the composing-rule as the editor marshaled the types into lines in his stick, and arrayed them in solid columns on the galley. Whatever might have been his opinion of the copy before him, there was no indication of it in his face, which wore the stolid indifference of his craft. Perhaps this was unfortunate, for as the day wore on and the level rays of the sun began to pierce the adjacent thicket, they sought out and discovered an anxious ambush figure drawn up beside the editor's window,— a figure that had sat there motionless for hours. Within, the editor worked on as steadily and impassively as Fate. And without, the born poet of Sierra Flat sat and watched him as waiting its decree.

The effect of the poem on Sierra Flat was remarkable and unprecedented. The absolute vileness of its doggerel, the gratuitous imbecility of its thought, and above all the crowning audacity of the fact that it was the work of a citizen and published in the county paper, brought it instantly into popularity. For many months Calaveras had languished for a sensation; since the last Vigilance Committee nothing had transpired to dispel the listless ennui begotten of stagnant business and growing civilization. In more prosperous moments the office of the "Record" would have been simply gutted and the editor deported; at present the paper was in such demand that the edition was speedily exhausted. In brief, the poem of Mr. Milton Chubbuck came like a special providence to Sierra Flat. It was read by camp-fires, in lonely cabins, in flaring barrooms and noisy saloons, and declaimed from the boxes of stage-coaches. It was sung in Poker Flat with the addition of a local chorus, and danced as an unhallowed rhythmic dance by the Pyrrhic phalanx of One Horse Gulch, known as "The Festive Stags of Calaveras." Some unhappy ambiguities of expression gave rise to many new readings, notes, and commentaries, which, I regret to state, were more often marked by ingenuity, than delicacy of thought or expression.

Never before did poet acquire such sudden local reputation. From the seclusion of McCorkle's cabin and the obscurity of culinary labors he was haled forth into the glowing sunshine of Fame. The name of Chubbuck was written in letters of chalk on unpainted walls and carved with a pick on the sides of tunnels. A drink known variously as "The Chubbuck Tranquilizer" or "The Chubbuck Exalter" was dispensed at the bars. For some weeks a rude design for a Chubbuck statue, made up of illustrations from circus and melodeon posters, representing the genius of Calaveras in brief skirts on a flying steed in the act of crowning the poet Chubbuck, was visible at Keeler's Ferry. The poet himself was overborne with invitations to drink and extravagant congratulations. The meeting between Colonel Starbottle of Siskiyou and Chubbuck, as previously arranged by our "Boston," late of Roaring Camp, is said to have been indescribably affecting. The Colonel embraced him unsteadily. "I could not return to my constituents at Siskiyou, sir, if this hand, which has grasped that of the gifted Prentice and the lamented Poe, should not have been honored by the touch of the godlike Chubbuck. Gentlemen, American literature is looking up. Thank you! I will take sugar in mine." It was "Boston" who indited letters of congratulations from H. W. Longfellow, Tennyson, and Browning to Mr. Chubbuck, deposited them in the Sierra Flat post-office, and obligingly consented to dictate the replies.

The simple faith and unaffected delight with which these manifestations were received by the poet and his patron might have touched the hearts of these grim masters of irony, but for the sudden and equal development in both of the variety of weak natures. Mr. McCorkle basked in the popularity of his protégé, and became alternately supercilious or patronizing toward the dwellers of Sierra Flat; while the poet, with hair carefully oiled and curled, and bedecked with cheap jewelry and flaunting neck-handkerchief, paraded himself before the single hotel. As may be imagined, this new disclosure of weakness afforded intense satisfaction to Sierra Flat, gave another lease of popularity to the poet, and suggested another idea to the facetious "Boston."

At that time a young lady popularly and professionally known as the "California Pet" was performing to enthusiastic audiences in the interior. Her specialty lay in the personation of youthful masculine character; as a *gamin* of the street she was irresistible, as a Negro-dancer she carried the honest miner's heart by storm. A saucy, pretty brunette, she had preserved a wonderful moral reputation even under the Jove-like advances of showers of gold that greeted her appearance on the stage at Sierra Flat. A prominent and delighted member of that audience was Milton Chubbuck. He attended every night. Every day he lingered at the door of the Union Hotel for a glimpse of the "California Pet." It was not long before he received a note from her,—in "Boston's" most popular and approved female hand,—acknowledging his admiration. It was not long before "Boston" was called upon to indite a suitable reply. At last, in furtherance of his facetious design, it became necessary for "Boston" to call upon the young actress herself and secure her personal participation. To her he unfolded a plan, the successful carrying out of which he felt would secure his fame to posterity as a practical humorist. The "California Pet's" black eyes sparkled approvingly and mischievously. She only stipulated that she should see the man first,—a concession to her feminine weakness which years of dancing Juba and wearing trousers and boots had not wholly eradicated from her willful breast. By all means, it should be done. And the interview was arranged for the next week.

It must not be supposed that during this interval of popularity Mr. Chubbuck had been unmindful of his poetic qualities. A certain portion of each day he was absent from town,—"a-communin' with natur'," as Mr. McCorkle expressed it,—and actually wandering in the mountain trails, or lying on his back under the trees, or gathering fragrant herbs and the bright-colored berries of the Manzanita. These and his company he generally brought to the editor's office late in the afternoon, often to that enterprising journalist's infinite weariness. Quiet and uncommunicative, he would sit there patiently watching him at his work until the hour for closing the office arrived, when he would as quietly depart. There was something so humble and unobtrusive in these visits, that the editor could not find it in his heart to deny them, and accepting them, like the woodpeckers, as a part of his sylvan surroundings, often forgot even his presence. Once or twice, moved by some beauty of expression in the moist, shy eyes, he felt like seriously admonishing his visitor of his idle folly; but his glance falling upon the oiled hair and the gorgeous necktie he invariably thought better of it. The case was evidently hopeless.

The interview between Mr. Chubbuck and the "California Pet" took place in a private room of the Union Hotel; propriety being respected by the presence of that arch-humorist, "Boston." To this gentleman we are indebted for the only true account of the meeting. However reticent Mr. Chubbuck might have been in the presence of his own sex, toward the fairer portion of humanity he was, like most poets, exceedingly voluble. Accustomed as the "California Pet" had been to excessive compliment, she was fairly embarrassed by the extravagant praises of her visitor. Her personation of boy characters, her dancing of the "champion jig," were particularly dwelt upon with fervid but unmistakable admiration. At last, recovering her audacity and emboldened by the presence of "Boston," the "California Pet" electrified her hearers by demanding, half jestingly, half viciously, if it were as a boy or a girl that she was the subject of his flattering admiration.

"That knocked him out o' time," said the delighted "Boston," in his subsequent account of the interview. "But do you believe the d—d fool actually asked her to take him with her; wanted to engage in the company."

The plan, as briefly unfolded by "Boston," was to prevail upon Mr. Chubbuck to make his appearance in costume (already designed and prepared by the inventor) before a Sierra Flat audience, and recite an original poem at the Hall immediately on the conclusion of the "California Pet's" performance. At a given signal the audience were to rise and deliver a volley of unsavory articles (previously provided by the originator of the scheme); then a select few were to rush on the stage, seize the poet, and, after marching him in triumphal procession through the town, were to deposit him beyond its uttermost limits, with strict injunctions never to enter it again. To the first part of the plan the poet was committed; for the latter portion it was easy enough to find participants.

The eventful night came, and with it an audience that packed the long narrow room with one dense mass of human beings. The "California Pet" never had been so joyous, so reckless, so fascinating and audacious before. But the applause was tame and weak compared to the ironical outburst that greeted the second rising of the curtain and the entrance of the born poet of Sierra Flat. Then there was a hush of expectancy, and the poet stepped to the footlights and stood with his manuscript in his hand.

His face was deadly pale. Either there was some suggestion of his fate in the faces of his audience, or some mysterious instinct told him of his danger. He attempted to speak, but faltered, tottered, and staggered to the wings.

Fearful of losing his prey, "Boston" gave the signal and leaped upon the stage. But at the same moment a light figure darted from behind the scenes, and delivering a kick that sent the discomfited humorist back among the musicians, cut a pigeon-wing, executed a double-shuffle, and then advancing to the footlights with that inimitable look, that audacious swagger and utter abandon which had so thrilled and fascinated them a moment before, uttered the characteristic speech, "Wot are you goin' to hit a man fur when he's down, s-a-a-y?"

The look, the drawl, the action, the readiness, and

above all the downright courage of the little woman, had an effect. A roar of sympathetic applause followed the act. "Cut and run while you can," she whispered hurriedly over her one shoulder, without altering the other's attitude of pert and saucy defiance toward the audience. But even as she spoke, the poet tottered and sank fainting upon the stage. Then she threw a despairing whisper behind the scenes, "Ring down the curtain."

There was a slight movement of opposition in the audience, but among them rose the burly shoulders of Yuba Bill, the tall, erect figure of Henry York, of Sandy Bar, and the colorless, determined face of John Oakhurst. The curtain came down.

Behind it knelt the "California Pet" beside the prostrate poet. "Bring me some water. Run for a doctor! Stop!! CLEAR OUT, ALL OF YOU!"

She had unloosed the gaudy cravat and opened the shirt-collar of the insensible figure before her. Then she burst into an hysterical laugh.

"Manuela!"

Her tiring-woman, a Mexican half-breed, came toward her.

"Help me with him to my dressing-room, quick; then stand outside and wait. If anyone questions you, tell them he's gone. Do you hear? HE's gone."

The old woman did as she was bade. In a few moments the audience had departed. Before morning so also had the "California Pet," Manuela, and the poet of Sierra Flat.

But, alas! with them also had departed the fair fame of the "California Pet." Only a few, and these, it is to be feared, of not best moral character them-

selves, still had faith in the stainless honor of their favorite actress. "It was a mighty foolish thing to do, but
it'll all come out right yet." On the other hand, a majority gave her full credit and approbation for her
undoubted pluck and gallantry, but deplored that she
should have thrown it away upon a worthless object.
To elect for a lover the despised and ridiculed vagrant
of Sierra Flat, who had not even the manliness to
stand up in his own defense, was not only evidence of
inherent moral depravity, but was an insult to the
community. Colonel Starbottle saw in it only another
instance of extreme frailty of the sex; he had known
similar cases; and remembered distinctly, sir, how a
well known Philadelphia heiress, one of the finest
women that ever rode in her kerridge, that, gad, sir!
had thrown over a Southern member of Congress to
consort with a d——d nigger. The Colonel had also noticed a singular look in the dog's eye which he did not
entirely fancy. He would not say anything against the
lady, sir, but he had noticed— And here, haply, the
Colonel became so mysterious and darkly confidential
as to be unintelligible and inaudible to the bystanders.

A few days after the disappearance of Mr. Chubbuck a singular report reached Sierra Flat, and it was
noticed that "Boston," who since the failure of his
elaborate joke had been even more depressed in spirits than is habitual with great humorists, suddenly
found that his presence was required in San Francisco.
But as yet nothing but the vaguest surmises were
afloat, and nothing definite was known.

It was a pleasant afternoon when the editor of the
"Sierra Flat Record" looked up from his case and beheld the figure of Mr. Morgan McCorkle standing in

the doorway. There was a distressed look on the face of that worthy gentleman that at once enlisted the editor's sympathizing attention. He held an open letter in his hand as he advanced toward the middle of the room.

"As a man as has allers borne a fair reputation," began Mr. McCorkle slowly, "I should like, if so be as I could, Mister Editor, to make a correction in the columns of your valooable paper."

Mr. Editor begged him to proceed.

"Ye may not disremember that about a month ago I fetched here what so be as we'll call a young man whose name might be as it were Milton—Milton Chubbuck."

Mr. Editor remembered perfectly.

"Thet same party I'd knowed better nor fower year, two on 'em campin' out together. Not that I'd known him all the time, fur he war shy and strange at spells, and had odd ways that I took war nat'ral to a borned poet. Ye may remember that I said he was a borned poet?"

The editor distinctly did.

"I picked this same party up in St. Jo., taking a fancy to his face, and kinder calklating he'd runned away from home; for I'm a married man, Mr. Editor, and hev children of my own,—and thinkin' belike he was a borned poet."

"Well," said the editor.

"And as I said before, I should like now to make a correction in the columns of your valooable paper."

"What correction?" asked the editor.

"I said, ef you remember my words, as how he was a borned poet."

"Yes."

"From statements in this yer letter it seems as how I war wrong."

"Well?"

"She war a woman."

COLONEL STARBOTTLE
FOR THE PLAINTIFF

It had been a day of triumph for Colonel Starbottle. First, for his personality, as it would have been
difficult to separate the Colonel's achievements from
his individuality; second, for his oratorical abilities as
a sympathetic pleader; and third, for his functions as
the leading legal counsel for the Eureka Ditch Company *versus* the State of California. On his strictly
legal performances in this issue I prefer not to speak;
there were those who denied them, although the jury
had accepted them in the face of the ruling of the
half-amused, half-cynical Judge himself. For an hour
they had laughed with the Colonel, wept with him,
been stirred to personal indignation or patriotic exaltation by his passionate and lofty periods,—what else
could they do than give him their verdict? If it was
alleged by some that the American eagle, Thomas
Jefferson, and the Resolutions of '98 had nothing
whatever to do with the contest of a ditch company
over a doubtfully worded legislative document; that
wholesale abuse of the State Attorney and his political
motives had not the slightest connection with the legal
question raised—it was, nevertheless, generally ac-

cepted that the losing party would have been only too
glad to have the Colonel on their side. And Colonel
Starbottle knew this, as, perspiring, florid, and panting, he rebuttoned the lower buttons of his blue frock-
coat, which had become loosed in an oratorical spasm,
and readjusted his old-fashioned, spotless shirt frill
above it as he strutted from the court-room amidst the
hand-shakings and acclamations of his friends.

And here an unprecedented thing occurred. The
Colonel absolutely declined spirituous refreshment at
the neighboring Palmetto Saloon, and declared his
intention of proceeding directly to his office in the adjoining square. Nevertheless, the Colonel quitted the
building alone, and apparently unarmed, except for
his faithful gold-headed stick, which hung as usual
from his forearm. The crowd gazed after him with un-
disguised admiration of this new evidence of his pluck.
It was remembered also that a mysterious note had
been handed to him at the conclusion of his speech,
—evidently a challenge from the State Attorney. It
was quite plain that the Colonel—a practiced duelist
—was hastening home to answer it.

But herein they were wrong. The note was in a female hand, and simply requested the Colonel to ac-
cord an interview with the writer at the Colonel's office as soon as he left the court. But it was an engagement that the Colonel—as devoted to the fair sex as
he was to the "code"—was no less prompt in accepting. He flicked away the dust from his spotless white
trousers and varnished boots with his handkerchief,
and settled his black cravat under his Byron collar as
he neared his office. He was surprised, however, on
opening the door of his private office, to find his visitor

already there; he was still more startled to find her somewhat past middle age and plainly attired. But the Colonel was brought up in a school of Southern politeness, already antique in the republic, and his bow of courtesy belonged to the epoch of his shirt frill and strapped trousers. No one could have detected his disappointment in his manner, albeit his sentences were short and incomplete. But the Colonel's colloquial speech was apt to be fragmentary incoherencies of his larger oratorical utterances.

"A thousand pardons—for—er—having kept a lady waiting—er! But—er—congratulations of friends —and—er—courtesy due to them—er—interfered with—though perhaps only heightened—by procrastination—the pleasure of—ha!" And the Colonel completed his sentence with a gallant wave of his fat but white and well-kept hand.

"Yes! I came to see you along o' that speech of yours. I was in court. When I heard you gettin' it off on that jury, I says to myself, 'That's the kind o' lawyer *I* want. A man that's flowery and convincin'! Just the man to take up our case.' "

"Ah! It's a matter of business, I see," said the Colonel, inwardly relieved, but externally careless. "And —er—may I ask the nature of the case?"

"Well! it's a breach-o'-promise suit," said the visitor calmly.

If the Colonel had been surprised before, he was now really startled, and with an added horror that required all his politeness to conceal. Breach-of-promise cases were his peculiar aversion. He had always held them to be a kind of litigation which could have been obviated by the prompt killing of the masculine offender—in which case he would have gladly defended the killer. But a suit for damages,—*damages!* —with the reading of love-letters before a hilarious jury and court, was against all his instincts. His chivalry was outraged; his sense of humor was small, and in the course of his career he had lost one or two important cases through an unexpected development of this quality in a jury.

The woman had evidently noticed his hesitation, but mistook its cause. "It ain't me—but my darter."

The Colonel recovered his politeness. "Ah! I am relieved, my dear madam! I could hardly conceive a man ignorant enough to—er—er—throw away such evident good fortune—or base enough to deceive the trustfulness of womanhood—matured and experienced only in the chivalry of our sex, ha!"

The woman smiled grimly. "Yes!—it's my darter, Zaidee Hooker—so ye might spare some of them pretty speeches for *her* before the jury."

The Colonel winced slightly before this doubtful prospect, but smiled. "Ha! Yes!—certainly—the jury. But—er—my dear lady, need we go as far as that? Cannot this affair be settled—er—out of court? Could not this—er—individual—be admonished—told that he must give satisfaction—personal satisfaction—for his dastardly conduct—to—er—near relative—or even valued personal friend? The—er—arrangements necessary for that purpose I myself would undertake."

He was quite sincere; indeed, his small black eyes shone with that fire which a pretty woman or an "affair of honor" could alone kindle. The visitor stared vacantly at him, and said slowly, "And what good is that goin' to do *us?*"

"Compel him to—er—perform his promise," said the Colonel, leaning back in his chair.

"Ketch him doin' it!" she exclaimed scornfully. "No—that ain't wot we're after. We must make him *pay!* Damages—and nothin' short o' *that*."

The Colonel bit his lip. "I suppose," he said gloomily, "you have documentary evidence—written promises and protestations—er—er—love-letters, in fact?"

"No—nary a letter! Ye see, that's jest it—and that's where *you* come in. You've got to convince that jury yourself. You've got to show what it is—tell the whole story your own way. Lord! to a man like you that's nothin'.'"

Startling as this admission might have been to any other lawyer, Starbottle was absolutely relieved by it. The absence of any mirth-provoking correspondence, and the appeal solely to his own powers of persuasion, actually struck his fancy. He lightly put aside the compliment with a wave of his white hand.

"Of course," he said confidently, "there is strongly presumptive and corroborative evidence? Perhaps you can give me—er—a brief outline of the affair?"

"Zaidee kin do that straight enough, I reckon," said the woman; "what I want to know first is, kin you take the case?"

The Colonel did not hesitate; his curiosity was piqued. "I certainly can. I have no doubt your daughter will put me in possession of sufficient facts and details—to constitute what we call—er—a brief."

"She kin be brief enough—or long enough—for the matter of that," said the woman, rising. The Colonel accepted this implied witticism with a smile.

"And when may I have the pleasure of seeing her?" he asked politely.

"Well, I reckon as soon as I can trot out and call her. She's just outside, meanderin' in the road—kinder shy, ye know, at first."

She walked to the door. The astounded Colonel nevertheless gallantly accompanied her as she stepped out into the street and called shrilly, "You Zaidee!"

A young girl here apparently detached herself from a tree and the ostentatious perusal of an old election poster, and sauntered down towards the office door. Like her mother, she was plainly dressed; unlike her, she had a pale, rather refined face, with a demure mouth and downcast eyes. This was all the Colonel saw as he bowed profoundly and led the way into his office, for she accepted his salutations without lifting her head. He helped her gallantly to a chair, on which she seated herself sideways, somewhat ceremoniously, with her eyes following the point of her parasol as she traced a pattern on the carpet. A second chair offered to the mother, that lady, however, declined. "I reckon to leave you and Zaidee together to talk it out," she said; turning to her daughter, she added, "Jest you tell him all, Zaidee," and before the Colonel could rise again, disappeared from the room. In spite of his professional experience, Starbottle was for a moment embarrassed. The young girl, however, broke the silence without looking up.

"Adoniram K. Hotchkiss," she began, in a monotonous voice, as if it were a recitation addressed to the public, "first began to take notice of me a year ago. Arter that—off and on"—

"One moment," interrupted the astounded Colonel; "do you mean Hotchkiss the President of the Ditch Company?" He had recognized the name of a prominent citizen—a rigid, ascetic, taciturn, middle-aged man—a deacon—and more than that, the head of the company he had just defended. It seemed inconceivable.

"That's him," she continued, with eyes still fixed on the parasol and without changing her monotonous tone—"off and on ever since. Most of the time at the Free-Will Baptist Church—at morning service, prayer-meetings, and such. And at home—outside—er—in the road."

"Is it this gentleman—Mr. Adoniram K. Hotchkiss who—er—promised marriage?" stammered the Colonel.

"Yes."

The Colonel shifted uneasily in his chair. "Most extraordinary! for—you see—my dear young lady—this becomes—a—er—most delicate affair."

"That's what maw said," returned the young woman simply, yet with the faintest smile playing around her demure lips and downcast cheek.

"I mean," said the Colonel, with a pained yet courteous smile, "that this—er—gentleman—is in fact —er—one of my clients."

"That's what maw said too, and of course your knowing him will make it all the easier for you."

A slight flush crossed the Colonel's cheek as he returned quickly and a little stiffly, "On the contrary— er—it may make it impossible for me to—er—act in this matter."

The girl lifted her eyes. The Colonel held his breath

as the long lashes were raised to his level. Even to an ordinary observer that sudden revelation of her eyes seemed to transform her face with subtle witchery. They were large, brown, and soft, yet filled with an extraordinary penetration and prescience. They were the eyes of an experienced woman of thirty fixed in the face of a child. What else the Colonel saw there Heaven only knows! He felt his inmost secrets plucked from him—his whole soul laid bare—his vanity, belligerency, gallantry—even his mediæval chivalry, penetrated, and yet illuminated, in that single glance. And when the eyelids fell again, he felt that a greater part of himself had been swallowed up in them.

"I beg your pardon," he said hurriedly. "I mean—this matter may be arranged—er—amicably. My interest with—and as you wisely say—my—er—knowledge of my client—er—Mr. Hotchkiss—may effect —a compromise."

"And *damages*," said the young girl, readdressing her parasol, as if she had never looked up.

The Colonel winced. "And—er—undoubtedly *compensation*—if you do not press a fulfillment of the promise. Unless," he said, with an attempted return to his former easy gallantry, which, however, the recollection of her eyes made difficult, "it is a question of—er—the affections."

"Which?" asked this fair client softly.

"If you still love him?" explained the Colonel, actually blushing.

Zaidee again looked up; again taking the Colonel's breath away with eyes that expressed not only the fullest perception of what he had *said*, but of what he thought and had not said, and with an added subtle suggestion of what he might have thought. "That's tellin'," she said, dropping her long lashes again.

The Colonel laughed vacantly. Then feeling himself growing imbecile, he forced an equally weak gravity. "Pardon me—I understand there are no letters; may I know the way in which he formulated his declaration and promises?"

"Hymn-books."

"I beg your pardon," said the mystified lawyer.

"Hymn-books—marked words in them with pencil —and passed 'em on to me," repeated Zaidee. "Like 'love,' 'dear,' 'precious,' 'sweet,' and 'blessed,'" she added, accenting each word with a push of her parasol on the carpet. "Sometimes a whole line outer Tate and Brady—and Solomon's Song, you know, and sich."

"I believe," said the Colonel loftily, "that the—er—phrases of sacred psalmody lend themselves to the language of the affections. But in regard to the distinct promise of marriage—was there—er—no *other* expression?"

"Marriage Service in the prayer-book—lines and words outer that—all marked," Zaidee replied.

The Colonel nodded naturally and approvingly. "Very good. Were others cognizant of this? Were there any witnesses?"

"Of course not," said the girl. "Only me and him. It was generally at church-time—or prayer-meeting. Once, in passing the plate, he slipped one o' them peppermint lozenges with the letters stamped on it 'I love you' for me to take."

The Colonel coughed slightly. "And you have the lozenge?"

"I ate it."

"Ah," said the Colonel. After a pause he added delicately, "But were these attentions—er—confined to—er—sacred precincts? Did he meet you elsewhere?"

"Useter pass our house on the road," returned the girl, dropping into her monotonous recital, "and useter signal."

"Ah, signal?" repeated the Colonel approvingly.

"Yes! He'd say 'Keerow,' and I'd say 'Keeree.' Suthing like a bird, you know."

Indeed, as she lifted her voice in imitation of the call, the Colonel thought it certainly very sweet and birdlike. At least as *she* gave it. With his remembrance of the grim deacon he had doubts as to the melodiousness of *his* utterance. He gravely made her repeat it.

"And after that signal?" he added suggestively.

"He'd pass on."

The Colonel again coughed slightly, and tapped his desk with his penholder.

"Were there any endearments—er—caresses—er —such as taking your hand—er—clasping your waist?" he suggested, with a gallant yet respectful sweep of his white hand and bowing of his head; "er —slight pressure of your fingers in the changes of a dance—I mean," he corrected himself, with an apologetic cough—"in the passing of the plate?"

"No; he was not what you'd call 'fond,'" returned the girl.

"Ah! Adoniram K. Hotchkiss was not 'fond' in the ordinary acceptance of the word," noted the Colonel, with professional gravity.

She lifted her disturbing eyes, and again absorbed

his in her own. She also said "Yes," although her eyes in their mysterious prescience of all he was thinking disclaimed the necessity of any answer at all. He smiled vacantly. There was a long pause; on which she slowly disengaged her parasol from the carpet pattern, and stood up.

"I reckon that's about all," she said.

"Er—yes—but one moment," began the Colonel vaguely. He would have liked to keep her longer, but with her strange premonition of him he felt powerless to detain her, or explain his reason for doing so. He instinctively knew she had told him all; his professional judgment told him that a more hopeless case had never come to his knowledge. Yet he was not daunted, only embarrassed. "No matter," he said. "Of course I shall have to consult with you again."

Her eyes again answered that she expected he would, and she added simply, "When?"

"In the course of a day or two," he replied quickly. "I will send you word."

She turned to go. In his eagerness to open the door for her, he upset his chair, and with some confusion, that was actually youthful, he almost impeded her movements in the hall, and knocked his broad-brimmed Panama hat from his bowing hand in a final gallant sweep. Yet as her small, trim, youthful figure, with its simple Leghorn straw hat confined by a blue bow under her round chin, passed away before him, she looked more like a child than ever.

The Colonel spent that afternoon in making diplomatic inquiries. He found his youthful client was the daughter of a widow who had a small ranch on the crossroads, near the new Free-Will Baptist Church

—the evident theatre of this pastoral. They led a secluded life, the girl being little known in the town, and her beauty and fascination apparently not yet being a recognized fact. The Colonel felt a pleasurable relief at this, and a general satisfaction he could not account for. His few inquiries concerning Mr. Hotchkiss only confirmed his own impressions of the alleged lover,—a serious-minded, practically abstracted man, abstentive of youthful society, and the last man apparently capable of levity of the affections or serious flirtation. The Colonel was mystified, but determined of purpose, whatever that purpose might have been.

The next day he was at his office at the same hour. He was alone—as usual—the Colonel's office being really his private lodgings, disposed in connecting rooms, a single apartment reserved for consultation. He had no clerk, his papers and briefs being taken by his faithful body-servant and ex-slave "Jim" to another firm who did his office work since the death of Major Stryker, the Colonel's only law partner, who fell in a duel some years previous. With a fine constancy the Colonel still retained his partner's name on his doorplate, and, it was alleged by the superstitious, kept a certain invincibility also through the *manes* of that lamented and somewhat feared man.

The Colonel consulted his watch, whose heavy gold case still showed the marks of a providential interference with a bullet destined for its owner, and replaced it with some difficulty and shortness of breath in his fob. At the same moment he heard a step in the passage, and the door opened to Adoniram K. Hotchkiss. The Colonel was impressed; he had a duelist's respect for punctuality.

The man entered with a nod and the expectant inquiring look of a busy man. As his feet crossed that sacred threshold the Colonel became all courtesy; he placed a chair for his visitor, and took his hat from his half-reluctant hand. He then opened a cupboard and brought out a bottle of whiskey and two glasses.

"A—er—slight refreshment, Mr. Hotchkiss," he suggested politely.

"I never drink," replied Hotchkiss, with the severe attitude of a total abstainer.

"Ah—er—not the finest Bourbon whiskey, selected by a Kentucky friend? No? Pardon me! A cigar, then —the mildest Havana."

"I do not use tobacco nor alcohol in any form," repeated Hotchkiss ascetically. "I have no foolish weaknesses."

The Colonel's moist, beady eyes swept silently over his client's sallow face. He leaned back comfortably in his chair, and half closing his eyes as in dreamy reminiscence, said slowly: "Your reply, Mr. Hotchkiss, reminds me of—er—sing'lar circumstance that—er—occurred, in point of fact—at the St. Charles Hotel, New Orleans. Pinkey Hornblower— personal friend—invited Senator Doolittle to join him in social glass. Received, sing'larly enough, reply similar to yours. 'Don't drink nor smoke?' said Pinkey. 'Gad, sir, you must be mighty sweet on the ladies.' Ha!" The Colonel paused long enough to allow the faint flush to pass from Hotchkiss's cheek, and went on, half closing his eyes: " 'I allow no man, sir, to discuss my personal habits,' declared Doolittle, over his shirt collar. 'Then I reckon shootin' must be one of those habits,' said Pinkey coolly. Both men drove out on the Shell Road back of cemetery next morning. Pinkey put bullet at twelve paces through Doolittle's temple. Poor Doo never spoke again. Left three wives and seven children, they say—two of 'em black."

"I got a note from you this morning," said Hotchkiss, with badly concealed impatience. "I suppose in reference to our case. You have taken judgment, I believe."

The Colonel, without replying, slowly filled a glass of whiskey and water. For a moment he held it dreamily before him, as if still engaged in gentle reminiscences called up by the act. Then tossing it off, he wiped his lips with a large white handkerchief, and leaning back comfortably in his chair, said, with a wave of his hand, "The interview I requested, Mr. Hotchkiss, concerns a subject—which I may say is—er—er—at present *not* of a public or business nature —although *later* it might become—er—er—both. It is an affair of some—er—delicacy."

The Colonel paused, and Mr. Hotchkiss regarded him with increased impatience. The Colonel, however, continued, with unchanted deliberation: "It concerns—er—er—a young lady—a beautiful, high-souled creature, sir, who, apart from her personal loveliness—er—er—I may say is of one of the first families of Missouri, and—er—not remotely connected by marriage with one of—er—er—my boyhood's dearest friends." The latter, I grieve to say, was a pure invention of the Colonel's—an oratorical addition to the scanty information he had obtained the previous day. "The young lady," he continued blandly, "enjoys the further distinction of being the object of such attention from you as would make this

interview—really—a confidential matter—er—er—
among friends and—er—er—relations in present
and future. I need not say that the lady I refer to is
Miss Zaidee Juno Hooker, only daughter of Almira
Ann Hooker, relict of Jefferson Brown Hooker, for-
merly of Bone County, Kentucky, and latterly of—
er—Pike County, Missouri."

The sallow, ascetic hue of Mr. Hotchkiss's face had
passed through a livid and then a greenish shade, and
finally settled into a sullen red. "What's all this
about?" he demanded roughly.

The least touch of belligerent fire came into Starbottle's eye, but his bland courtesy did not change. "I
believe," he said politely, "I have made myself clear
as between—er—gentlemen, though perhaps not as
clear as I should to—er—er—jury."

Mr. Hotchkiss was apparently stuck with some
significance in the lawyer's reply. "I don't know," he
said, in a lower and more cautious voice, "what you
mean by what you call 'my attentions' to—anyone—
or how it concerns you. I have not exchanged half a
dozen words with—the person you name—have never
written her a line—nor even called at her house.

He rose with an assumption of ease, pulled down
his waistcoat, buttoned his coat, and took up his hat.
The Colonel did not move.

"I believe I have already indicated my meaning in
what I have called 'your attentions,' " said the Colonel blandly, "and given you my 'concern' for speaking as—er—er—mutal friend. As to *your* statement
of your relations with Miss Hooker, I may state that it
is fully corroborated by the statement of the young
lady herself in this very office yesterday."

"Then what does this impertinent nonsense mean? Why am I summoned here?" demanded Hotchkiss furiously.

"Because," said the Colonel deliberately, "that statement is infamously—yes, damnably to your discredit, sir!"

Mr. Hotchkiss was here seized by one of those impotent and inconsistent rages which occasionally betray the habitually cautious and timid man. He caught up the Colonel's stick, which was lying on the table. At the same moment the Colonel, without any apparent effort, grasped it by the handle. To Mr. Hotchkiss's astonishment, the stick separated in two pieces, leaving the handle and about two feet of narrow glittering steel in the Colonel's hand. The man recoiled, dropping the useless fragment. The Colonel picked it up, fitted the shining blade in it, clicked the spring, and then rising with a face of courtesy yet of unmistakeably genuine pain, and with even a slight tremor in his voice, said gravely,—

"Mr. Hotchkiss, I owe you a thousand apologies, sir, that—er—a weapon should be drawn by me— even through your own inadvertence—under the sacred protection of my roof, and upon an unarmed man. I beg your pardon, sir, and I even withdraw the expressions which provoked that inadvertence. Nor does this apology prevent you from holding me responsible—personally reponsible *elsewhere* for an indiscretion committed in behalf of a lady—my—er— client."

"Your client? Do you mean you have taken her case? You, the counsel for the Ditch Company?" asked Mr. Hotchkiss, in trembling indignation.

"Having won *your* case, sir," replied the Colonel coolly, "the—er—usages of advocacy do not prevent me from espousing the cause of the weak and unprotected."

"We shall see, sir," said Hotchkiss, grasping the handle of the door and backing into the passage. "There are other lawyers who"—

"Permit me to see you out," interrupted the Colonel, rising politely.

—"will be ready to resist the attacks of blackmail," continued Hotchkiss, retreating along the passage.

"And then you will be able to repeat your remarks to me *in the street*," continued the Colonel, bowing, as he persisted in following his visitor to the door.

But here Mr. Hotchkiss quickly slammed it behind him, and hurried away. The Colonel returned to his office, and sitting down, took a sheet of letter-paper bearing the inscription "Starbottle and Stryker, Attorneys and Counselors," and wrote the following lines:—

HOOKER *versus* HOTCHKISS.

DEAR MADAM,—Having had a visit from the defendant in above, we should be pleased to have an interview with you at two P. M. to-morrow.

> Your obedient servants,
> STARBOTTLE AND STRYKER.

This he sealed and dispatched by his trusted servant Jim, and then devoted a few moments to reflection. It was the custom of the Colonel to act first, and justify the action by reason afterwards.

He knew that Hotchkiss would at once lay the matter before rival counsel. He knew that they would advise him that Miss Hooker had "no case"—that she would be non-suited on her own evidence, and he ought not to compromise, but be ready to stand trial. He believed, however, that Hotchkiss feared such exposure, and although his own instincts had been at first against this remedy, he was now instinctively in favor of it. He remembered his own power with a jury; his vanity and his chivalry alike approved of this heroic method; he was bound by no prosaic facts— he had his own theory of the case, which no mere evidence could gainsay. In fact, Mrs. Hooker's admission that he was to "tell the story in his own way" actually appeared to him an inspiration and a prophecy.

Perhaps there was something else, due possibly to the lady's wonderful eyes, of which he had thought much. Yet it was not her simplicity that affected him solely; on the contrary, it was her apparent intelligent reading of the character of her recreant lover—and of his own! Of all the Colonel's previous "light" or "serious" loves, none had ever before flattered him in that way. And it was this, combined with the respect which he had held for their professional relations, that precluded his having a more familiar knowledge of his client, through serious questioning or playful gallantry. I am not sure it was not part of the charm to have a rustic *femme incomprise* as a client.

Nothing could exceed the respect with which he greeted her as she entered his office the next day. He even affected not to notice that she had put on her best clothes, and, he made no doubt, appeared as when she had first attracted the mature yet faithless attentions of Deacon Hotchkiss at church. A white virginal muslin was belted around her slim figure by a blue ribbon, and her Leghorn hat was drawn around her oval cheek by a bow of the same color. She had a Southern girl's narrow feet, encased in white stockings and kid slippers, which were crossed primly before her as she sat in a chair, supporting her arm by her faithful parasol planted firmly on the floor. A faint odor of southernwood exhaled from her, and, oddly enough, stirred the Colonel with a far-off recollection of a pine-shaded Sunday-school on a Georgia hillside, and of his first love, aged ten, in a short starched frock. Possibly it was the same recollection that revived something of the awkwardness he had felt then.

He, however, smiled vaguely, and sitting down, coughed slightly, and placed his finger-tips together. "I have had an—er—interview with Mr. Hotchkiss, but—I—er—regret to say there seems to be no prospect of—er—compromise."

He paused, and to his surprise her listless "company" face lit up with an adorable smile. "Of course! —ketch him!" she said. "Was he mad when you told him?" She put her knees comfortably together and leaned forward for a reply.

For all that, wild horses could not have torn from the Colonel a word about Hotchkiss's anger. "He expressed his intention of employing counsel—and defending a suit," returned the Colonel, affably basking in her smile.

She dragged her chair nearer his desk. "Then you'll fight him tooth and nail?" she asked eagerly;

"you'll show him up? You'll tell the whole story your own way? You'll give him fits?—and you'll make him pay? Sure?" she went on breathlessly.

"I—er—will," said the Colonel almost as breathlessly.

She caught his fat white hand, which was lying on the table, between her own and lifted it to her lips. He felt her soft young fingers even through the isle-thread gloves that encased them, and the warm moisture of her lips upon his skin. He felt himself flushing—but was unable to break the silence or change his position. The next moment she had scuttled back with her chair to her old position.

"I—er—certainly shall do my best," stammered the Colonel, in an attempt to recover his dignity and composure.

"That's enough! You'll *do* it," said she enthusiastically. "Lordy! Just you talk for *me* as ye did for *his* old Ditch Company, and you'll fetch it—every time! Why, when you made that jury sit up the other day —when you got that off about the Merrikan flag waving equally over the rights of honest citizens banded together in peaceful commercial pursuits, as well as over the fortress of official proflig—"

"Oligarchy," murmured the Colonel courteously.

—"oligarchy," repeated the girl quickly, "my breath was just took away. I said to maw, 'Ain't he too sweet for anything!' I did, honest Injin! And when you rolled it all off at the end—never missing a word (you didn't need to mark 'em in a lesson-book, but had 'em all ready on your tongue)—and walked out— Well! I didn't know you nor the Ditch Company 'from Adam, but I could have just run over and kissed you there before the whole court!"

She laughed, with her face glowing, although her strange eyes were cast down. Alack! The Colonel's face was equally flushed, and his own beady eyes were on his desk. To any other woman he would have voiced the banal gallantry that he should now, himself, look forward to that reward, but the words never reached his lips. He laughed, coughed slightly, and when he looked up again she had fallen into the same attitude as on her first visit, with her parasol point on the floor.

"I must ask you to—er—direct your memory to—er—another point: the breaking off of the—er—er—er—engagement. Did he—er—give any reason for it? Or show any cause?"

"No; he never said anything," returned the girl.

"Not in his usual way?—er—no reproaches out of the hymnbook?—or the sacred writings?"

"No; he just *quit*."

"Er—ceased his attentions," said the Colonel gravely. "And naturally you—er—were not conscious of any cause for his doing so."

The girl raised her wonderful eyes so suddenly and so penetratingly without replying in any other way that the Colonel could only hurriedly say: "I see! None, of course!"

At which she rose, the Colonel rising also. "We—shall begin proceedings at once. I must, however, caution you to answer no questions, nor say anything about this case to anyone until you are in court."

She answered his request with another intelligent

look and a nod. He accompanied her to the door. As he took her proffered hand, he raised the lisle-thread fingers to his lips with old-fashioned gallantry. As if that act had condoned for his first omissions and awkwardness, he became his old-fashioned self again, buttoned his coat, pulled out his shirt frill, and strutted back to his desk.

A day or two later it was known throughout the town that Zaidee Hooker had sued Adoniram Hotchkiss for breach of promise, and that the damages were laid at five thousand dollars. As in those bucolic days the Western press was under the secure censorship of a revolver, a cautious tone of criticism prevailed, and any gossip was confined to personal expression, and even then at the risk of the gossiper. Nevertheless, the situation provoked the intensest curiosity. The Colonel was approached—until his statement that he should consider any attempt to overcome his professional secrecy a personal reflection withheld further advances. The community were left to the more ostentatious information of the defendant's counsel, Messrs. Kitcham and Bilser, that the case was "ridiculous" and "rotten," that the plaintiff would be nonsuited, and the fire-eating Starbottle would be taught a lesson that he could not "bully" the law, and there were some dark hints of a conspiracy. It was even hinted that the "case" was the revengeful and preposterous outcome of the refusal of Hotchkiss to pay Starbottle an extravagant fee for his late services to the Ditch Company. It is unnecessary to say that these words were not reported to the Colonel. It was, however, an unfortunate circumstance for the calmer, ethical consideration of the subject that the Church sided with Hotchkiss, as this provoked an equal adherence to the plaintiff and Starbottle on the part of the larger body of non-church-goers, who were delighted at a possible exposure of the weakness of religious rectitude. "I've allus had my suspicions o' them early candle-light meetings down at that gospel shop," said one critic, "and I reckon Deacon Hotchkiss didn't rope in the gals to attend jest for psalm-singing." "Then for him to get up and leave the board afore the game's finished and try to sneak out of it," said another,—"I suppose that's what they call *religious*."

It was therefore not remarkable that the courthouse three weeks later was crowded with an excited multitude of the curious and sympathizing. The fair plaintiff, with her mother, was early in attendance, and under the Colonel's advice appeared in the same modest garb in which she had first visited his office. This and her downcast, modest demeanor were perhaps at first disappointing to the crowd, who had evidently expected a paragon of loveliness in this Circe of that grim, ascetic defendant, who sat beside his counsel. But presently all eyes were fixed on the Colonel, who certainly made up in *his* appearance any deficiency of his fair client. His portly figure was clothed in a blue dress coat with brass buttons, a buff waistcoat which permitted his frilled shirt-front to become erectible above it, a black satin stock which confined a boyish turned-down collar around his full neck, and immaculate drill trousers, strapped over varnished boots. A murmur ran round the court. "Old 'Personally Responsible' has got his war-point on"; "The Old War-Horse is smelling powder," were whispered comments. Yet for all that, the most irreverent among them recognized vaguely, in this bizarre figure, something of an honored past in their country's history, and possibly felt the spell of old deeds and old names that had once thrilled their boyish pulses. The new District Judge returned Colonel Starbottle's profoundly punctilious bow. The Colonel was followed by his Negro servant, carrying a parcel of hymn-books and Bibles, who, with a courtesy evidently imitated from his master, placed one before the opposite counsel. This, after a first curious glance, the lawyer somewhat superciliously tossed aside. But when Jim, proceeding to the jury-box, placed with equal politeness the remaining copies before the jury, the opposite counsel sprang to his feet.

"I want to direct the attention of the Court to this unprecedented tampering with the jury, by this gratuitous exhibition of matter impertinent and irrelevant to the issue."

The Judge cast an inquiring look at Colonel Starbottle.

"May it please the Court," returned Colonel Starbottle with dignity, ignoring the counsel, "the defendant's counsel will observe that he is already furnished with the matter—which I regret to say he has treated—in the presence of the Court—and of his client, a deacon of the church—with—er—great superciliousness. When I state to Your Honor that the books in question are hymn-books and copies of the Holy Scriptures, and that they are for the instruction of the jury, to whom I shall have to refer them in the course of my opening, I believe I am within my rights."

"The act is certainly unprecedented," said the Judge dryly, "but unless the counsel for the plaintiff expects the jury to *sing* from these hymn-books, their introduction is not improper, and I cannot admit the objection. As defendant's counsel are furnished with copies also, they cannot plead 'surprise,' as in the introduction of new matter, and as plaintiff's counsel relies evidently upon the jury's attention to his opening, he would not be the first person to distract it." After a pause he added, addressing the Colonel, who remained standing, "The Court is with you, sir; proceed."

But the Colonel remained motionless and statuesque, with folded arms.

"I have overruled the objection," repeated the Judge; "you may go on."

"I am waiting, Your Honor, for the—er—withdrawal by the defendant's counsel of the word 'tampering,' as refers to myself, and of 'impertinent,' as refers to the sacred volumes."

"The request is a proper one, and I have no doubt will be acceded to," returned the Judge quietly. The defendant's counsel rose and mumbled a few words of apology, and the incident closed. There was, however, a general feeling that the Colonel had in some way "scored," and if his object had been to excite the greatest curiosity about the books, he had made his point.

But impassive of his victory, he inflated his chest, with his right hand in the breast of his buttoned coat, and began. His usual high color had paled slightly, but the small pupils of his prominent eyes glittered like steel. The young girl leaned forward in her chair with an attention so breathless, a sympathy so quick, and an admiration so artless and unconscious that in an instant she divided with the speaker the attention of the whole assemblage. It was very hot; the court was crowded to suffocation; even the open windows revealed a crowd of faces outside the building, eagerly following the Colonel's words.

He would remind the jury that only a few weeks ago he stood there as the advocate of a powerful Company, then represented by the present defendant. He spoke then as the champion of strict justice against legal oppression; no less should he to-day champion the cause of the unprotected and the comparatively defenseless—save for that paramount power which surrounds beauty and innocence—even though the plaintiff of yesterday was the defendant of to-day. As he approached the court a moment ago he had raised his eyes and beheld the starry flag flying from its dome, and he knew that glorious banner was a symbol of the perfect equality, under the Constitution, of the rich and the poor, the strong and the weak —an equality which made the simple citizen taken from the plough in the field, the pick in the gulch, or from behind the counter in the mining town, who served on that jury, the equal arbiters of justice with that highest legal luminary whom they were proud to welcome on the bench to-day. The Colonel paused, with a stately bow to the impassive Judge. It was this, he continued, which lifted his heart as he approached the building. And yet—he had entered it with an uncertain—he might almost say—a timid step. And why? He knew, gentlemen, he was about to confront a profound—ay! a sacred responsibility! Those hymn-books and holy writings handed to the jury were *not,* as His Honor had surmised, for the purpose of enabling the jury to indulge in—er—preliminary choral exercise! He might, indeed, say, "Alas, not!" They were the damning, incontrovertible proofs of the perfidy of the defendant. And they would prove as terrible a warning to him as the fatal characters upon Belshazzar's wall. There was a strong sensation. Hotchkiss turned a sallow green. His lawyers assumed a careless smile.

It was his duty to tell them that this was not one of those ordinary "breach-of-promise" cases which were too often the occasion of ruthless mirth and indecent levity in the court-room. The jury would find nothing of that here. There were no love-letters with the epithets of endearment, nor those mystic crosses and ciphers which, he had been credibly informed, chastely hid the exchange of those mutual caresses known as "kisses." There was no cruel tearing of the veil from those sacred privacies of the human affection; there was no forensic shouting out of those fond confidences meant only for *one.* But there was, he was shocked to say, a new sacrilegious intrusion. The weak pipings of Cupid were mingled with the chorus of the saints,—the sanctity of the temple known as the "meeting-house" was desecrated by proceedings more in keeping with the shrine of Venus; and the inspired writings themselves were used as the medium of amatory and wanton flirtation by the defendant in his sacred capacity as deacon.

The Colonel artistically paused after this thunderous denunciation. The jury turned eagerly to the leaves of the hymn-books, but the larger gaze of the audience remained fixed upon the speaker and the girl, who sat in rapt admiration of his periods. After the hush, the Colonel continued in a lower and sadder voice: "There are, perhaps, few of us here, gentlemen, —with the exception of the defendant,—who can arrogate to themselves the title of regular church-goers, or to whom these humbler functions of the prayer-meeting, the Sunday-school, and the Bible-class are habitually familiar. Yet"—more solemnly—"down in our hearts is the deep conviction of our shortcomings and failings, and a laudable desire that others, at least, should profit by the teachings we neglect. Perhaps," he continued, closing his eyes dreamily, "there is not a man here who does not recall the happy days of his boyhood, the rustic village spire, the lessons shared with some artless village maiden, with whom he later sauntered, hand in hand, through the woods, as the simple rhyme rose upon their lips—

> *'Always make it a point to have it a rule,*
> *Never to be late at the Sabbath-school.'*

He would recall the strawberry feasts, the welcome annual picnic, redolent with hunks of gingerbread and sarsaparilla. How would they feel to know that these scared recollections were now forever profaned in their memory by the knowledge that the defendant was capable of using such occasions to make love to the larger girls and teachers, whilst his artless companions were innocently—the Court will pardon me for introducing what I am credibly informed is the local expression—'doing gooseberry'?" The tremulous flicker of a smile passed over the faces of the listening crowd, and the Colonel slightly winced. But he recovered himself instantly, and continued,—

"My client, the only daughter of a widowed mother —who has for years stemmed the varying tides of adversity, in the western precincts of this town—stands before you to-day invested only in her own innocence. She wears no—er—rich gifts of her faithless admirer—is panoplied in no jewels, rings, nor mementos of affection such as lovers delight to hang upon the shrine of their affections; hers is not the glory with which Solomon decorated the Queen of Sheba, though the defendant, as I shall show later, clothed her in the less expensive flowers of the king's poetry. No, gentlemen! The defendant exhibited in this affair a certain frugality of—er—percuniary investment, which I am willing to admit may be commendable in his class. His only gift was characteristic alike of his methods and his economy. There is, I understand, a certain not unimportant feature of religious exercise known as 'taking a collection.' The defendant, on this occasion, by the mute presentation of a tin plate covered with baize, solicited the pecuniary contributions of the faithful. On approaching the plaintiff, however, he himself slipped a love-token upon the plate and pushed it towards her. That love-token was a lozenge—a small disk, I have reason to believe, concocted of peppermint and sugar, bearing upon its reverse surface the simple words, 'I love you!' I have since ascertained that these disks may be bought for five cents a dozen —or at considerably less than one half cent for the single lozenge. Yes, gentlemen, the words 'I love you!' —the oldest legend of all; the refrain 'when the morning stars sang together'—were presented to the plaintiff by a medium so insignificant that there is, happily, no coin in the republic low enough to represent its value.

"I shall prove to you, gentlemen of the jury," said the Colonel solemnly, drawing a Bible from his coat-tail pocket, "that the defendant for the last twelve months conducted an amatory correspondence with the plaintiff by means of underlined words of Sacred Writ and church psalmody, such as 'beloved,' 'precious,' and 'dearest,' occasionally appropriating whole passages which seemed apposite to his tender passion. I shall call your attention to one of them. The defendant, while professing to be a total abstainer,—a man who, in my own knowledge, has refused spirituous refreshment as an inordinate weakness of the flesh,—with shameless hypocrisy underscores with his pencil the following passage, and presents it to the plaintiff. The gentlemen of the jury will find it in the Song of Solomon, page 548, chapter ii., verse 5." After a pause, in which the rapid rustling of leaves was heard in the jury-box, Colonel Starbottle declaimed in a pleading, stentorian voice, " 'Stay me with—er—*flagons*, comfort me with—er—apples —for I am—er—sick of love.' Yes, gentlemen!—yes, you may well turn from those accusing pages and look at the double-faced defendant. He desires—to—er— be—'stayed with flagons'! I am not aware at present what kind of liquor is habitually dispensed at these meetings, and for which the defendant so urgently clamored; but it will be my duty, before this trial is over, to discover it, if I have to summon every bar-keeper in this district. For the moment I will simply call your attention to the *quantity*. It is not a single drink that the defendant asks for—not a glass of light and generous wine, to be shared with his inamorata, but a number of flagons or vessels, each possibly holding a pint measure—*for himself!*"

The smile of the audience had become a laugh. The Judge looked up warningly, when his eye caught the fact that the Colonel had again winced at this mirth. He regarded him seriously. Mr. Hotchkiss's counsel had joined in the laugh affectedly, but Hotchkiss himself sat ashy pale. There was also a commotion in the jury-box, a hurried turning over of leaves, and an excited discussion.

"The gentlemen of the jury," said the Judge, with official gravity, "will please keep order and attend only to the speeches of counsel. Any discussion *here* is irregular and premature, and must be reserved for the jury-room after they have retired."

The foreman of the jury struggled to his feet. He was a powerful man, with a good-humored face, and, in spite of his unfelicitous nickname of "The Bone-Breaker," had a kindly, simple but somewhat emotional nature. Nevertheless, it appeared as if he were laboring under some powerful indignation.

"Can we ask a question, Judge?" he said respectfully, although his voice had the unmistakable Western ring in it, as of one who was unconscious that he could be addressing any but his peers.

"Yes," said the Judge good-humoredly.

"We're finding in this yere piece, out o' which the Kernel hes just bin a-quotin', some language that me and my pardners allow hadn't orter be read out afore a young lady in court, and we want to know of you—ez a fa'r-minded and impartial man—ef this is the reg'lar kind o' book given to gals and babies down at the meetin'-house."

"The jury will please follow the counsel's speech without comment," said the Judge briefly, fully aware that the defendant's counsel would spring to his feet, as he did promptly.

"The Court will allow us to explain to the gentlemen that the language they seem to object to has been accepted by the best theologians for the last thousand years as being purely mystic. As I will explain later, those are merely symbols of the Church"—

"Of wot?" interrupted the foreman, in deep scorn. "Of the Church!"

"We ain't askin' any questions o' *you*, and we ain't takin' any answers," said the foreman, sitting down abruptly.

"I must insist," said the Judge sternly, "that the plaintiff's counsel be allowed to continue his opening without interruption. You" (to defendant's counsel) "will have your opportunity to reply later."

The counsel sank down in his seat with the bitter conviction that the jury was manifestly against him, and the case as good as lost. But his face was scarcely as disturbed as his client's, who, in great agitation, had begun to argue with him wildly, and was apparently pressing some point against the lawyer's vehement opposal. The Colonel's murky eyes brightened as he still stood erect, with his hand thrust in his breast.

"It will be put to you, gentlemen, when the counsel on the other side refrains from mere interruption and confines himself to reply, that my unfortunate client has no action—no remedy at law—because there were no spoken words of endearment. But, gentlemen, it will depend upon *you* to say what are and what are not articulate expressions of love. We all know that among the lower animals, with whom you may possibly be called upon to classify the defendant, there are certain signals more or less harmonious, as the case may be. The ass brays, the horse neighs, the sheep bleats—the feathered denizens of the grove call to their mates in more musical roundelays. These are recognized facts, gentlemen, which you yourselves, as dwellers among nature in this beautiful land, are all cognizant of. They are facts that no one would deny—and we should have a poor opinion of the ass who, at—er—such a supreme moment, would attempt to suggest that his call was unthinking and without significance. But, gentlemen, I shall prove to you that such was the foolish, self-convicting custom of the defendant. With the greatest reluctance, and the—er—greatest pain, I succeeded in wresting from the maidenly modesty of my fair client the innocent confession that the defendant had induced her to correspond with him in these methods. Picture to yourself, gentlemen, the lonely moonlight road beside the widow's humble cottage. It is a beautiful night, sanctified to the affections, and the innocent girl is leaning from her casement. Presently there appears upon the road a slinking, stealthy figure, the defendant on his way to church. True to the instruction she has received from him, her lips part in the musical utterance" (the Colonel lowered his voice in a faint falsetto, presumably in fond imitation of his fair client), "'Keeree!' Instantly the night becomes resonant with the impassioned reply" (the Colonel here lifted his voice in stentorian tones), " 'Keerow.' Again, as he passes, rises the soft 'Keeree'; again, as his form is lost in the distance, comes back the deep "Keerow.' "

A burst of laughter, long, loud, and irrepressible, struck the whole court-room, and before the Judge could lift his half-composed face and take his handkerchief from his mouth, a faint "Keeree" from some unrecognized obscurity of the court-room was followed by a loud "Keerow" from some opposite locality. "The Sheriff will clear the court," said the Judge sternly; but, alas! as the embarrassed and choking officials rushed hither and thither, a soft "Keeree" from the spectators at the window, *outside* the court-house, was answered by a loud chorus of "Keerows" from the opposite windows, filled with onlookers. Again the laughter arose everywhere,—even the fair plaintiff herself sat convulsed behind her handkerchief.

The figure of Colonel Starbottle alone remained erect—white and rigid. And then the Judge, looking up, saw—what no one else in the court had seen—that the Colonel was sincere and in earnest; that what he had conceived to be the pleader's most perfect acting and most elaborate irony were the deep, serious, mirthless *convictions* of a man without the least sense of humor. There was the respect of this conviction in the Judge's voice as he said to him gently, "You may proceed, Colonel Starbottle."

"I thank Your Honor," said the Colonel slowly, "for recognizing and doing all in your power to prevent an interruption that, during my thirty years' experience at the bar, I have never been subjected to without the privilege of holding the instigators thereof responsible—*personally* responsible. It is possibly my fault that I have failed, oratorically, to convey to the gentlemen of the jury the full force and significance of the defendant's signals. I am aware that my voice is singularly deficient in producing either the dulcet tones of my fair client or the impassioned vehemence of the defendant's response. I will," continued the Colonel, with a fatigued but blind fatuity that ignored the hurriedly knit brows and warning eye of the Judge, "try again. The note uttered by my client" (lowering his voice to the faintest of falsettos) "was 'Keeree'; the response was 'Keerowow.'" And the Colonel's voice fairly shook the dome above him.

Another uproar of laughter followed this apparently audacious repetition, but was interrupted by an unlooked-for incident. The defendant rose abruptly, and tearing himself away from the withholding hand and pleading protestations of his counsel, absolutely fled from the court-room, his appearance outside being recognized by a prolonged "Kee-row" from the bystanders, which again and again followed him in the distance.

In the momentary silence which followed, the Colonel's voice was heard saying, "We rest here, Your Honor," and he sat down. No less white, but more agitated, was the face of the defendant's counsel, who instantly rose.

"For some unexplained reason, Your Honor, my client desires to suspend further proceedings, with a view to effect a peaceable compromise with the plaintiff. As he is a man of wealth and position, he is able and willing to pay liberally for that privilege. While I, as his counsel, am still convinced of his legal irresponsibility, as he has chosen publicly to abandon his rights here, I can only ask Your Honor's permission to suspend further proceedings until I can confer with Colonel Starbottle."

"As far as I can follow the pleadings," said the Judge gravely, "the case seems to be hardly one for litigation, and I approve of the defendant's course, while I strongly urge the plaintiff to accept it."

Colonel Starbottle bent over his fair client. Presently he rose, unchanged in look or demeanor. "I yield, Your Honor, to the wishes of my client, and—er—lady. We accept."

Before the court adjourned that day it was known throughout the town that Adoniram K. Hotchkiss had compromised the suit for four thousand dollars and costs.

Colonel Starbottle had so far recovered his equanimity as to strut jauntily towards his office, where he was to meet his fair client. He was surprised, however, to find her already there, and in company with a somewhat sheepish-looking young man—a stranger. If the Colonel had any disappointment in meeting a third party to the interview, his old-fashioned courtesy did not permit him to show it. He bowed graciously, and politely motioned them each to a seat.

"I reckoned I'd bring Hiram round with me," said the young lady, lifting her searching eyes, after a pause, to the Colonel's, "though he *was* awful shy, and allowed that you didn't know him from Adam, or even suspect his existence. But I said, 'That's just where you slip up, Hiram; a pow'ful man like the Colonel knows everything—and I've seen it in his eye.' Lordy!" she continued, with a laugh, leaning forward over her parasol, as her eyes again sought the Colonel's, "don't you remember when you asked me if I loved that old Hotchkiss, and I told you, 'That's tellin',' and you looked at me—Lordy! I knew *then* you suspected there was a Hiram *somewhere,* as good as if I'd told you. Now you jest get up, Hiram, and give the Colonel a good handshake. For if it wasn't for *him* and *his* searchin' ways, and *his* awful power of language, I wouldn't hev got that four thousand dollars out o' that flirty fool Hotchkiss—enough to buy a farm, so as you and me could get married! That's what you owe to *him.* Don't stand there like a stuck fool starin' at him. He won't eat you—though he's killed many a better man. Come, have *I* got to do *all* the kissin'?"

It is of record that the Colonel bowed so courteously and so profoundly that he managed not merely to evade the proffered hand of the shy Hiram, but to only lightly touch the franker and more impulsive finger-tips of the gentle Zaidee. "I—er—offer my sincerest congratulations—though I think you—er—overestimate—my—er—powers of penetration. Unfortunately, a pressing engagement, which may oblige me also to leave town to-night, forbids my saying more. I have—er—left the—er—business settlement of this—er—case in the hands of the lawyers who do my office work, and who will show you every attention. And now let me wish you a very good afternoon."

Nevertheless, the Colonel returned to his private room, and it was nearly twilight when the faithful Jim entered, to find him sitting meditatively before his desk. " 'Fo' God! Kernel, I hope dey ain't nuffin de matter, but you's lookin' mighty solemn! I ain't seen you look dat way, Kernel, since de day pooh Massa Stryker was fetched home shot froo de head."

"Hand me down the whiskey, Jim," said the Colonel, rising slowly.

The Negro flew to the closet joyfully, and brought out the bottle. The Colonel poured out a glass of the spirit and drank it with his old deliberation.

"You're quite right, Jim," he said, putting down his glass, "but I'm—er—getting old—and—somehow—I am missing poor Stryker damnably!"

A PASSAGE IN THE LIFE OF
MR. JOHN OAKHURST

He always thought it must have been Fate. Certainly nothing could have been more inconsistent with his habits than to have been in the Plaza at seven o'clock of that midsummer morning. The sight of his colorless face in Sacramento was rare at that season, and indeed at any season, anywhere, publicly, before two o'clock in the afternoon. Looking back upon it in after years, in the light of a chanceful life, he determined, with the characteristic philosophy of his profession, that it must have been Fate.

Yet it is my duty as a strict chronicler of facts to state that Mr. Oakhurst's presence there that morning was due to a very simple cause. At exactly half past six, the bank being then a winner to the amount of twenty thousand dollars, he had risen from the faro table, relinquished his seat to an accomplished assistant, and withdrawn quietly, without attracting a glance from the silent, anxious faces bowed over the table. But when he entered his luxurious sleeping room, across the passageway, he was a little shocked at finding the sun streaming through an inadvertently opened window. Something in the rare beauty of the morning, perhaps something in the novelty of the idea, struck him as he was about to close the blinds, and he hesitated. Then, taking his hat from the table, he stepped down a private staircase into the street.

The people who were abroad at that early hour were of a class quite unknown to Mr. Oakhurst. There were milkmen and hucksters delivering their wares, small tradespeople opening their shops, housemaids sweeping doorsteps, and occasionally a child. These Mr. Oakhurst regarded with a certain cold curiosity, perhaps quite free from the cynical disfavor with which he generally looked upon the more pretentious of his race whom he was in the habit of meeting. Indeed, I think he was not altogether displeased with the admiring glances which these humble women threw after his handsome face and figure, conspicuous even in a country of fine-looking men. While it is very probable that this wicked vagabond, in the pride of his social isolation, would have been coldly indifferent to the advances of a fine lady, a little girl who ran admiringly by his side in a ragged dress had the power to call a faint flush into his colorless cheek. He dismissed her at last, but not until she had found out—what sooner or later her large-hearted and discriminating sex inevitably did—that he was exceedingly free and openhanded with his money, and also—what perhaps none other of her sex ever did—that the bold black eyes of this fine gentleman were in reality of a brownish and even tender gray.

There was a small garden before a white cottage in a side street that attracted Mr. Oakhurst's attention. It was filled with roses, heliotrope, and verbena—flowers familiar enough to him in the expensive and more portable form of bouquets, but as it seemed to him then, never before so notably lovely. Perhaps it was because the dew was yet fresh upon them, perhaps it was because they were unplucked, but Mr. Oakhurst admired them, not as a possible future tribute to the fascinating and accomplished Miss Ethelinda, then performing at the Varieties, for Mr. Oakhurst's especial benefit, as she had often assured him; nor yet as a *douceur* to the enthralling Miss Montmorrissy, with whom Mr. Oakhurst expected to sup that evening, but simply for himself, and mayhap for the flowers' sake. Howbeit, he passed on, and so out into the open plaza, where, finding a bench under a cottonwood tree, he first dusted the seat with his handkerchief, and then sat down.

It was a fine morning. The air was so still and calm that a sigh from the sycamores seemed like the deep-drawn breath of the just awakening tree, and the faint rustle of its boughs as the outstretching of cramped and reviving limbs. Far away the Sierras stood out against a sky so remote as to be of no positive color—so remote that even the sun despaired of ever reaching it, and so expended its strength recklessly on the whole landscape, until it fairly glittered in a white and vivid contrast. With a very rare impulse, Mr. Oakhurst took off his hat, and half reclined on the bench, with his face to the sky. Certain birds who had taken a critical attitude on a spray above him apparently began an animated discussion regarding his possible malevolent intentions. One or two, emboldened by the silence, hopped on the ground at his feet, until the sound of wheels on the gravel walk frightened them away.

Looking up, he saw a man coming slowly towards him, wheeling a nondescript vehicle in which a woman was partly sitting, partly reclining. Without knowing why, Mr. Oakhurst instantly conceived that the carriage was the invention and workmanship of the man, partly from its oddity, partly from the strong, mechanical hand that grasped it, and partly from a certain pride and visible consciousness in the manner in which the man handled it. Then Mr. Oakhurst saw something more—the man's face was familiar. With that regal faculty of not forgetting a face that had ever given him professional audience, he instantly classified it under the following mental formula: "At 'Frisco, Polka Saloon. Lost his week's wages. I reckon seventy dollars—on red. Never came again." There was, however, no trace of this in the calm eyes and unmoved face that he turned upon the stranger, who, on the contrary, blushed, looked embarrassed, hesitated, and then stopped with an involuntary motion that brought the carriage and its fair occupant face to face with Mr. Oakhurst.

I should hardly do justice to the position she will occupy in this veracious chronicle by describing the lady now—if, indeed, I am able to do it at all. Certainly, the popular estimate was conflicting. The late Colonel Starbottle—to whose large experience of a charming sex I have before been indebted for many valuable suggestions—had, I regret to say, depreciated her fascinations. "A yellow-faced cripple, by dash—a sick woman, with mahogany eyes. One of your blanked spiritual creatures, with no flesh on her bones." On the other hand, however, she enjoyed later much complimentary disparagement from her own sex. Miss Celestina Howard, second leader in the ballet at the Varieties, had, with great alliterative directness, in after years, denominated her as an "aquiline asp." Mlle. Brimborion remembered that she had always warned "Mr. Jack" that this woman would "empoison" him. But Mr. Oakhurst, whose impressions are perhaps the most important, only saw a pale, thin, deep-eyed woman, raised above the level of her companion by the refinement of long suffering and isolation, and a certain shy virginity of manner. There was a suggestion of physical purity in the folds of her fresh-looking robe, and a certain picturesque tastefulness in the details, that, without knowing why, made him think that the robe was her invention and handiwork, even as the carriage she occupied was evidently the work of her companion. Her own hand, a trifle too thin, but well-shaped, subtle-fingered, and gentlewomanly, rested on the side of the carriage, the counterpart of the strong mechanical grasp of her companion's.

There was some obstruction to the progress of the vehicle, and Mr. Oakhurst stepped forward to assist. While the wheel was being lifted over the curbstone, it was necessary that she should hold his arm, and for a moment her thin hand rested there, light and cold as a snowflake, and then—as it seemed to him—like a snowflake melted away. Then there was a pause, and then conversation—the lady joining occasionally and shyly.

It appeared that they were man and wife. That for the past two years she had been a great invalid, and had lost the use of her lower limbs from rheumatism. That until lately she had been confined to her bed, until her husband—who was a master carpenter—had bethought himself to make her this carriage. He took her out regularly for an airing before going to work, because it was his only time, and—they attracted less attention. They had tried many doctors, but without avail. They had been advised to go to the Sulphur Springs, but it was expensive. Mr. Decker, the husband, had once saved eighty dollars for that purpose, but while in San Francisco had his pocket picked— Mr. Decker was so senseless. (The intelligent reader need not be told that it is the lady who is speaking.) They had never been able to make up the sum again, and they had given up the idea. It was a dreadful thing to have one's pocket picked. Did he not think so?

Her husband's face was crimson, but Mr. Oakhurst's countenance was quite calm and unmoved, as he gravely agreed with her, and walked by her side until they passed the little garden that he had admired. Here Mr. Oakhurst commanded a halt, and going to the door, astounded the proprietor by a preposterously extravagant offer for a choice of the flowers. Presently he returned to the carriage with his arms full of roses, heliotrope, and verbena, and cast them in the lap of the invalid. While she was bending over them with childish delight, Mr. Oakhurst took the opportunity of drawing her husband aside.

"Perhaps," he said in a low voice, and a manner quite free from any personal annoyance—"perhaps it's just as well that you lied to her as you did. You can say now that the pickpocket was arrested the other day, and you got your money back." Mr. Oakhurst quietly slipped four twenty-dollar gold pieces into the broad hand of the bewildered Mr. Decker. "Say that—or anything you like—but the truth. Promise me you won't say that!"

The man promised. Mr. Oakhurst quietly returned to the front of the little carriage. The sick woman was still eagerly occupied with the flowers, and as she raised her eyes to his, her faded cheeks seemed to have caught some color from the roses, and her eyes some of their dewy freshness. But at that instant Mr. Oakhurst lifted his hat, and before she could thank him was gone.

I grieve to say that Mr. Decker shamelessly broke his promise. That night, in the very goodness of his heart and uxorious self-abnegation, he, like all devoted husbands, not only offered himself, but his friend and benefactor, as a sacrifice on the family altar. It is only fair, however, to add that he spoke with great fervor of the generosity of Mr. Oakhurst, and dealt with an enthusiasm quite common with his class on the mysterious fame and prodigal vices of the gambler.

"And now, Elsie, dear, say that you'll forgive me," said Mr. Decker, dropping on one knee beside his wife's couch. "I did it for the best. It was for you, dearey, that I put that money on them cards that night in 'Frisco. I thought to win a heap—enough to take you away, and enough left to get you a new dress."

Mrs. Decker smiled and pressed her husband's hand. "I do forgive you, Joe, dear," she said, still smiling, with eyes abstractedly fixed on the ceiling; "and you ought to be whipped for deceiving me so, you bad boy, and making me make such a speech.

There, say no more about it. If you'll be very good hereafter, and will just now hand me that cluster of roses, I'll forgive you." She took the branch in her fingers, lifted the roses to her face, and presently said, behind their leaves—

"Joe!"

"What is it, lovey?"

"Do you think that this Mr.—what do you call him?—Jack Oakhurst would have given that money back to you if I hadn't made that speech?"

"Yes."

"If he hadn't seen me at all?"

Mr. Decker looked up. His wife had managed in some way to cover up her whole face with the roses, except her eyes, which were dangerously bright.

"No; it was you, Elsie—it was all along of seeing you that made him do it."

"A poor sick woman like me?"

"A sweet, little, lovely, pooty Elsie—Joe's own little wifey! How could he help it?"

Mrs. Decker fondly cast one arm around her husband's neck, still keeping the roses to her face with the other. From behind them she began to murmur gently and idiotically, "Dear, ole square Joey. Elsie's oney booful big bear." But, really, I do not see that my duty as a chronicler of facts compels me to continue this little lady's speech any further, and out of respect to the unmarried reader I stop.

Nevertheless, the next morning Mrs. Decker betrayed some slight and apparently uncalled-for irritability on reaching the plaza, and presently desired her husband to wheel her back home. Moreover, she was very much astonished at meeting Mr. Oakhurst just as they were returning, and even doubted if it were he, and questioned her husband as to his identity with the stranger of yesterday as he approached. Her manner to Mr. Oakhurst, also, was quite in contrast with her husband's frank welcome. Mr. Oakhurst instantly detected it. "Her husband has told her all, and she dislikes me," he said to himself, with that fatal appreciation of the half-truths of a woman's motives that causes the wisest masculine critic to stumble. He lingered only long enough to take the business address of the husband, and then, lifting his hat gravely, without looking at the lady, went his way. It struck the honest master carpenter as one of the charming anomalies of his wife's character that, although the meeting was evidently very much constrained and unpleasant, instantly afterward his wife's spirits began to rise. "You was hard on him—a leetle hard, wasn't you Elsie?" said Mr. Decker deprecatingly. "I'm afraid he may think I've broke my promise." "Ah, indeed," said the lady indifferently. Mr. Decker instantly stepped round to the front of the vehicle. "You look like an A-1 first-class lady riding down Broadway in her own carriage, Elsie," said he; "I never seed you lookin' so peart and sassy before."

A few days later the proprietor of the San Isabel Sulphur Springs received the following note in Mr. Oakhurst's well-known dainty hand:

DEAR STEVE,—I've been thinking over your proposition to buy Nichols's quarter interest and have concluded to go in. But I don't see how the thing will pay until you have more accommodation down there, and for the best class—I mean *my* customers. What we want is an extension to the main building, and two or three cottages put up. I send down a builder to take hold of the job at once. He takes his sick wife with him, and you are to look after them as you would for one of us.

I may run down there myself after the races, just to look after things; but I sha'n't set upon any game this season.

Yours always,

JOHN OAKHURST

It was only the last sentence of this letter that provoked criticism. "I can understand," said Mr. Hamlin, a professional brother to whom Mr. Oakhurst's letter was shown—"I can understand why Jack goes in heavy and builds, for it's a sure spec, and is bound to be a mighty soft thing in time, if he comes here regularly. But why in blank he don't set up a bank this season and take the chance of getting some of the money back that he puts into circulation in building is what gets me. I wonder now," he mused deeply, "what *is* his little game."

The season had been a prosperous one to Mr. Oakhurst, and proportionally disastrous to several members of the legislature, judges, colonels, and others who had enjoyed but briefly the pleasure of Mr. Oakhurst's midnight society. And yet Sacramento had become very dull to him. He had lately formed a habit of early morning walks—so unusual and startling to his friends, both male and female, as to occasion the intensest curiosity. Two or three of the latter set spies upon his track, but the inquisition resulted only in the discovery that Mr. Oakhurst walked to the plaza, sat down upon one particular bench for a few moments, and then returned without seeing anybody, and the theory that there was a woman in the case was abandoned. A few superstitious gentlemen of his own profession believed that he did it for "luck." Some others, more practical, declared that he went out to "study points."

After the races at Marysville, Mr. Oakhurst went to San Francisco; from that place he returned to Marysville, but a few days after was seen at San José, Santa Cruz, and Oakland. Those who met him declared that his manner was restless and feverish, and quite unlike his ordinary calmness and phlegm. Colonel Starbottle pointed out the fact that at San Francisco, at the Club, Jack had declined to deal. "Hand shaky, sir—depend upon it; don't stimulate enough —blank him!"

From San José he started to go to Oregon by land with a rather expensive outfit of horses and camp equipage, but on reaching Stockton he suddenly diverged, and four hours later found him, with a single horse, entering the canyon of the San Isabel Warm Sulphur Springs.

It was a pretty triangular valley lying at the foot of three sloping mountains, dark with pines and fantastic with madrono and manzanita. Nestling against the mountainside, the straggling buildings and long piazza of the hotel glittered through the leaves; and here and there shone a white toylike cottage. Mr. Oakhurst was not an admirer of nature, but he felt something of the same novel satisfaction in the view that he experienced in his first morning walk in Sacramento. And now carriages began to pass him on the road filled with gaily dressed women, and the cold California outlines of the landscape began to take upon themselves somewhat of a human warmth and color. And then the long hotel piazza came in view, efflorescent with the full-toileted fair. Mr. Oakhurst, a good rider after the California fashion, did not check his speed as he approached his destination, but charged the hotel at a gallop, threw his horse on his haunches within a foot of the piazza, and then quietly emerged from the cloud of dust that veiled his dismounting.

Whatever feverish excitement might have raged within, all his habitual calm returned as he stepped upon the piazza. With the instinct of long habit he turned and faced the battery of eyes with the same cold indifference with which he had for years encountered the half-hidden sneers of men and the half-frightened admiration of women. Only one person stepped forward to welcome him. Oddly enough, it was Dick Hamilton, perhaps the only one present who, by birth, education, and position, might have satisfied the most fastidious social critic. Happily for Mr. Oakhurst's reputation, he was also a very rich banker and social leader. "Do you know who that is you spoke to?" asked young Parker, with an alarmed expression. "Yes," replied Hamilton, with charatcetistic effrontery; "the man you lost a thousand dollars to last week. *I* only know him *socially*." "But isn't he a gambler?" queried the youngest Miss Smith. "He is," replied Hamilton; "but I wish, my dear young lady, that we all played as open and honest a game as our friend yonder, and were as willing as he is to abide by its fortunes."

But Mr. Oakhurst was happily out of hearing of this colloquy, and was even then lounging listlessly, yet watchfully, along the upper hall. Suddenly he heard a light footstep behind him, and then his name called in a familiar voice that drew the blood quickly to his heart. He turned, and she stood before him.

But how transformed! If I have hesitated to describe the hollow-eyed cripple—the quaintly dressed artisan's wife, a few pages ago—what shall I do with this graceful, shapely, elegantly attired gentlewoman into whom she has been merged within these two months? In good faith, she was very pretty. You and I, my dear madam, would have been quick to see that those charming dimples were misplaced for true beauty, and too fixed in their quality for honest mirthfulness; that the delicate lines around those aquiline nostrils were cruel and selfish; that the sweet, virginal surprise of those lovely eyes was as apt to be opened on her plate as upon the gallant speeches of her dinner partner; that her sympathetic color came and went more with her own spirits than yours. But you and I are not in love with her, dear madam, and Mr. Oakhurst is. And even in the folds of her Parisian gown, I am afraid this poor fellow saw the same subtle strokes of purity that he had seen in her homespun robe. And then there was the delightful revelation that she could walk, and that she had dear little feet of her own in the tiniest slippers of her French shoemaker, with such preposterous blue bows, and Chappell's own stamp, Rue de something or other, Paris, on the narrow sole.

He ran towards her with a heightened color and outstretched hands. But she whipped her own behind her, glanced rapidly up and down the long hall, and stood looking at him with a half-audacious, half-mischievous admiration in utter contrast to her old reserve.

"I've a great mind not to shake hands with you at all. You passed me just now on the piazza without speaking, and I ran after you, as I suppose many another poor woman has done."

Mr. Oakhurst stammered that she was so changed.

"The more reason why you should know me. Who changed me? You. You have re-created me. You found a helpless, crippled, sick, poverty-stricken woman, with one dress to her back, and that her own make, and you gave her life, health, strength, and fortune. You did, and you know it, sir. How do you like your work?" She caught the side seams of her gown in either hand and dropped him a playful courtesy. Then, with a sudden, relenting gesture, she gave him both her hands.

Outrageous as this speech was, and unfeminine, as I trust every fair reader will deem it, I fear it pleased Mr. Oakhurst. Not but that he was accustomed to a certain frank female admiration; but then it was of the coulisses and not of the cloister with which he always persisted in associating Mrs. Decker. To be addressed in this way by an invalid Puritan, a sick saint, with the austerity of suffering still clothing her—a woman who had a Bible on the dressing table, who went to church three times a day, and was devoted to her husband, completely bowled him over. He still held her hands as she went on—

"Why didn't you come before? What were you doing in Marysville, in San José, in Oakland? You see I have followed you. I saw you as you came down the canyon, and knew you at once. I saw your letter to Joseph, and knew you were coming. Why didn't you write to me? You will sometime! Good evening, Mr. Hamilton."

She had withdrawn her hands, but not until Hamilton, ascending the staircase, was nearly abreast of them. He raised his hat to her with well-bred composure, nodded familiarly to Oakhurst, and passed on. When he had gone Mrs. Decker lifted her eyes to Mr. Oakhurst. "Some day I shall ask a great favor of you!"

Mr. Oakhurst begged that it should be now. "No, not until you know me better. Then, some day, I shall want you to—kill that man!"

She laughed, such a pleasant little ringing laugh, such a display of dimples—albeit a little fixed in the corners of her mouth—such an innocent light in her brown eyes, and such a lovely color in her cheeks, that Mr. Oakhurst—who seldom laughed—was fain to laugh too. It was as if a lamb had proposed to a fox a foray into a neighboring sheepfold.

A few evenings after this, Mrs. Decker arose from a charmed circle of her admirers on the hotel piazza, excused herself for a few moments, laughingly declined an escort, and ran over to her little cottage— one of her husband's creation—across the road. Perhaps from the sudden and unwonted exercise in her still convalescent state, she breathed hurriedly and feverishly as she entered her boudoir, and once or twice placed her hand upon her breast. She was startled on turning up the light to find her husband lying on the sofa.

"You look hot and excited, Elsie, love," said Mr. Decker; "you ain't took worse, are you?"

Mrs. Decker's face had paled, but now flushed again. "No," she said, "only a little pain here," as she again placed her hand upon her corsage.

"Can I do anything for you?" said Mr. Decker, rising with affectionate concern.

"Run over to the hotel and get me some brandy, quick!"

Mr. Decker ran. Mrs. Decker closed and bolted the door, and then putting her hand to her bosom, drew out the pain. It was folded foursquare, and was, I grieve to say, in Mr. Oakhurst's handwriting.

She devoured it with burning eyes and cheeks until there came a step upon the porch. Then she hurriedly replaced it in her bosom and unbolted the door. Her husband entered; she raised the spirits to her lips and declared herself better.

"Are you going over there again tonight?" asked Mr. Decker submissively.

"No," said Mrs. Decker, with her eyes fixed dreamily on the floor.

"I wouldn't if I was you," said Mr. Decker with a sigh of relief. After a pause he took a seat on the sofa, and drawing his wife to his side, said, "Do you know what I was thinking of when you came in, Elsie?" Mrs. Decker ran her fingers through his stiff black hair, and couldn't imagine.

"I was thinking of old times, Elsie; I was thinking of the days when I built that kerridge for you, Elsie—when I used to take you out to ride, and was both hoss and driver! We was poor then, and you was sick, Elsie, but we was happy. We've got money now, and a house, and you're quite another woman. I may say, dear, that you're a *new* woman. And that's where the trouble comes in. I could build you a kerridge, Elsie; I could build you a house, Elsie—but there I stopped. I couldn't build up *you*. You're strong and pretty, Elsie, and fresh and new. But somehow, Elsie, you ain't no work of mine!"

He paused. With one hand laid gently on his forehead and the other pressed upon her bosom as if to feel certain of the presence of her pain, she said sweetly and soothingly:

"But it was your work, dear."

Mr. Decker shook his head sorrowfully. "No, Elsie, not mine. I had the chance to do it once and I let it go. It's done now; but not by me."

Mrs. Decker raised her surprised, innocent eyes to his. He kissed her tenderly, and then went on in a more cheerful voice.

"That ain't all I was thinking of, Elsie. I was thinking that maybe you give too much of your company to that Mr. Hamilton. Not that there's any wrong in it, to you or him. But it might make people talk. You're the only one here, Elsie," said the master carpenter, looking fondly at his wife, "who isn't talked about; whose work ain't inspected or condemned."

Mrs. Decker was glad he had spoken about it. She had thought so, too, but she could not well be uncivil to Mr. Hamilton, who was a fine gentleman, without making a powerful enemy. "And he's always treated me as if I was a born lady in his own circle," added the little woman, with a certain pride that made her husband fondly smile. "But I have thought of a plan. He will not stay here if I should go away. If, for instance,

I went to San Francisco to visit ma for a few days, he would be gone before I should return."

Mr. Decker was delighted. "By all means," he said; "go tomorrow. Jack Oakhurst is going down, and I'll put you in his charge."

Mrs. Decker did not think it was prudent. "Mr. Oakhurst is our friend, Joseph, but you know his reputation." In fact, she did not know that she ought to go now, knowing that he was going the same day; but with a kiss Mr. Decker overcame her scruples. She yielded gracefully. Few women, in fact, knew how to give up a point as charmingly as she.

She stayed a week in San Francisco. When she returned she was a trifle thinner and paler than she had been. This she explained as the result of perhaps too active exercise and excitement. "I was out-of-doors nearly all the time, as ma will tell you," she said to her husband, "and always alone. I am getting quite independent now," she added gaily. "I don't want any escort—I believe, Joey dear, I could get along even without you—I'm so brave!"

But her visit, apparently, had not been productive of her impelling design. Mr. Hamilton had not gone, but had remained, and called upon them that very evening. "I've thought of a plan, Joey, dear," said Mrs. Decker when he had departed. "Poor Mr. Oakhurst has a miserable room at the hotel—suppose you ask him when he returns from San Francisco to stop with us. He can have our spare room. I don't think," she added archly, "that Mr. Hamilton will call often." Her husband laughed, intimated that she was a little coquette, pinched her cheek, and complied. "The queer thing about a woman," he said afterwards confidentially to Mr. Oakhurst, "is that without having any plan of her own, she'll take anybody's and build a house on it entirely different to suit herself. And dern my skin, if you'll be able to say whether or not you didn't give the scale and measurements yourself. That's what gets me."

The next week Mr. Oakhurst was installed in the Deckers' cottage. The business relations of her husband and himself were known to all, and her own reputation was above suspicion. Indeed, few women were more popular. She was domestic, she was prudent, she was pious. In a country of great feminine freedom and latitude, she never rode or walked with anybody but her husband; in an epoch of slang and ambiguous expression, she was always precise and formal in her speech; in the midst of a fashion of ostentatious decoration she never wore a diamond, nor a single valuable jewel. She never permitted an indecorum in public; she never countenanced the familiarities of California society. She declaimed against the prevailing tone of infidelity and skepticism in religion. Few people who were present will ever forget the dignified yet stately manner with which she rebuked Mr. Hamilton in the public parlor for entering upon the discussion of a work on materialism, lately published; and some among them, also, will not forget the expression of amused surprise on Mr. Hamilton's face that gradually changed to sardonic gravity as he courteously waived his point. Certainly, not Mr. Oakhurst, who from that moment began to be uneasily impatient of his friend, and even—if such a term could be applied to any moral quality in Mr. Oakhurst—to fear him.

For, during this time, Mr. Oakhurst had begun to show symptoms of a change in his usual habits. He was seldom, if ever, seen in his old haunts, in a barroom, or with his old associates. Pink and white notes, in distracted handwriting, accumulated on the dressing table in his rooms at Sacramento. It was given out in San Francisco that he had some organic disease of the heart, for which his physician had prescribed perfect rest. He read more, he took long walks, he sold his fast horses, he went to church.

I have a very vivid recollection of his first appearance there. He did not accompany the Deckers, nor did he go into their pew, but came in as the service commenced, and took a seat quietly in one of the back pews. By some mysterious instinct his presence became presently known to the congregation, some of whom so far forgot themselves, in their curiosity, as to face around and apparently address their responses to him. Before the service was over it was pretty well understood that "miserable sinners" meant Mr. Oakhurst. Nor did this mysterious influence fail to affect the officiating clergyman, who introduced an allusion to Mr. Oakhurst's calling and habits in a sermon on the architecture of Solomon's Temple, and in a manner so pointed and yet labored as to cause the youngest of us to flame with indignation. Happily, however, it was lost upon Jack; I do not think he even heard it. His handsome, colorless face—albeit a trifle worn and thoughtful—was inscrutable. Only once, during the singing of a hymn, at a certain note in the contralto's voice, there crept into his dark eyes a look of wistful tenderness, so yearning and yet so hopeless that those who were watching him felt their own glisten. Yet I retain a very vivid remembrance of his standing up to receive benediction, with the suggestion in his manner and tightly buttoned coat of taking the fire of his adversary at ten paces. After church he disappeared as quietly as he entered, and fortunately escaped hearing the comments on his rash act. His appearance was generally considered as an impertinence—attributable only to some wanton fancy —or possibly a bet. One or two thought that the sexton was exceedingly remiss in not turning him out after discovering who he was; and a prominent pewholder remarked that if he couldn't take his wife and daughters to that church without exposing them to such an influence, he would try to find some church where he could. Another traced Mr. Oakhurst's presence to certain Broad Church radical tendencies, which he regretted to say he had lately noted in their pastor. Deacon Sawyer, whose delicately organized, sickly wife had already borne him eleven children, and died in an ambitious attempt to complete the dozen, avowed that the presence of a person of Mr. Oakhurst's various and indiscriminate gallantries was an insult to the memory of the deceased that, as a man, he could not brook.

It was about this time that Mr. Oakhurst, contrasting himself with a conventional world in which he had hitherto rarely mingled, became aware that there was something in his face, figure, and carriage quite unlike other men—something that if it did not betray his former career, at least showed an individuality and originality that was suspicious. In this belief he shaved off his long, silken mustache, and religiously brushed out his clustering curls every morning. He even went so far as to affect a negligence of dress, and hid his small, slim, arched feet in the largest and heaviest walking shoes. There is a story told that he went to his tailor in Sacramento, and asked him to make him a suit of clothes like everybody else. The tailor, familiar with Mr. Oakhurst's fastidiousness, did not know what he meant. "I mean," said Mr. Oakhurst savagely, "something *respectable*—something that doesn't exactly fit me, you know." But however Mr. Oakhurst might hide his shapely limbs in homespun and homemade garments, there was something in his carriage, something in the pose of his beautiful head, something in the strong and fine manliness of his presence, something in the perfect and utter discipline and control of his muscles, something in the high repose of his nature—a repose not so much a matter of intellectual ruling as of his very nature—that go where he would, and with whom, he was always a notable man in ten thousand. Perhaps this was never so clearly intimated to Mr. Oakhurst as when, emboldened by Mr. Hamilton's advice and assistance and his predilections, he became a San Francisco broker. Even before objection was made to his presence in the Board—the objection, I remember, was urged very eloquently by Watt Sanders, who was supposed to be the inventor of the "freezing out" system of disposing of poor stockholders, and who also enjoyed the reputation of having been the impelling cause of Briggs of Tuolumne's ruin and suicide—even before this formal protest of respectability against lawlessness, the aquiline suggestions of Mr. Oakhurst's mien and countenance not only prematurely fluttered the pigeons, but absolutely occasioned much uneasiness among the fish hawks, who circled below him with their booty. "Dash me! but he's as likely to go after us as anybody," said Joe Fielding.

It wanted but a few days before the close of the brief summer season at San Isabel Warm Springs. Already there had been some migration of the more fashionable, and there was an uncomfortable suggestion of dregs and lees in the social life that remained. Mr. Oakhurst was moody; it was hinted that even the secure reputation of Mrs. Decker could no longer protect her from the gossip which his presence excited. It is but fair to her to say that during the last few weeks of this trying ordeal she looked like a sweet, pale martyr, and conducted herself toward her traducers with the gentle, forgiving manner of one who relied not upon the idle homage of the crowd, but upon the security of a principle that was dearer than popular favor. "They talk about myself and Mr. Oakhurst, my dear," she said to a friend, "but Heaven and my husband can best answer their calumny. It never shall be said that my husband ever turned his back upon a friend in the moment of his adversity because the position was changed, because his friend was poor and he was rich." This was the first intimation to the public that Jack had lost money, although it was known generally that the Deckers had lately bought some valuable property in San Francisco.

A few evenings after this an incident occurred which seemed to unpleasantly discord with the general social harmony that had always existed at San Isabel. It was at dinner, and Mr. Oakhurst and Mr. Hamilton, who sat together at a separate table, were observed to rise in some agitation. When they reached the hall, by a common instinct they stepped into a little breakfast-room which was vacant, and closed the door. Then Mr. Hamilton turned, with a half-amused, half-serious smile, toward his friend, and said—

"If we are to quarrel, Jack Oakhurst—you and I —in the name of all that is ridiculous, don't let it be about a—"

I do not know what was the epithet intended. It was either unspoken or lost. For at that very instant Mr. Oakhurst raised a wine glass and dashed its contents into Hamilton's face.

As they faced each other the men seemed to have changed natures. Mr. Oakhurst was trembling with excitement, and the wine glass that he returned to the table shivered between his fingers. Mr. Hamilton stood there, grayish white, erect, and dripping. After a pause he said coldly—

"So be it. But remember! our quarrel commences here. If I fall by your hand, you shall not use it to clear her character; if you fall by mine, you shall not be called a martyr. I am sorry it has come to this, but amen!—the sooner now the better."

He turned proudly, dropped his lids over his cold steel-blue eyes, as if sheathing a rapier, bowed, and passed coldly out.

They met twelve hours later in a little hollow two miles from the hotel, on the Stockton road. As Mr. Oakhurst received his pistol from Colonel Starbottle's hands he said to him in a low voice, "Whatever turns up or down I shall not return to the hotel. You will find some directions in my room. Go there—" but his voice suddenly faltered, and he turned his glistening eyes away, to his second's intense astonishment.

"I've been out a dozen times with Jack Oakhurst," said Colonel Starbottle afterwards, "and I never saw him anyways cut before. Blank me if I didn't think he was losing his sand, till he walked to position."

The two reports were almost simultaneous. Mr. Oakhurst's right arm dropped suddenly to his side, and his pistol would have fallen from his paralyzed fingers, but the discipline of trained nerve and muscle prevailed, and he kept his grasp until he had shifted it to the other hand, without changing his position. Then there was a silence that seemed interminable, a gathering of two or three dark figures where a smoke curl still lazily floated, and then the hurried, husky, panting voice of Colonel Starbottle in his ear, "He's hit hard—through the lungs—you must run for it!"

Jack turned his dark, questioning eyes upon his second, but did not seem to listen; rather seemed to hear some other voice, remoter in the distance. He hesitated, and then made a step forward in the direction of the distant group. Then he paused again as the figures separated, and the surgeon came hastily toward him.

"He would like to speak with you a moment," said the man. "You have little time to lose, I know; but," he added in a lower voice, "it is my duty to tell you he has still less."

A look of despair so hopeless in its intensity swept over Mr. Oakhurst's usually impassive face that the surgeon started. "You are hit," he said, glancing at Jack's helpless arm.

"Nothing—a mere scratch," said Jack hastily. Then he added, with a bitter laugh, "I'm not in luck today. But come! We'll see what he wants."

His long feverish stride outstripped the surgeon's, and in another moment he stood where the dying man lay—like most dying men—the one calm, composed, central figure of an anxious group. Mr. Oakhurst's face was less calm as he dropped on one knee beside him and took his hand. "I want to speak with this gentleman alone," said Hamilton, with something of his old imperious manner, as he turned to those about him. When they drew back, he looked up in Oakhurst's face.

His own face was white, but not so white as that which Mr. Oakhurst bent over him—a face so ghastly, with haunting doubts and a hopeless presentiment of coming evil, a face so piteous in its infinite weariness and envy of death, that the dying man was touched, even in the languor of dissolution, with a pang of compassion, and the cynical smile faded from his lips.

"Forgive me, Jack," he whispered more feebly, "for what I have to say. I don't say it in anger, but only because it must be said. I could not do my duty to you—I could not die contented until you knew it all. It's a miserable business at best, all around. But it can't be helped now. Only I ought to have fallen by Decker's pistol and not yours."

A flush like fire came into Jack's cheek, and he would have risen, but Hamilton held him fast.

"Listen! in my pocket you will find two letters. Take them—there! You will know the handwriting. But promise you will not read them until you are in a place of safety. Promise me!"

Jack did not speak, but held the letters between his fingers as if they had been burning coals.

"Promise me," said Hamilton faintly.

"Why?" asked Oakhurst, dropping his friend's hand coldly.

"Because," said the dying man with a bitter smile—"because—when you have read them—you—will—go back—to capture—and death!"

They were his last words. He pressed Jack's hand faintly. Then his grasp relaxed, and he fell back a corpse.

It was nearly ten o'clock at night, and Mrs. Decker reclined languidly upon the sofa with a novel in her hand, while her husband discussed the politics of the country in the barroom of the hotel. It was a warm night, and the French window looking out upon a little balcony was partly open. Suddenly she heard a foot upon the balcony, and she raised her eyes from the book with a slight start. The next moment the window was hurriedly thrust wide and a man entered.

Mrs. Decker rose to her feet with a little cry of alarm.

"For Heaven's sake, Jack, are you mad? He has only gone for a little while—he may return at any moment. Come an hour later—tomorrow—any time when I can get rid of him—but go, now, dear, at once."

Mr. Oakhurst walked toward the door, bolted it, and then faced her without a word. His face was haggard, his coat sleeve hung loosely over an arm that was bandaged and bloody.

Nevertheless, her voice did not falter as she turned again toward him. "What has happened, Jack? Why are you here?"

He opened his coat, and threw two letters in her lap.

"To return your lover's letters—to kill you—and then myself," he said in a voice so low as to be almost inaudible.

Among the many virtues of this admirable woman was invincible courage. She did not faint, she did not cry out. She sat quietly down again, folded her hands in her lap, and said calmly—

"And why should you not?"

Had she recoiled, had she shown any fear or contrition, had she essayed an explanation or apology, Mr. Oakhurst would have looked upon it as an evidence of guilt. But there is no quality that courage recognizes so quickly as courage, there is no condition that desperation bows before but desperation; and Mr. Oakhurst's power of analysis was not so keen as to prevent him from confounding her courage with a moral quality. Even in this fury he could not help admiring this dauntless invalid.

"Why should you not?" she repeated with a smile. "You gave me life, health, and happiness, Jack. You gave me your love. Why should you not take what you have given? Go on. I am ready."

She held out her hands with that same infinite grace of yielding with which she had taken his own on the first day of their meeting at the hotel. Jack raised his head, looked at her for one wild moment, dropped upon his knees beside her, and raised the folds of her dress to his feverish lips. But she was too clever not to instantly see her victory; she was too much of a woman, with all her cleverness, to refrain from pressing that victory home. At the same moment, as with the impulse of an outraged and wounded woman, she rose, and with an imperious gesture pointed to the window. Mr. Oakhurst rose in his turn, cast one glance upon her, and without another word passed out of her presence forever.

When he had gone, she closed the window and bolted it, and going to the chimney piece placed the letters, one by one, in the flame of the candle until they were consumed. I would not have the reader think that during this painful operation she was unmoved. Her hand trembled and—not being a brute—for some minutes (perhaps longer) she felt very badly, and the corners of her sensitive mouth were depressed. When her husband arrived it was with a genuine joy that she ran to him, and nestled against his broad breast with a feeling of security that thrilled the honest fellow to the core.

"But I've heard dreadful news tonight, Elsie," said Mr. Decker, after a few endearments were exchanged.

"Don't tell me anything dreadful, dear; I'm not well tonight," she pleaded sweetly.

"But it's about Mr. Oakhurst and Hamilton."

"Please!" Mr. Decker could not resist the petitionary grace of those white hands and that sensitive mouth, and took her to his arms. Suddenly he said, "What's that?"

He was pointing to the bosom of her white dress. Where Mr. Oakhurst had touched her there was a spot of blood.

It was nothing; she had slightly cut her hand in closing the window; it shut so hard! If Mr. Decker had remembered to close and bolt the shutter before he went out, he might have saved her this. There was such a genuine irritability and force in this remark that Mr. Decker was quite overcome by remorse. But Mrs. Decker forgave him with that graciousness which I have before pointed out in these pages, and with the halo of that forgiveness and marital confidence still lingering above the pair, with the reader's permission we will leave them and return to Mr. Oakhurst.

But not for two weeks. At the end of that time he walked into his rooms in Sacramento, and in his old manner took his seat at the faro table.

"How's your arm, Jack?" asked an incautious player.

There was a smile followed the question, which, however, ceased as Jack looked up quietly at the speaker.

"It bothers my dealing a little, but I can shoot as well with my left."

The game was continued in that decorous silence which usually distinguished the table at which Mr. John Oakhurst presided.

WAN LEE,
THE PAGAN

As I opened Hop Sing's letter there fluttered to the ground a square strip of yellow paper covered with hieroglyphics, which at first glance I innocently took to be the label from a pack of Chinese firecrackers. But the same envelope also contained a smaller strip of rice paper, with two Chinese characters traced in India ink, that I at once knew to be Hop Sing's visiting card. The whole, as afterwards literally translated, ran as follows:

To the stranger the gates of my house are not closed; the rice jar is on the left, and the sweetmeats on the right, as you enter.

Two sayings of the Master:

Hospitality is the virtue of the son and the wisdom of the ancestor.

The superior man is lighthearted after the cropgathering; he makes a festival.

When the stranger is in your melon patch observe him not too closely; inattention is often the highest form of civility.

Happiness, Peace, and Prosperity.

HOP SING

Admirable, certainly, as was this morality and proverbial wisdom, and although this last axiom was very characteristic of my friend Hop Sing, who was that most somber of all humorists, a Chinese philosopher, I must confess that even after a very free translation I was at a loss to make any immediate application of the message. Luckily I discovered a third enclosure in the shape of a little note in English and Hop Sing's own commercial hand. It ran thus:

The pleasure of your company is requested at No. — Sacramento Street, on Friday evening at eight o'clock. A cup of tea at nine—sharp.   HOP SING

This explained all. It meant a visit to Hop Sing's warehouse, the opening and exhibition of some rare Chinese novelties and curios, a chat in the back office, a cup of tea of a perfection unknown beyond these sacred precincts, cigars, and a visit to the Chinese Theater or Temple. This was in fact the favorite program of Hop Sing when he exercised his functions of hospitality as the chief factor or superintendent of the Ning Foo Company.

At eight o'clock on Friday evening I entered the warehouse of Hop Sing. There was that deliciously commingled mysterious foreign odor that I had so often noticed; there was the old array of uncouth-looking objects, the long procession of jars and crockery, the same singular blending of the grotesque and the mathematically neat and exact, the same endless suggestions of frivolity and fragility, the same want of harmony in colors that were each, in themselves, beautiful and rare. Kites in the shape of enormous dragons and gigantic butterflies; kites so ingeniously arranged as to utter at intervals, when facing the wind, the cry of a hawk; kites so large as to be beyond any boy's power of restraint—so large that you understood why kite-flying in China was an amusement for adults; gods of china and bronze so gratuitously ugly as to be beyond any human interest or sympathy from their very impossibility; jars of sweetmeats covered all over with moral sentiments from Confucius; hats that looked like baskets, and baskets that looked like hats; silk so light that I hesitate to record the incredible number of square yards that you might pass through the ring on your little finger—these and a great many other indescribable objects were all familiar to me. I pushed my way through the dimly lighted warehouse until I reached the back office or parlor, where I found Hop Sing waiting to receive me.

Before I describe him I want the average reader to discharge from his mind any idea of a Chinaman that he may have gathered from the pantomime. He did not wear beautifully scalloped drawers fringed with little bells—I never met a Chinaman who did; he did not habitually carry his forefinger extended before him at right angles with his body, nor did I ever hear him utter the mysterious sentence, "Ching a ring a ring chaw," nor dance under any provocation. He was, on the whole, a rather grave, decorous, handsome gentleman. His complexion, which extended all over his head except where his long pigtail grew, was like a very nice piece of glazed brown paper-muslin. His eyes were black and bright, and his eyelids set at an angle of 15°; his nose straight and delicately formed, his mouth small, and his teeth white and clean. He wore a dark blue silk blouse, and in the streets on cold days a short jacket of astrakhan fur. He wore also a pair of drawers of blue brocade gathered tightly over his calves and ankles, offering a general sort of suggestion that he had forgotten his trousers that morning, but that, so gentlemanly were his manners, his friends had forborne to mention the fact to him. His manner was urbane, although quite serious. He spoke French and English fluently. In brief, I doubt if you could have found the equal of this Pagan shopkeeper among the Christian traders of San Francisco.

There were a few others present: a judge of the federal court, an editor, a high government official, and a prominent merchant. After we had drunk our tea, and tasted a few sweetmeats from a mysterious jar that looked as if it might contain a preserved mouse among its other nondescript treasures, Hop Sing arose, and gravely beckoning us to follow him, began to descend to the basement. When we got there, we were amazed at finding it brilliantly lighted, and that a number of chairs were arranged in a half circle on the asphalt pavement. When he had courteously seated us, he said—

"I have invited you to witness a performance which I can at least promise you no other foreigners but yourselves have ever seen. Wang, the court juggler, arrived here yesterday morning. He has never given a performance outside of the palace before. I have asked him to entertain my friends this evening. He requires no theater, stage, accessories, or any confederate—nothing more than you see here. Will you be pleased to examine the ground yourselves, gentlemen."

Of course we examined the premises. It was the ordinary basement or cellar of the San Francisco storehouse, cemented to keep out the damp. We poked our sticks into the pavement and rapped on the walls to satisfy our polite host, but for no other purpose. We were quite content to be the victims of any clever deception. For myself, I knew I was ready to be deluded to any extent, and if I had been offered an explanation of what followed, I should have probably declined it.

Although I am satisfied that Wang's general performance was the first of that kind ever given on American soil, it has probably since become so familiar to many of my readers that I shall not bore them with it here. He began by setting to flight, with the aid of his fan, the usual number of butterflies made before our eyes of little bits of tissue paper, and kept them in the air during the remainder of the performance. I have a vivid recollection of the judge trying to catch one that had lit on his knee, and of its evading him with the pertinacity of a living insect. And even at this time Wang, still plying his fan, was taking chickens out of hats, making oranges disappear, pulling endless yards of silk from his sleeve, apparently filling the whole area of the basement with goods that appeared mysteriously from the ground, from his own sleeves, from nowhere! He swallowed knives to the ruin of his digestion for years to come; he dislocated every limb of his body; he reclined in the air, apparently upon nothing. But his crowning performance, which I have never yet seen repeated, was the most weird, mysterious, and astounding. It is my apology for this long introduction, my sole excuse for writing this article, the genesis of this veracious history.

He cleared the ground of its encumbering articles for a space of about fifteen feet square, and then invited us all to walk forward and again examine it. We did so gravely; there was nothing but the cemented pavement below to be seen or felt. He then asked for the loan of a handkerchief, and as I chanced to be nearest him, I offered mine. He took it and spread it open upon the floor. Over this he spread a large square of silk, and over this again a large shawl nearly covering the space he had cleared. He then took a position at one of the points of this rectangle, and began a monotonous chant, rocking his body to and fro in time with the somewhat lugubrious air.

We sat still and waited. Above the chant we could hear the striking of the city clocks, and the occasional rattle of a cart in the street overhead. The absolute watchfulness and expectation, the dim, mysterious half-light of the cellar, falling in a gruesome way upon the misshapen bulk of a Chinese deity in the background, a faint smell of opium smoke mingling with spice, and the dreadful uncertainty of what we were really waiting for, sent an uncomfortable thrill down our backs, and made us look at each other with a forced and unnatural smile. This feeling was heightened when Hop Sing slowly rose, and without a word, pointed with his finger to the center of the shawl.

There was something beneath the shawl! Surely— and something that was not there before. At first a mere suggestion in relief, a faint outline, but growing more and more distinct and visible every moment. The chant still continued, the perspiration began to roll from the singer's face, gradually the hidden object took upon itself a shape and bulk that raised the shawl in its center some five or six inches. It was now unmistakably the outline of a small but perfect human figure, with extended arms and legs. One of two of us turned pale; there was a feeling of general uneasiness, until the editor broke the silence by a gibe that, poor as it was, was received with spontaneous enthusiasm. Then the chant suddenly ceased, Wang arose, and with a quick, dexterous movement, stripped both shawl and silk away, and discovered, sleeping peacefully upon my handkerchief, a tiny Chinese baby!

The applause and uproar which followed this revelation ought to have satisfied Wang, even if his audience was a small one; it was loud enough to awaken the baby—a pretty little boy about a year old, looking like a Cupid cut out of sandalwood. He was whisked away almost as mysteriously as he appeared. When Hop Sing returned my handkerchief to me with a bow, I asked if the juggler was the father of the baby. "No sabe!" said the imperturbable Hop Sing, taking refuge in that Spanish form of noncommittalism so common in California.

"But does he have a new baby for every performance?" I asked.

"Perhaps; who knows?"

"But what will become of this one?"

"Whatever you choose, gentlemen," replied Hop Sing, with a courteous inclination; "it was born here—you are its godfathers."

There were two characteristic peculiarities of any Californian assemblage in 1865: it was quick to take a hint, and generous to the point of prodigality in its response to any charitable appeal. No matter how sordid or avaricious the individual, he could not resist the infection of sympathy. I doubled the points of my handkerchief into a bag, dropped a coin into it, and without a word, passed it to the judge. He quietly added a twenty-dollar gold piece, and passed it to the next; when it was returned to me it contained over a hundred dollars. I knotted the money in the handkerchief, and gave it to Hop Sing.

"For the baby, from its godfathers."

"But what name?" said the judge. There was a running fire of "Erebus," "Nox," "Plutus," "Terra Cotta," "Antæus," etc., etc. Finally the question was referred to our host.

"Why not keep his own name," he said quietly— "Wan Lee?" And he did.

And thus was Wan Lee, on the night of Friday the 5th of March, 1856, born into this veracious chronicle.

The last form of the *Northern Star* for the 19th of July, 1865—the only daily paper published in Klamath County—had just gone to press, and at 3 A.M. I was putting aside my proofs and manuscripts, preparatory to going home, when I discovered a letter lying under some sheets of paper which I must have overlooked. The envelope was considerably soiled, it had no postmark, but I had no difficulty in recognizing the hand of my friend Hop Sing. I opened it hurriedly, and read as follows:

MY DEAR SIR,—I do not know whether the bearer will suit you, but unless the office of "devil" in your newspaper is a purely technical one, I think he has all the qualities required. He is very quick, active and intelligent; understands English better than he speaks it, and makes up for any defect by his habits of observation and imitation. You have only to show him how to do a thing once, and he will repeat it, whether it is an offense or a virtue. But you certainly know him already; you are one of his godfathers, for is he not Wan Lee, the reputed son of Wang the conjurer, to whose performances I had the honor to introduce you? But perhaps you have forgotten it.

I shall send him with a gang of coolies to Stockton, thence by express to your town. If you can use him there, you will do me a favor, and probably save his life, which is at present in great peril from the hands of the younger members of your Christian and highly civilized race who attend the enlightened schools in San Francisco.

He has acquired some singular habits and customs from his experience of Wang's profession, which he followed for some years, until he became too large to go in a hat, or be produced from his father's sleeve. The money you left with me has been expended on his education; he has gone through the triliteral classics, but, I think, without much benefit. He knows but little of Confucius, and absolutely nothing of Mencius. Owing to the negligence of his father, he associated, perhaps, too much with American children.

I should have answered your letter before, by post, but I thought that Wan Lee himself would be a better messenger for this.

Yours respectfully,

HOP SING

And this was the long-delayed answer to my letter to Hop Sing. But where was "the bearer"? How was the letter delivered? I summoned hastily the foreman, printers, and office boy, but without eliciting anything; no one had seen the letter delivered, nor knew anything of the bearer. A few days later I had a visit from my laundryman, Ah Ri.

"You wantee debbil? All lightee; me catchee him."

He returned in a few moments with a bright-looking Chinese boy, about ten years old, with whose appearance and general intelligence I was so greatly impressed that I engaged him on the spot. When the business was concluded, I asked his name.

"Wan Lee," said the boy.

"What! Are you the boy sent out by Hop Sing? What the devil do you mean by not coming here before, and how did you deliver that letter?"

Wan Lee looked at me and laughed. "Me pitchee in top side window."

I did not understand. He looked for a moment perplexed, and then, snatching the letter out of my hand, ran down the stairs. After a moment's pause, to my great astonishment, the letter came flying in at the window, circled twice around the room, and then dropped gently like a bird upon my table. Before I had got over my surprise Wan Lee reappeared, smiled, looked at the letter and then at me, said, "So, John," and then remained gravely silent. I said nothing further, but it was understood that this was his first official act.

His next performance, I grieve to say, was not attended with equal success. One of our regular paper-carriers fell sick, and, at a pinch, Wan Lee was ordered to fill his place. To prevent mistakes he was shown over the route the previous evening, and supplied at about daylight with the usual number of subscribers' copies. He returned after an hour, in good spirits and without the papers. He had delivered them all he said.

Unfortunately for Wan Lee, at about eight o'clock indignant subscribers began to arrive at the office. They had received their copies; but how? In the form of hard-pressed cannon balls, delivered by a single shot and a mere tour de force through the glass of bedroom windows. They had received them full in the face, like a baseball, if they happened to be up and stirring; they had received them in quarter sheets, tucked in at separate windows; they had found them in the chimney, pinned against the door, shot through attic windows, delivered in long slips through convenient keyholes, stuffed into ventilators, and occupying the same can with the morning's milk. One subscriber, who waited for some time at the office door to have a personal interview with Wan Lee (then comfortably locked in my bedroom), told me, with tears of rage in his eyes, that he had been awakened at five o'clock by a most hideous yelling below his windows; that on rising, in great agitation, he was startled by the sudden appearance of the *Northern Star*, rolled hard and bent into the form of a boomerang or East Indian club that sailed into the window, described a number of fiendish circles in the room, knocked over the light, slapped the baby's face, "took" him (the subscriber) "in the jaw," and then returned out of the window, and dropped helplessly in the area. During the rest of the day wads and strips

of soiled paper, purporting to be copies of the
Northern Star of that morning's issue, were brought
indignantly to the office. An admirable editorial on
"The Resources of Humboldt County," which I had
constructed the evening before, and which, I have
reason to believe, might have changed the whole balance of trade during the ensuing year, and left San
Francisco bankrupt at her wharves, was in this way
lost to the public.

It was deemed advisable for the next three weeks
to keep Wan Lee closely confined to the printing office and the purely mechanical part of the business.
Here he developed a surprising quickness and adapta-
bility, winning even the favor and good will of the
printers and foreman, who at first looked upon his
introduction into the secrets of their trade as fraught
with the gravest political significance. He learned to
set type readily and neatly, his wonderful skill in manipulation aiding him in the mere mechanical act,
and his ignorance of the language confining him simply to the mechanical effort—confirming the printer's axiom that the printer who considers or follows
the ideas of his copy makes a poor compositor. He
would set up deliberately long diatribes against himself, composed by his fellow printers, and hung on his
hook as copy, and even such short sentences as "Wan
Lee is the devil's own imp," "Wan Lee is a Mongolian
rascal," and bring the proof to me with happiness
beaming from every tooth and satisfaction shining
in his huckleberry eyes.

It was not long, however, before he learned to re-
taliate on his mischievous persecutors. I remember
one instance in which his reprisal came very near in-

volving me in a serious misunderstanding. Our fore-man's name was Webster, and Wan Lee presently learned to know and recognize the individual and combined letters of his name. It was during a political campaign, and the eloquent and fiery Colonel Star-bottle of Siskiyou had delivered an effective speech, which was reported especially for the *Northern Star.* In a very sublime peroration Colonel Starbottle had said, "In the language of the godlike Webster, I re-peat—" and here followed the quotation, which I have forgotten. Now, it chanced that Wan Lee, look-ing over the galley after it had been revised, saw the name of his chief persecutor, and, of course, imagined the quotation his. After the form was locked up, Wan Lee took advantage of Webster's absence to remove the quotation, and substitute a thin piece of lead of the same size as the type, engraved with Chinese char-acters making a sentence which, I had reason to be-lieve, was an utter and abject confession of the incapacity and offensiveness of the Webster family generally, and exceedingly eulogistic of Wan Lee himself personally.

The next morning's paper contained Colonel Star-bottle's speech in full, in which it appeared that the "godlike" Webster had on one occasion uttered his thoughts in excellent but perfectly enigmatical Chi-nese. The rage of Colonel Starbottle knew no bounds. I have a vivid recollection of that admirable man walking into my office and demanding a retraction of the statement.

"But, my dear sir," I asked, "are you willing to deny, over your own signature, that Webster ever ut-tered such a sentence? Dare you deny that, with Mr.

Webster's well-known attainments, a knowledge of Chinese might not have been among the number? Are you willing to submit a translation suitable to the capacity of our readers, and deny, upon your honor as a gentleman, that the late Mr. Webster ever uttered such a sentiment? If you are, sir, I am willing to publish your denial."

The Colonel was not, and left highly indignant.

Webster, the foreman, took it more coolly. Happily he was unaware that for two days after, Chinamen from the laundries, from the gulches, from the kitchens, looked in the front office door with faces beaming with sardonic delight; that three hundred extra copies of the *Star* were ordered for the washhouses on the river. He only knew that during the day Wan Lee occasionally went off into convulsive spasms, and that he was obliged to kick him into consciousness again. A week after the occurrence I called Wan Lee into my office.

"Wan," I said gravely, "I should like you to give me, for my own personal satisfaction, a translation of that Chinese sentence which my gifted countryman, the late godlike Webster, uttered upon a public occasion." Wan Lee looked at me intently, and then the slightest possible twinkle crept into his black eyes. Then he replied, with equal gravity—

"Mishtel Webstel—he say: 'China boy makee me belly much foolee. China boy makee me heap sick.' " Which I have reason to think was true.

But I fear I am giving but one side, and not the best, of Wan Lee's character. As he imparted it to me, his had been a hard life. He had known scarcely any childhood—he had no recollection of a father or

mother. The conjurer Wang had brought him up.
He had spent the first seven years of his life in appear-
ing from baskets, in dropping out of hats, in climb-
ing ladders, in putting his little limbs out of joint in
posturing. He had lived in an atmosphere of trickery
and deception; he had learned to look upon mankind
as dupes of their senses; in fine, if he had thought at
all, he would have been a skeptic; if he had been a little older, he would have been a cynic; if he had been
older still, he would have been a philosopher. As it
was, he was a little imp! A good-natured imp it was,
too—an imp whose moral nature had never been
awakened, an imp up for a holiday, and willing to
try virtue as a diversion. I don't know that he had
any spiritual nature; he was very superstitious; he carried about with him a hideous little porcelain god,
which he was in the habit of alternately reviling and
propitiating. He was too intelligent for the commoner
Chinese vices of stealing or gratuitous lying. Whatever discipline he practiced was taught by his intellect.

I am inclined to think that his feelings were not altogether unimpressible—although it was almost impossible to extract an expression from him—and I
conscientiously believe he became attached to those
that were good to him. What he might have become
under more favorable conditions than the bondsman
of an overworked, underpaid literary man, I don't
know; I only know that the scant, irregular, impulsive kindnesses that I showed him were gratefully received. He was very loyal and patient—two qualities
rare in the average American servant. He was like
Malvolio, "sad and civil" with me; only once, and

then under great provocation, do I remember of his exhibiting any impatience. It was my habit after leaving the office at night to take him with me to my rooms, as the bearer of any supplemental or happy afterthought in the editorial way that might occur to me before the paper went to press. One night I had been scribbling away past the usual hour of dismissing Wan Lee, and had become quite oblivious of his presence in a chair near my door, when suddenly I became aware of a voice saying, in plaintive accents, something that sounded like "Chy Lee."

I faced around sternly.

"What did you say?"

"Me say, 'Chy Lee.' "

"Well?" I said impatiently.

"You sabe, 'How do, John'?"

"Yes."

"You sabe, 'So long, John'?"

"Yes."

"Well, 'Chy Lee' allee same!"

I understood him quite plainly. It appeared that "Chy Lee" was a form of "good night," and that Wan Lee was anxious to go home. But an instinct of mischief which I fear I possessed in common with him impelled me to act as if oblivious of the hint. I muttered something about not understanding him, and again bent over my work. In a few minutes I heard his wooden shoes pattering pathetically over the floor. I looked up. He was standing near the door.

"You no sabe, 'Chy Lee'?"

"No," I said sternly.

"You sabe muchee big foolee!—allee same!"

And with this audacity upon his lips he fled. The

next morning, however, he was as meek and patient as before, and I did not recall his offense. As a probable peace-offering, he blacked all my boots—a duty never required of him—including a pair of buff deerskin slippers and an immense pair of horseman's jack boots, on which he indulged his remorse for two hours.

I have spoken of his honesty as being a quality of his intellect rather than his principle, but I recall about this time two exceptions to the rule. I was anxious to get some fresh eggs as a change to the heavy diet of a mining town, and knowing that Wan Lee's countrymen were great poultry-raisers, I applied to him. He furnished me with them regularly every morning, but refused to take any pay, saying that the man did not sell them—a remarkable instance of self-abnegation, as eggs were then worth half a dollar apiece. One morning, my neighbor, Foster, dropped in upon me at breakfast, and took occasion to bewail his own ill fortune, as his hens had lately stopped laying, or wandered off in the bush. Wan Lee, who was present during our colloquy, preserved his characteristic sad taciturnity. When my neighbor had gone, he turned to me with a slight chuckle—"Flostel's hens—Wan Lee's hens—allee same!" His other offense was more serious and ambitious. It was a season of great irregularities in the mails, and Wan Lee had heard me deplore the delay in the delivery of my letters and newspapers. On arriving at my office one day, I was amazed to find my table covered with letters, evidently just from the post office, but unfortunately not one addressed to me. I turned to Wan Lee, who was surveying them with a calm satisfaction, and demanded an explanation. To my horror he pointed to an empty mailbag in the corner, and said, "Postman he say, 'No lettee, John—no lettee, John.' Postman plentee lie! Postman no good. Me catchee lettee last night—allee same!" Luckily it was still early; the mails had not been distributed; I had a hurried interview with the postmaster, and Wan Lee's bold attempt at robbing the U. S. mail was finally condoned, by the purchase of a new mailbag, and the whole affair thus kept a secret.

If my liking for my little pagan page had not been sufficient, my duty to Hop Sing was enough to cause me to take Wan Lee with me when I returned to San Francisco, after my two years' experience with the *Northern Star.* I do not think he contemplated the change with pleasure. I attributed his feelings to a nervous dread of crowded public streets—when he had to go across town for me on an errand, he always made a long circuit of the outskirts; to his dislike for the discipline of the Chinese and English school to which I proposed to send him; to his fondness for the free, vagrant life of the mines; to sheer willfulness! That it might have been a superstitious premonition did not occur to me until long after.

Nevertheless it really seemed as if the opportunity I had long looked for and confidently expected had come—the opportunity of placing Wan Lee under gently restraining influences, of subjecting him to a life and experience that would draw out of him what good my superficial care and ill-regulated kindness could not reach. Wan Lee was placed at the school of a Chinese missionary—an intelligent and kind-hearted clergyman, who had shown great interest in the boy, and who, better than all, had a wonderful faith in him. A home was found for him in the family of a widow, who had a bright and interesting daughter about two years younger than Wan Lee. It was this bright, cheery, innocent, and artless child that hitherto had been unsuspected—that awakened a moral susceptibility which had lain for years insensible alike to the teachings of society or the ethics of the theologian.

These few brief months, bright with a promise that we never saw fulfilled, must have been happy ones to Wan Lee. He worshiped his little friend with something of the same superstition, but without any of the caprice, that he bestowed upon his porcelain pagan god. It was his delight to walk behind her to school, carrying her books—a service always fraught with danger to him from the little hands of his Caucasian Christian brothers. He made her the most marvelous toys; he would cut out of carrots and turnips the most astonishing roses and tulips; he made lifelike chickens out of melon seeds; he constructed fans and kites, and was singularly proficient in the making of dolls' paper dresses. On the other hand she played and sang to him; taught him a thousand little prettinesses and refinements only known to girls; gave him a yellow ribbon for his pigtail, as best suiting his complexion; read to him; showed him wherein he was original and valuable; took him to Sunday school with her, against the precedents of the school, and small-womanlike, triumphed. I wish I could add here that she effected his conversion, and made him give up his porcelain idol, but I am telling a true story, and this little girl was quite content to fill him with her own Christian goodness, without letting him know that he was changed. So they got along very well together—this little Christian girl, with her shining cross hanging around her plump, white little neck, and this dark little pagan, with his hideous porcelain god hidden away in his blouse.

There were two days of that eventful year which will long be remembered in San Francisco—two days when a mob of her citizens set upon and killed unarmed, defenseless foreigners, because they were foreigners and of another race, religion, and color, and worked for what wages they could get. There were some public men so timid that, seeing this, they thought that the end of the world had come; there were some eminent statesmen, whose names I am ashamed to write here, who began to think that the passage in the Constitution which guarantees civil and religious liberty to every citizen or foreigner was a mistake. But there were also some men who were not so easily frightened, and in twenty-four hours we had things so arranged that the timid men could wring their hands in safety, and the eminent statesman utter their doubts without hurting anybody or anything. And in the midst of this I got a note from Hop Sing, asking me to come to him immediately.

I found his warehouse closed and strongly guarded by the police against any possible attack of the rioters. Hop Sing admitted me through a barred grating with his usual imperturbable calm, but as it seemed to me, with more than his usual seriousness. Without a word he took my hand and led me to the rear of the room, and thence downstairs into the basement. It was dimly lighted, but there was something lying on the floor covered by a shawl. As I approached, he drew the shawl away with a sudden gesture, and revealed Wan Lee, the pagan, lying there dead!

Dead, my reverend friends, dead! Stoned to death in the streets of San Francisco, in the year of grace, eighteen hundred and sixty-nine, by a mob of half-grown boys and Christian school children!

As I put my hand reverently upon his breast, I felt something crumbling beneath his blouse. I looked inquiringly at Hop Sing. He put his hand between the folds of silk, and drew out something with the first bitter smile I had ever seen on the face of that pagan gentleman.

It was Wan Lee's porcelain god, crushed by a stone from the hands of those Christian iconoclasts!

AN INGÉNUE OF THE SIERRAS

ONE

We all held our breath as the coach rushed through the semidarkness of Galloper's Ridge. The vehicle itself was only a huge lumbering shadow; its side lights were carefully extinguished, and Yuba Bill had just politely removed from the lips of an outside passenger even the cigar with which he had been ostentatiously exhibiting his coolness. For it had been rumored that the Ramon Martinez gang of "road agents" were "laying" for us on the second grade, and would time the passage of our lights across Galloper's in order to intercept us in the "brush" beyond. If we could cross the ridge without being seen, and so get through the brush before they reached it, we were safe. If they followed, it would only be a stern chase with the odds in our favor.

The huge vehicle swayed from side to side, rolled, dipped, and plunged, but Bill kept the track, as if, in the whispered words of the expressman, he could "feel and smell" the road he could no longer see. We knew that at times we hung perilously over the edge of slopes that eventually dropped a thousand feet sheer to the tops of the sugar pines below, but we knew that

Bill knew it also. The half visible heads of the horses, drawn wedgewise together by the tightened reins, appeared to cleave the darkness like a plowshare, held between his rigid hands. Even the hoofbeats of the six horses had fallen into a vague, monotonous, distant roll. Then the ridge was crossed, and we plunged into the still blacker obscurity of the brush. Rather we no longer seemed to move—it was only the phantom night that rushed by us. The horses might have been submerged in some swift Lethean stream; nothing but the top of the coach and the rigid bulk of Yuba Bill arose above them. Yet even in that awful moment our speed was unslackened; it was as if Bill cared no longer to *guide* but only to drive, or as if the direction of his huge machine was determined by other hands than his. An incautious whisperer hazarded the paralyzing suggestion of our "meeting another team." To our great astonishment Bill overheard it; to our greater astonishment he replied. "It 'ud be only a neck and neck race which would get to h—ll first," he said quietly. But we were relieved—for he had *spoken!* Almost simultaneously the wider turnpike began to glimmer faintly as a visible track before us; the wayside trees fell out of line, opened up, and dropped off one after another; we were on the broader tableland, out of danger, and apparently unperceived and unpursued.

Nevertheless in the conversation that broke out again with the relighting of the lamps, and the comments, congratulations, and reminiscences that were freely exchanged, Yuba Bill preserved a dissatisfied and even resentful silence. The most generous praise of his skill and courage awoke no response. "I reckon the old man waz just spilin' for a fight, and is feelin' disappointed," said a passenger. But those who knew that Bill had the true fighter's scorn for any purely purposeless conflict were more or less concerned and watchful of him. He would drive steadily for four or five minutes with thoughtfully knitted brows, but eyes still keenly observant under his slouched hat, and then, relaxing his strained attitude, would give way to a movement of impatience. "You ain't uneasy about anything, Bill, are you?" asked the expressman confidentially. Bill lifted his eyes with a slightly contemptuous surprise. "Not about anything ter *come*. It's what *hez* happened that I don't exackly *sabe*. I don't see no signs of Ramon's gang ever havin' been out at all, and ef they were out I don't see why they didn't go for us."

"The simple fact is that our ruse was successful," said an outside passenger. "They waited to see our lights on the ridge, and not seeing them, missed us until we had passed. That's my opinion."

"You ain't puttin' any price on that opinion, air ye?" inquired Bill politely.

"No."

" 'Cos thar's a comic paper in 'Frisco pays for them things, and I've seen worse things in it."

"Come off, Bill," retorted the passenger, slightly nettled by the tittering of his companions. "Then what did you put out the lights for?"

"Well," returned Bill grimly, "it mout have been because I didn't keer to hev you chaps blazin' away at the first bush you *thought* you saw move in your skeer, and bringin' down their fire on us."

The explanation, though unsatisfactory, was by no

means an improbable one, and we thought it better to accept it with a laugh. Bill, however, resumed his abstracted manner.

"Who got in at the Summit?" he at last asked abruptly of the expressman.

"Derrick and Simpson of Cold Spring, and one of the 'Excelsior' boys," responded the expressman.

"And that Pike County girl from Dow's Flat, with her bundles. Don't forget her," added the outside passenger ironically.

"Does anybody here know her?" continued Bill, ignoring the irony.

"You'd better ask Judge Thompson; he was mighty attentive to her; gettin' her a seat by the off window, and lookin' after her bundles and things."

"Gettin' her a seat by the *window?*" repeated Bill.

"Yes, she wanted to see everything, and wasn't afraid of the shooting."

"Yes," broke in a third passenger, "and he was so d—d civil that when she dropped her ring in the straw, he struck a match agin all your rules, you know, and held it for her to find it. And it was just as we were crossin' through the brush, too. I saw the hull thing through the window, for I was hanging over the wheels with my gun ready for action. And it wasn't no fault of Judge Thompson's if his d—d foolishness hadn't shown us up, and got us a shot from the gang."

Bill gave a short grunt, but drove steadily on without further comment or even turning his eyes to the speaker.

We were now not more than a mile from the station at the crossroads where we were to change horses. The lights already glimmered in the distance, and there was a faint suggestion of the coming dawn on the summits of the ridge to the west. We had plunged into a belt of timber, when suddenly a horseman emerged at a sharp canter from a trail that seemed to be parallel with our own. We were all slightly startled, Yuba Bill alone preserving his moody calm.

"Hullo!" he said.

The stranger wheeled to our side as Bill slackened his speed. He seemed to be a "packer" or freight muleteer.

"Ye didn't get 'held up' on the Divide?" continued Bill cheerfully.

"No," returned the packer, with a laugh; "*I* don't carry treasure. But I see you're all right, too. I saw you crossin' over Galloper's."

"*Saw* us?" said Bill sharply. "We had our lights out."

"Yes, but there was suthin' white—a handkerchief or woman's veil, I reckon—hangin' from the window. It was only a movin' spot agin the hillside, but ez I was lookin' out for ye I knew it was you by that. Good night!"

He cantered away. We tried to look at each other's faces, and at Bill's expression in the darkness, but he neither spoke nor stirred until he threw down the reins when we stopped before the station. The passengers quickly descended from the roof; the expressman was about to follow, but Bill plucked his sleeve.

"I'm goin' to take a look over this yer stage and these yer passengers with ye, afore we start."

"Why, what's up?"

"Well," said Bill, slowly disengaging himself from one of his enormous gloves, "when we waltzed down into the brush up there I saw a man, ez plain ez I see you, rise up from it. I thought our time had come and the band was goin' to play, when he sorter drew back, made a sign, and we just scooted past him."

"Well?"

"Well," said Bill, "it means that this yer coach was *passed through free* tonight."

"You don't object to *that*—surely? I think we were deucedly lucky."

Bill slowly drew off his other glove. "I've been riskin' my everlastin' life on this d——d line three times a week," he said with mock humility, "and I'm allus thankful for small mercies. *But,*" he added grimly, "when it comes down to being passed free by some pal of a hoss thief, and thet called a speshal Providence, *I ain't in it!* No, sir, I ain't in it!"

TWO

It was with mixed emotions that the passengers heard that a delay of fifteen minutes to tighten certain screw bolts had been ordered by the autocratic Bill. Some were anxious to get their breakfast at Sugar Pine, but others were not averse to linger for the daylight that promised greater safety on the road. The expressman, knowing the real cause of Bill's delay, was nevertheless at a loss to understand the object of it. The passengers were all well-known; any idea of complicity with the road agents was wild and impossible, and even if there was a confederate of the gang among them, he would have been more likely to precipitate a robbery than to check it. Again, the discovery of such a confederate—to whom they clearly owed their safety—and his arrest would have been quite against the Californian sense of justice, if not actually illegal. It seemed evident that Bill's quixotic sense of honor was leading him astray.

The station consisted of a stable, a wagon shed, and a building containing three rooms. The first was fitted up with "bunks" or sleeping berths for the employees; the second was the kitchen; and the third and larger apartment was dining room or sitting room, and was used as general waiting room for the passengers. It was not a refreshment station, and there was no "bar." But a mysterious command from the omnipotent Bill produced a demijohn of whiskey, with which he hospitably treated the company. The seductive influence of the liquor loosened the tongue of the gallant Judge Thompson. He admitted to having stuck a match to enable the fair Pike Countian to find her ring, which, however, proved to have fallen in her lap. She was "a fine, healthy young woman—a type of the Far West, sir; in fact, quite a prairie blossom! yet simple and guileless as a child." She was on her way to Marysville, he believed, "although she expected to meet friends—a friend, in fact—later on." It was her first visit to a large town—in fact, any civilized center—since she crossed the plains three years ago. Her girlish curiosity was quite touching, and her innocence irresistible. In fact, in a country whose tendency was to produce "frivolity and forwardness in young girls, he found her a most interesting young person." She was even then out in the stable yard watching the horses being harnessed, "preferring to indulge a pardonable healthy young curiosity than to listen to the empty compliments of the younger passengers."

The figure which Bill saw thus engaged, without being otherwise distinguished, certainly seemed to justify the Judge's opinion. She appeared to be a well-matured country girl, whose frank gray eyes and large laughing mouth expressed a wholesome and abiding gratification in her life and surroundings. She was watching the replacing of luggage in the boot. A little feminine start, as one of her own parcels was thrown somewhat roughly on the roof, gave Bill his opportunity. "Now there," he growled to the helper, "ye ain't carting stone! Look out, will yer! Some of your things, miss?" he added, with gruff courtesy, turning to her. "These yer trunks, for instance?"

She smiled a pleasant assent, and Bill, pushing aside the helper, seized a large square trunk in his arms. But from excess of zeal, or some other mischance, his foot slipped, and he came down heavily, striking the corner of the trunk on the ground and loosening its hinges and fastenings. It was a cheap, common-looking affair, but the accident discovered in its yawning lid a quantity of white, lace-edged feminine apparel of an apparently superior quality. The young lady uttered another cry and came quickly forward, but Bill was profuse in his apologies, himself girded the broken box with a strap, and declared his intention of having the company "make it good" to her with a new one. Then he casually accompanied her to the door of the waiting room, entered, made a place for her before the fire by simply lifting the nearest and most youthful passenger by the coat collar from the stool that he was occupying, and having installed the lady in it, displaced another man who was standing before the chimney, and drawing himself up to his full six feet of height in front of her, glanced down upon his fair passenger as he took his waybill from his pocket.

"You name is down here as Miss Mullins?" he said.

She looked up, became suddenly aware that she and her questioner were the center of interest to the whole circle of passengers, and with a slight rise of color, returned, "Yes."

"Well, Miss Mullins, I've got a question or two to ask ye. I ask it straight out afore this crowd. It's in my rights to take ye aside and ask it—but that ain't my style; I'm no detective. I needn't ask it at all, but act as ef I knowed the answer, or I might leave it to be asked by others. Ye needn't answer it ef ye don't like; ye've got a friend over ther—Judge Thompson—who is a friend to ye, right or wrong, jest as any other man here is—as though ye'd packed your own jury. Well, the simple question I've got to ask ye is *this:* Did you signal to anybody from the coach when we passed Galloper's an hour ago?"

We all thought that Bill's courage and audacity had reached its climax here. To openly and publicly accuse a "lady" before a group of chivalrous Californians, and that lady possessing the further attractions of youth, good looks, and innocence, was little short of desperation. There was an evident movement of adhesion towards the fair stranger, a slight muttering broke out on the right, but the very boldness of the act held them in stupefied surprise. Judge Thompson, with a bland propitiatory smile began: "Really, Bill, I must protest on behalf of this young lady"— when the fair accused, raising her eyes to her accuser, to the consternation of everybody answered with the slight but convincing hesitation of conscientious truthfulness:

"I did."

"Ahem!" interposed the Judge hastily, "er—that is—er—you allowed your handkerchief to flutter from the window—I noticed it myself—casually—one might say even playfully—but without any particular significance."

The girl, regarding her apologist with a singular mingling of pride and impatience, returned briefly: "I signaled."

"Who did you signal to?" asked Bill gravely.

"The young gentleman I'm going to marry."

A start, followed by a slight titter from the younger passengers, was instantly suppressed by a savage glance from Bill.

"What did you signal to him for?" he continued.

"To tell him I was here, and that it was all right," returned the young girl, with a steadily rising pride and color.

"Wot was all right?" demanded Bill.

"That I wasn't followed, and that he could meet me on the road beyond Cass's Ridge Station." She hesitated a moment, and then, with a still greater pride, in which a youthful defiance was still mingled, said: "I've run away from home to marry him. And I mean to! No one can stop me. Dad didn't like him just because he was poor, and dad's got money. Dad wanted me to marry a man I hate, and got a lot of dresses and things to bribe me."

"And you're taking them in your trunk to the other feller?" said Bill grimly.

"Yes, he's poor," returned the girl defiantly.

"Then your father's name is Mullins?" asked Bill.

"It's not Mullins. I—I—took that name," she hesitated, with her first exhibition of self-consciousness.

"Wot *is* his name?"

"Eli Hemmings."

A smile of relief and significance went round the circle. The fame of Eli or "Skinner" Hemmings as a notorious miser and usurer had passed even beyond Galloper's Ridge.

"The step that you're taking, Miss Mullins, I need not tell you, is one of great gravity," said Judge Thompson, with a certain paternal seriousness of manner, in which, however, we were glad to detect a glaring affectation; "and I trust that you and your affianced have fully weighed it. Far be it from me to interfere with or question the natural affections of two young people, but may I ask you what you know of the—er—young gentleman for whom you are sacrificing so much, and perhaps imperiling your whole future? For instance, have you known him long?"

The slightly troubled air of trying to understand—not unlike the vague wonderment of childhood—with which Miss Mullins had received the beginning of this exordium, changed to a relieved smile of comprehension as she said quickly, "Oh yes, nearly a whole year."

"And," said the Judge, smiling, "has he a vocation —is he in business?"

"Oh yes," she returned; "he's a collector."

"A collector?"

"Yes; he collects bills, you know—money," she went on, with childish eagerness, "not for himself— *he* never has any money, poor Charley—but for his firm. It's dreadful hard work, too; keeps him out for days and nights, over bad roads and baddest weather. Sometimes, when he's stole over to the ranch just to see me, he's been so bad he could scarcely keep his seat in the saddle, much less stand. And he's got to take mighty big risks, too. Times the folks are cross with him and won't pay; once they shot him in the arm, and he came to me, and I helped do it up for him. But he don't mind. He's real brave—jest as brave as he's good." There was such a wholesome ring of truth in this pretty praise that we were touched in sympathy with the speaker.

"What firm does he collect for?" asked the Judge gently.

"I don't know exactly—he won't tell me; but I think it's a Spanish firm. You see"—she took us all into her confidence with a sweeping smile of innocent yet half-mischievous artfulness—"I only know because I peeped over a letter he once got from his firm, telling him he must hustle up and be ready for the road the next day; but I think the name was Martinez—yes, Ramon Martinez."

In the dead silence that ensued—a silence so profound that we could hear the horses in the distant stable yard rattling their harness—one of the younger "Excelsior" boys burst into a hysteric laugh, but the fierce eye of Yuba Bill was down upon him, and seemed to instantly stiffen him into a silent, grinning mask. The young girl, however, took no note of it. Following out, with loverlike diffusiveness, the reminiscences thus awakened, she went on:

"Yes, it's mighty hard work, but he says it's all for me, and as soon as we're married he'll quit it. He might have quit it before, but he won't take no money of me, nor what I told him I could get out of dad! That ain't his style. He's mighty proud—if he is poor —is Charley. Why, thar's all ma's money which she left me in the Savin's Bank that I wanted to draw out— for I had the right—and give it to him, but he wouldn't hear of it! Why, he wouldn't take one of the things I've got with me, if he knew it. And so he goes on ridin' and ridin', here and there and everywhere, and gettin' more and more played out and sad, and thin and pale as a spirit, and always so uneasy about his business, and startin' up at times when we're meetin' out in the South Woods or in the far clearin', and sayin': 'I must be goin' now, Polly,' and yet always tryin' to be chiffle and chipper afore me. Why, he must have rid miles and miles to have watched for me thar in the brush at the foot of Galloper's tonight, jest to see if all was safe; and Lordy! I'd have given him the signal and showed a light if I'd died for it the next minit. There! That's what I know of Charley —that's what I'm running away from home for— that's what I'm running to him for, and I don't care who knows it! And I only wish I'd done it afore—and

I would—if—if—if—he'd only *asked me!* There now!" She stopped, panted, and choked. Then one of the sudden transitions of youthful emotion overtook the eager, laughing face; it clouded up with the swift change of childhood, a lightning quiver of expression broke over it, and—then came the rain!

I think this simple act completed our utter demoralization! We smiled feebly at each other with that assumption of masculine superiority which is miserably conscious of its own helplessness at such moments. We looked out of the window, blew our noses, said: "Eh—what?" and "I say," vaguely to each other, and were greatly relieved, and yet apparently astonished, when Yuba Bill, who had turned his back upon the fair speaker, and was kicking the logs in the fireplace, suddenly swept down upon us and bundled us all into the road, leaving Miss Mullins alone. Then he walked aside with Judge Thompson for a few moments; returned to us, autocratically demanded of the party a complete reticence towards Miss Mullins on the subject matter under discussion, reentered the station, reappeared with the young lady, suppressed a faint idiotic cheer which broke from us at the spectacle of her innocent face once more cleared and rosy, climbed the box, and in another moment we were under way.

"Then she don't know what her lover is yet?" asked the expressman eagerly.

"No."

"Are *you* certain it's one of the gang?"

"Can't say *for sure*. It mout be a young chap from Yolo who bucked again the tiger[1] at Sacramento, got

[1] Gambled at faro.

regularly cleaned out and busted, and joined the gang for a flier. They say thar was a new hand in that job over at Keeley's—and a mighty game one, too; and ez there was some buckshot onloaded that trip, he might hev got his share, and that would tally with what the girl said about his arm. See! Ef that's the man, I've heered he was the son of some big preacher in the States, and a college sharp to boot, who ran wild in 'Frisco, and played himself for all he was worth. They're the wust kind to kick when they once get a foot over the traces. For stiddy, comf'ble kempany," added Bill reflectively, "give *me* the son of a man that was *hanged!*"

"But what are you going to do about this?"

"That depends upon the feller who comes to meet her."

"But you ain't going to try to take him? That would be playing it pretty low down on them both."

"Keep your hair on, Jimmy! The Judge and me are only going to rastle with the sperrit of that gay young galoot when he drops down for his girl—and exhort him pow'ful! Ef he allows he's convicted of sin and will find the Lord, we'll marry him and the gal off-hand at the next station, and the Judge will officiate himself for nothin'. We're goin' to have this yer elope-ment done on the square—and our waybill clean—you bet!"

"But you don't suppose he'll trust himself in your hands?"

"Polly will signal to him that it's all square."

"Ah!" said the expressman. Nevertheless in those few moments the men seemed to have exchanged dis-positions. The expressman looked doubtfully, critically, and even cynically before him. Bill's face had relaxed, and something like a bland smile beamed across it, as he drove confidently and unhesitatingly forward.

Day, meantime, although full blown and radiant on the mountain summits around us, was yet nebulous and uncertain in the valleys into which we were plunging. Lights still glimmered in the cabins and few ranch buildings which began to indicate the thicker settlements. And the shadows were heaviest in a little copse, where a note from Judge Thompson in the coach was handed up to Yuba Bill, who at once slowly began to draw up his horses. The coach stopped finally near the junction of a small crossroad. At the same moment Miss Mullins slipped down from the vehicle, and with a parting wave of her hand to the Judge, who had assisted her from the steps, tripped down the crossroad, and disappeared in its semiobscurity. To our surprise the stage waited, Bill holding the reins listlessly in his hands. Five minutes passed— an eternity of expectation, and as there was that in Yuba Bill's face which forbade idle questioning, an aching void of silence also! This was at last broken by a strange voice from the road:

"Go on—we'll follow."

The coach started forward. Presently we heard the sound of other wheels behind us. We all craned our necks backward to get a view of the unknown, but by the growing light we could only see that we were followed at a distance by a buggy with two figures in it. Evidently Polly Mullins and her lover! We hoped that they would pass us. But the vehicle, although drawn by a fast horse, preserved its distance always, and it was plain that its driver had no desire to satisfy our curiosity. The expressman had recourse to Bill.

"Is it the man you thought of?" he asked eagerly.

"I reckon," said Bill briefly.

"But," continued the expressman, returning to his former skepticism, "what's to keep them both from levanting together now?"

Bill jerked his hand towards the boot with a grim smile.

"Their baggage."

"Oh!" said the expressman.

"Yes," continued Bill. "We'll hang on to that gal's little frills and fixin's until this yer job's settled and the ceremony's over, jest as ef we waz her own father. And, what's more, young man," he added, suddenly turning to the expressman, "*you'll* express them trunks of hers *through to Sacramento* with your kempany's labels, and hand her the receipts and checks for them so she *can get 'em there*. That'll keep *him* outer temptation and the reach o' the gang, until they get away among white men and civilization again. When your hoary-headed ole grandfather, or to speak plainer, that partikler old whiskey-soaker known as Yuba Bill, wot sits on this box," he continued, with a diabolical wink at the expressman, "waltzes in to pervided for a young couple jest startin' in life, thar's nothin' mean about his style, you bet. He fills the bill every time! Speshul Providences take a back seat when he's around."

When the station hotel and straggling settlement of Sugar Pine, now distinct and clear in the growing light, at last rose within rifleshot on the plateau, the buggy suddenly darted swiftly by us, so swiftly that the faces of the two occupants were barely distinguishable as they passed, and keeping the lead by a dozen lengths, reached the door of the hotel. The young girl and her companion leaped down and vanished within as we drew up. They had evidently determined to elude our curiosity, and were successful.

But the material appetites of the passengers, sharpened by the keen mountain air, were more potent than their curiosity, and as the breakfast bell rang out at the moment the stage stopped, a majority of them rushed into the dining room and scrambled for places without giving much heed to the vanished couple or to the Judge and Yuba Bill, who had disappeared also. The through coach to Marysville and Sacramento was likewise waiting, for Sugar Pine was the limit of Bill's ministration, and the coach which we had just left went no farther. In the course of twenty minutes, however, there was a slight and somewhat ceremonious bustling in the hall and on the veranda, and Yuba Bill and the Judge reappeared. The latter was leading, with some elaboration of manner and detail, the shapely figure of Miss Mullins, and Yuba Bill was accompanying her companion to the buggy. We all rushed to the windows to get a good view of the mysterious stranger and probable ex-brigand whose life was now linked with our fair fellow passenger. I am afraid, however, that we all participated in a certain impression of disappointment and doubt. Handsome and even cultivated-looking, he assuredly was—young and vigorous in appearance. But there was a certain half-shamed, half-defiant suggestion in his expression, yet coupled with a watch-ful lurking uneasiness which was not pleasant and hardly becoming in a bridegroom—and the pos-sessor of such a bride. But the frank, joyous, inno-cent face of Polly Mullins, resplendent with a simple, happy confidence, melted our hearts again, and con-doned the fellow's shortcomings. We waved our hands; I think we would have given three rousing cheers as they drove away if the omnipotent eye of Yuba Bill had not been upon us. It was well, for the next moment we were summoned to the presence of that soft-hearted autocrat.

We found him alone with the Judge in a private sitting room, standing before a table on which there were a decanter and glasses. As we filed expectantly into the room and the door closed behind us, he cast a glance of hesitating tolerance over the group.

"Gentlemen," he said slowly, "you was all present at the beginnin' of a little game this mornin', and the Judge thar thinks that you oughter be let in at the fin-ish. *I* don't see that it's any of *your* d—d business—so to speak; but ez the Judge here allows you're all in the secret, I've called you in to take a partin' drink to the health of Mr. and Mrs. Charley Byng—ez is now comf'ably off on their bridal tower. What *you* know or what *you* suspects of the young galoot that's married the gal ain't worth shucks to anybody, and I wouldn't give it to a yaller pup to play with, but the Judge thinks you ought all to promise right here that you'll keep it dark. That's his opinion. Ez far as my opinion goes, gen'l'men," continued Bill, with greater blandness and apparent cordiality, "I wanter simply remark, in a keerless, offhand gin'ral way, that ef I ketch any God-forsaken, lop-eared, chuckled-headed blatherin' idjet airin' *his* opinion——"

"One moment, Bill," interposed Judge Thompson with a grave smile; "let me explain. You understand, gentlemen," he said, turning to us, "the singular, and I may say affecting, situation which our good-hearted friend here has done so much to bring to what we hope will be a happy termination. I want to give here, as my professional opinion, that there is nothing in his request which, in your capacity as good citizens and law-abiding men, you may not grant. I want to tell you, also, that you are condoning no offense against the statutes; that there is not a particle of legal evidence before us of the criminal antecedents of Mr. Charles Byng, except that which has been told you by the innocent lips of his betrothed, which the law of the land has now sealed forever in the mouth of his wife, and that our own actual experience of his acts has been in the main exculpatory of any previous irregularity—if not incompatible with it. Briefly, no judge would charge, no jury convict, on such evidence. When I add that the young girl is of legal age, that there is no evidence of any previous undue influence, but rather of the reverse, on the part of the bridegroom, and that I was content, as a magistrate, to perform the ceremony, I think you will be satisfied to give your promise, for the sake of the bride, and drink a happy life to them both."

I need not say that we did this cheerfully, and even extorted from Bill a grunt of satisfaction. The majority of the company, however, who were going with the through coach to Sacramento, then took their leave, and as we accompanied them to the veranda, we could see that Miss Polly Mullins's trunks were already transferred to the other vehicle under the protecting seals and labels of the all-potent Express Company. Then the whip cracked, the coach rolled away, and the last traces of the adventurous young couple disappeared in the hanging red dust of its wheels.

But Yuba Bill's grim satisfaction at the happy issue of the episode seemed to suffer no abatement. He even exceeded his usual deliberately regulated potations, and standing comfortably with his back to the center of the now deserted barroom, was more than usually loquacious with the expressman. "You see," he said, in bland reminiscence, "when your old Uncle Bill takes hold of a job like this, he puts it straight through without changin' hosses. Yet thar was a moment, young feller, when I thought I was stompt! It was when we'd made up our mind to make that chap tell the gal fust all what he was! Ef she'd rared or kicked in the traces, or hung back only ez much ez that, we'd hev given him jest five minits' law to get up and get and leave her, and we'd hev toted that gal and her fixin's back to her dad again! But she jest gave a little scream and start, and then went off inter hysterics, right on his buzzum, laughin' and cryin' and sayin' that nothin' should part 'em. Gosh! if I didn't think *he* woz more cut up than she about it; a minit it looked as ef *he* didn't allow to marry her arter all, but that passed, and they was married hard and fast—you bet! I reckon he's had enough of stayin' out o' nights to last him, and ef the valley settlements hevn't got hold of a very shinin' member, at least the foothills hev got shut of one more of the Ramon Martinez gang."

"What's that about the Ramon Martinez gang?" said a quiet potential voice.

Bill turned quickly. It was the voice of the Divisional Superintendent of the Express Company—a man of eccentric determination of character, and one of the few whom the autocratic Bill recognized as an equal—who had just entered the barroom. His dusty pongee cloak and soft hat indicated that he had that morning arrived on a round of inspection.

"Don't care if I do, Bill," he continued, in response to Bill's invitatory gesture, walking to the bar. "It's a little raw out on the road. Well, what were you saying about the Ramon Martinez gang? You haven't come across one of 'em, have you?"

"No," said Bill, with a slight blinking of his eye, as he ostentatiously lifted his glass to the light.

"And you *won't,*" added the Superintendent, leisurely sipping his liquor. "For the fact is, the gang is about played out. Not from want of a job now and then, but from the difficulty of disposing of the results of their work. Since the new instructions to the agents to identify and trace all dust and bullion offered to them went into force, you see, they can't get rid of their swag. All the gang are spotted at the offices, and it costs too much for them to pay a fence or a middleman of any standing. Why, all that flaky river gold they took from the Excelsior Company can be identified as easy as if it was stamped with the company's mark. They can't melt it down themselves;

they can't get others to do it for them; they can't ship it to the mint or assay offices in Marysville and 'Frisco, for they won't take it without our certificate and seals; and *we* don't take any undeclared freight *within* the lines that we've drawn around their beat, except from people and agents known. Why, *you* know that well enough, Jim," he said, suddenly appealing to the expressman, "don't you?"

Possibly the suddenness of the appeal caused the expressman to swallow his liquor the wrong way, for he was overtaken with a fit of coughing, and stammered hastily as he laid down his glass, "Yes—of course—certainly."

"No, sir," resumed the Superintendent cheerfully, "they're pretty well played out. And the best proof of it is that they've lately been robbing ordinary passengers' trunks. There was a freight wagon 'held up' near Dow's Flat the other day, and a lot of baggage gone through. I had to go down there to look into it. Darned if they hadn't lifted a lot o' woman's wedding things from that rich couple who got married the other day out at Marysville. Looks as if they were playing it rather low-down, don't it? Coming down to hardpan and the bedrock—eh?"

The expressman's face was turned anxiously towards Bill, who, after a hurried gulp of his remaining liquor, still stood staring at the window. Then he slowly drew on one of his large gloves. "Ye didn't," he said, with a slow, drawling, but perfectly distinct, articulation, "happen to know old 'Skinner' Hemmings when you were over there?"

"Yes."

"And his daughter?"

"He hasn't got any."

"A sort o' mild, innocent, guileless child of nature?" persisted Bill, with a yellow face, a deadly calm, and Satanic deliberation.

"No. I tell you he *hasn't* any daughter. Old man Hemmings is a confirmed old bachelor. He's too mean to support more than one."

"And you didn't happen to know any o' that gang, did ye?" continued Bill, with infinite protraction.

"Yes. Knew 'em all. There was French Pete, Cherokee Bob, Kanaka Joe, One-eyed Stillson, Softly Brown, Spanish Jack, and two or three Greasers."

"And ye didn't know a man by the name of Charley Byng?"

"No," returned the Superintendent, with a slight suggestion of weariness and a distraught glance towards the door.

"A dark, stylish chap, with shifty black eyes and a curled-up merstache?" continued Bill, with dry, colorless persistence.

"No. Look here, Bill, I'm in a little bit of a hurry— but I suppose you must have your little joke before we part. Now, what *is* your little game?"

"Wot you mean?" demanded Bill, with sudden brusqueness.

"Mean? Well, old man, you know as well as I do. You're giving me the very description of Ramon Martinez himself, ha! ha! No—Bill! you didn't play me this time. You're mighty spry and clever, but you didn't catch on just then."

He nodded and moved away with a light laugh. Bill turned a stony face to the expressman. Suddenly a gleam of mirth came into his gloomy eyes. He bent over the young man, and said in a hoarse, chuckling whisper:

"But I got even after all!"

"How?"

"He's tied up to that lying little she-devil, hard and fast!"

HOW SANTA CLAUS CAME
TO SIMPSON'S BAR

It had been raining in the valley of the Sacramento. The North Fork had overflowed its banks, and Rattlesnake Creek was impassable. The few boulders that had marked the summer ford at Simpson's Crossing were obliterated by a vast sheet of water stretching to the foothills. The up stage was stopped at Granger's; the last mail had been abandoned in the tules, the rider swimming for his life. "An area," remarked the *Sierra Avalanche,* with pensive local pride, "as large as the State of Massachusetts is now under water."

Nor was the weather any better in the foothills. The mud lay deep on the mountain road; wagons that neither physical force nor moral objurgation could move from the evil ways into which they had fallen encumbered the track, and the way to Simpson's Bar was indicated by broken-down teams and hard swearing. And further on, cut off and inaccessible, rained upon and bedraggled, smitten by high winds and threatened by high water, Simpson's Bar, on the eve of Christmas Day, 1862, clung like a swallow's nest to the rocky entablature and splintered capitals of Table Mountain, and shook in the blast.

As night shut down on the settlement, a few lights gleamed through the mist from the windows of cabins on either side of the highway, now crossed and gullied by lawless streams and swept by marauding winds. Happily most of the population were gathered at Thompson's store, clustered around a red-hot stove, at which they silently spat in some accepted sense of social communion that perhaps rendered conversation unnecessary. Indeed, most methods of diversion had long since been exhausted on Simpson's Bar; high water had suspended the regular occupations on gulch and on river, and a consequent lack of money and whiskey had taken the zest from most illegitimate recreation. Even Mr. Hamin was fain to leave the Bar with fifty dollars in his pocket—the only amount actually realized of the large sums won by him in the successful exercise of his arduous profession. "Ef I was asked," he remarked somewhat later—"ef I was asked to pint out a purty little village where a retired sport as didn't care for money could exercise hisself, frequent and lively, I'd say Simpson's Bar; but for a young man with a large family depending on his exertions, it don't pay." As Mr. Hamlin's family consisted mainly of female adults, this remark is quoted rather to show the breadth of his humor than the exact extent of his responsibilities.

Howbeit, the unconscious objects of this satire sat that evening in the listless apathy begotten of idleness and lack of excitement. Even the sudden splashing of hoofs before the door did not arouse them. Dick Bullen alone paused in the act of scraping out his pipe, and lifted his head, but no other one of the group indicated any interest in, or recognition of, the man who entered.

It was a figure familiar enough to the company, and known in Simpson's Bar as "The Old Man." A man of perhaps fifty years; grizzled and scant of hair, but still fresh and youthful of complexion. A face full of ready but not very powerful sympathy, with a chameleonlike aptitude for taking on the shade and color of contiguous moods and feelings. He had evidently just left some hilarious companions, and did not at first notice the gravity of the group, but clapped the shoulder of the nearest man jocularly, and threw himself into a vacant chair.

"Jest heard the best thing out, boys! Ye know Smiley, over yar—Jim Smiley—funniest man in the Bar? Well, Jim was jest telling the richest yarn about"—

"Smiley's a —— fool," interrupted a gloomy voice.

"A particular —— skunk," added another in sepulchral accents.

A silence followed these positive statements. The Old Man glanced quickly around the group. Then his face slowly changed. "That's so," he said reflectively, after a pause, "certainly a sort of a skunk and suthin' of a fool. In course." He was silent for a moment, as in painful contemplation of the unsavoriness and folly of the unpopular Smiley. "Dismal weather, ain't it?" he added, now fully embarked on the current of prevailing sentiment. "Mighty rough papers on the boys, and no show for money this season. And tomorrow's Christmas."

There was a movement among the men at this announcement, but whether of satisfaction or disgust was not plain. "Yes," continued the Old Man in the lugubrious tone he had within the last few moments unconsciously adopted,—"yes, Christmas, and to-night's Christmas Eve. Ye see, boys, I kinder thought—that is, I sorter had an idee, jest passin' like, you know—that maybe ye'd all like to come over to my house tonight and have a sort of tear round. But I suppose, now, you wouldn't? Don't feel like it, maybe?" he added with anxious sympathy, peering into the faces of his companions.

"Well, I don't know," responded Tom Flynn with some cheerfulness. "P'r'aps we may. But how about your wife, Old Man? What does *she* say to it?"

The Old Man hesitated. His conjugal experience had not been a happy one, and the fact was known to Simpson's Bar. His first wife, a delicate, pretty little woman, had suffered keenly and secretly from the jealous suspicions of her husband, until one day he invited the whole Bar to his house to expose her infidelity. On arriving, the party found the shy, petite creature quietly engaged in her household duties, and retired abashed and discomfited. But the sensitive woman did not easily recover from the shock of this extraordinary outrage. It was with difficulty she regained her equanimity sufficiently to release her lover from the closet in which he was concealed, and escape with him. She left a boy of three years to comfort her bereaved husband. The Old Man's present wife had been his cook. She was large, loyal, and aggressive.

Before he could reply, Joe Dimmick suggested with great directness that it was the "Old Man's house," and that, invoking the Divine Power, if the case were his own, he would invite whom he pleased, even if in so doing he imperiled his salvation. The Powers of Evil, he further remarked, should contend against him vainly. All this delivered with a terseness and vigor lost in this necessary translation.

"In course. Certainly. Thet's it," said the Old Man with a sympathetic frown. "Thar's no trouble about thet. It's my own house, built every stick on it myself. Don't you be afeard o' her, boys. She *may* cut up a trifle rough—ez wimmin do—but she'll come round." Secretly the Old Man trusted to the exaltation of liquor and the power of courageous example to sustain him in such an emergency.

As yet, Dick Bullen, the oracle and leader of Simpson's Bar, had not spoken. He now took his pipe from his lips. "Old Man, how's that yer Johnny gettin' on? Seems to me he didn't look so peart last time I seed him on the bluff heavin' rocks at Chinamen. Didn't seem to take much interest in it. Thar was a gang of 'em by yar yesterday—drownded out up the river —and I kinder thought o' Johnny, and how he'd miss 'em! Maybe now, we'd be in the way ef he wus sick?"

The father, evidently touched not only by this pathetic picture of Johnny's deprivation, but by the considerate delicacy of the speaker, hastened to assure him that Johnny was better, and that a "little fun might, 'liven him up." Whereupon Dick arose, shook himself, and saying, "I'm ready. Lead the way, Old Man: here goes," himself led the way with a leap, a characteristic howl, and darted out into the night. As he passed through the outer room he caught up a blazing brand from the hearth. The action was repeated by the rest of the party, closely following and elbowing each other, and before the astonished proprietor of Thompson's grocery was aware of the intention of his guests, the room was deserted.

The night was pitchy dark. In the first gust of wind their temporary torches were extinguished, and only the red brands dancing and flitting in the gloom like drunken will-o'-the-wisps indicated their whereabouts. Their way led up Pine Tree Canyon, at the head of which a broad, low, bark-thatched cabin burrowed in the mountainside. It was the home of the Old Man, and the entrance to the tunnel in which he worked when he worked at all. Here the crowd paused for a moment, out of delicate deference to their host, who came up panting in the rear.

"P'r'aps ye'd better hold on a second out yer, whilst I go in and see that things is all right," said the Old Man, with an indifference he was far from feeling. The suggestion was graciously accepted, the door opened and closed on the host, and the crowd, leaning their backs against the wall and cowering under the eaves, waited and listened.

For a few moments there was no sound but the dripping of water from the eaves and the stir and rustle of wrestling boughs above them. Then the men became uneasy, and whispered suggestion and suspicion passed from the one to the other. "Reckon she's caved in his head the first lick!" "Decoyed him inter the tunnel and barred him up, likely." "Got him down and sittin' on him." "Prob'ly biling suthin' to heave on us: stand clear the door, boys!" For just then the latch clicked, the door slowly opened, and a voice said, "Come in out o' the wet."

The voice was neither that of the Old Man nor of

his wife. It was the voice of a small boy, its weak treble broken by that preternatural hoarseness which only vagabondage and the habit of premature self-assertion can give. It was the face of a small boy that looked up at theirs—a face that might have been pretty, and even refined, but that it was darkened by evil knowledge from within, and dirt and hard experience from without. He had a blanket around his shoulders, and had evidently just risen from his bed. "Come in," he repeated, "and don't make no noise. The Old Man's in there talking to mar," he continued, pointing to an adjacent room which seemed to be a kitchen, from which the Old Man's voice came in deprecating accents. "Let me be," he added querulously to Dick Bullen, who had caught him up, blanket and all, and was affecting to toss him into the fire, "let go o' me, you d—d old fool, d'ye hear?"

Thus adjured, Dick Bullen lowered Johnny to the ground with a smothered laugh, while the men, entering quietly, ranged themselves around a long table of rough boards which occupied the center of the room. Johnny then gravely proceeded to a cupboard and brought out several articles, which he deposited on the table. "Thar's whiskey. And crackers. And red herons. And cheese." He took a bite of the latter on his way to the table. "And sugar." He scooped up a mouthful en route with a small and very dirty hand. "And terbacker. Thar's dried appils too on the shelf, but I don't admire 'em. Appils is swellin'. Thar," he concluded, "now wade in, and don't be afeard. I don't mind the old woman. She don't b'long to me. S'long."

He had stepped to the threshold of a small room,

scarcely larger than a closet, partitioned off from the main apartment, and holding in its dim recess a small bed. He stood there a moment looking at the company, his bare feet peeping from the blanket, and nodded.

"Hello, Johnny! You ain't goin' to turn in again, are ye?" said Dick.

"Yes, I are," responded Johnny decidedly.

"Why, wot's up, old fellow?"

"I'm sick."

"How sick?"

"I've got a fevier. And childblains. And roomatiz," returned Johnny, and vanished within. After a moment's pause, he added in the dark, apparently from under the bedclothes—"And biles!"

There was an embarrassing silence. The men looked at each other and at the fire. Even with the appetizing banquet before them, it seemed as if they might again fall into the despondency of Thompson's grocery, when the voice of the Old Man, incautiously lifted, came deprecatingly from the kitchen.

"Certainly! Thet's so. In course they is. A gang o' lazy, drunken loafers, and that ar Dick Bullen's the ornariest of all. Didn't hev no more *sabe* than to come round yar with sickness in the house and no provision. Thet's what I said: 'Bullen,' sez I, 'it's crazy drunk you are, or a fool,' sez I, 'to think o' such a thing.' 'Staples,' I sez, 'be you a man, Staples, and 'spect to raise h—ll under my roof and invalids lyin' round?' But they would come—they would. Thet's wot you must 'spect o' such trash as lays round the Bar."

A burst of laughter from the men followed this unfortunate exposure. Whether it was overheard in the kitchen, or whether the Old Man's irate companion had just then exhausted all other modes of expressing her contemptuous indignation, I cannot say, but a back door was suddenly slammed with great violence. A moment later and the Old Man reappeared, haply unconscious of the cause of the late hilarious outburst, and smiled blandly.

"The old woman thought she'd jest run over to Mrs. MacFadden's for a sociable call," he explained with jaunty indifference, as he took a seat at the board.

Oddly enough it needed this untoward incident to relieve the embarrassment that was beginning to be felt by the party, and their natural audacity returned with their host. I do not propose to record convivialities of that evening. The inquisitive reader will accept the statement that the conversation was characterized by the same intellectual exaltation, the same cautious reverence, the same fastidious delicacy, the same rhetorical precision, and the same logical and coherent discourse somewhat later in the evening, which distinguish similar gatherings of the masculine sex in more civilized localities and under more favorable auspices. No glasses were broken in the absence of any; no liquor was uselessly spilt on the floor or table in the scarcity of that article.

It was nearly midnight when the festivities were interrupted. "Hush," said Dick Bullen, holding up his hand. It was the querulous voice of Johnny from his adjacent closet: "O dad!"

The Old Man arose hurriedly and disappeared in the closet. Presently he reappeared. "His rheumatiz is coming on agin bad," he explained, "and he wants rubbin'.'" He lifted the demijohn of whiskey from the table and shook it. It was empty. Dick Bullen put down his tin cup with an embarrassed laugh. So did the others. The Old Man examined their contents and said hopefully, "I reckon that's enough; he don't need much. You hold on all o' you for a spell, and I'll be back;" and vanished in the closet with an old flannel shirt and the whiskey. The door closed but imperfectly, and the following dialogue was distinctly audible:

"Now, sonny, whar does she ache worst?"

"Sometimes over yar and sometimes under yer; but it's most powerful from yer to yer. Rub yer, dad."

A silence seemed to indicate a brisk rubbing. Then Johnny:

"Hevin' a good time out yer, Dad?"

"Yes, sonny."

"Tomorrer's Chrismiss—ain't it?"

"Yes, sonny. How does she feel now?"

"Better. Rub a little furder down. Wot's Chrismiss, anyway? Wot's it all about?"

"Oh, it's a day."

This exhaustive definition was apparently satisfactory, for there was a silent interval of rubbing. Presently Johnny again:

"Mar sez that everywhere else but yelr everybody gives things to everybody Chrismiss, and then she jist waded inter you. She sez thar's a man they call Sandy Claws, not a white man, you know, but a kind o' Chinemin, comes down the chimbley night afore Chrismiss and gives things to chillern—boys like me. Puts 'em in their butes! Thet's what she tried to play upon me. Easy now, pop, whar are you rubbin' to—

thet's a mile from the place. She jest made that up, didn't she, jest to aggrewate me and you? Don't rub thar. . . . Why, Dad!"

In the great quiet that seemed to have fallen upon the house the sigh of the near pines and the drip of leaves without was very distinct. Johnny's voice, too, was lowered as he went on, "Don't you take on now, for I'm gettin' all right fast. Wot's the boys doin' out thar?"

The Old Man partly opened the door and peered through. His guests were sitting there sociably enough, and there were a few silver coins and a lean buckskin purse on the table. "Bettin' on suthin'— some little game or 'nother. They're all right," he replied to Johnny, and recommenced his rubbing.

"I'd like to take a hand and win some money," said Johnny reflectively after a pause.

The Old Man glibly repeated what was evidently a familiar formula, that if Johnny would wait until he struck it rich in the tunnel he'd have lots of money, etc., etc.

"Yes," said Johnny, "but you don't. And whether you strike it or I win it, it's about the same. It's all luck. But it's mighty cur'o's about Chrismiss—ain't it? Why do they call it Chrismiss?"

Perhaps from some instinctive deference to the overhearing of his guests, or from some vague sense of incongruity, the Old Man's reply was so low as to be inaudible beyond the room.

"Yes," said Johnny, with some slight abatement of interest, "I've heard o' *him* before. Thar, that'll do, dad. I don't ache near so bad as I did. Now wrap me tight in this yer blanket. So. Now," he added in a

muffled whisper, "sit down yer by me till I go asleep."
To assure himself of obedience, he disengaged one
hand from the blanket, and grasping his father's
sleeve, again composed himself to rest.

For some moments the Old Man waited patiently.
Then the unwonted stillness of the house excited
his curiosity, and without moving from the bed he
cautiously opened the door with his disengaged hand,
and looked into the main room. To his infinite surprise it was dark and deserted. But even then a smol-
dering log on the hearth broke, and by the upspring-
ing blaze he saw the figure of Dick Bullen sitting by
the dying embers.

"Hello!"

Dick started, rose, and came somewhat unsteadily
toward him.

"Whar's the boys?" said the Old Man.

"Gone up the canyon on a little *pasear*. They're
coming back for me in a minit. I'm waitin' round for
'em. What are you starin' at, Old Man?" he added, with
a forced laugh; "do you think I'm drunk?"

The Old Man might have been pardoned the sup-
position, for Dick's eyes were humid and his face
flushed. He loitered and lounged back to the chimney, yawned, shook himself, buttoned up his coat,
and laughed. "Liquor ain't so plenty as that, Old
Man. Now don't you git up," he continued, as the
Old Man made a movement to release his sleeve from
Johnny's hand. "Don't you mind manners. Sit jest
whar you be; I'm goin' in a jiffy. Thar, that's them
now."

There was a low tap at the door. Dick Bullen
opened it quickly, nodded "good night" to his host,

and disappeared. The Old Man would have followed him but for the hand that still unconsciously grasped his sleeve. He could have easily disengaged it: it was small, weak, and emaciated. But perhaps because it *was* small, weak, and emaciated he changed his mind, and drawing his chair closer to the bed, rested his head upon it. In this defenseless attitude the potency of his earlier potations surprised him. The room flickered and faded before his eyes, reappeared, faded again, went out, and left him—asleep.

Meantime Dick Bullen, closing the door, confronted his companions. "Are you ready?" said Staples. "Ready," said Dick; "what's the time?" "Past twelve," was the reply; "can you make it?—it's nigh on fifty miles, the round trip hither and yon." "I reckon," returned Dick shortly. "Whar's the mare?" "Bill and Jack's holdin' her at the crossin'." "Let 'em hold on a minit longer," said Dick.

He turned and re-entered the house softly. By the light of the guttering candle and dying fire he saw that the door of the little room was open. He stepped toward it on tiptoe and looked in. The Old Man had fallen back in his chair, snoring, his helpless feet thrust out in a line with his collapsed shoulders, and his hat pulled over his eyes. Beside him, on a narrow wooden bedstead, lay Johnny, muffled tightly in a blanket that hid all save a strip of forehead and a few curls damp with perspiration. Dick Bullen made a step forward, hesitated, and glanced over his shoulder into the deserted room. Everything was quiet. With a sudden resolution he parted his huge mustaches with both hands and stooped over the sleeping boy. But even as he did so a mischievous blast, lying in wait, swooped down the chimney, rekindled the hearth, and lit up the room with a shameless glow from which Dick fled in bashful terror.

His companions were already waiting for him at the crossing. Two of them were struggling in the darkness with some strange misshapen bulk, which as Dick came nearer took the semblance of a great yellow horse.

It was the mare. She was not a pretty picture. From her Roman nose to her rising haunches, from her arched spine hidden by the stiff *machillas* of a Mexican saddle, to her thick, straight bony legs, there was not a line of equine grace. In her half-blind but wholly vicious white eyes, in her protruding underlip, in her monstrous color, there was nothing but ugliness and vice.

"Now then," said Staples, "stand cl'ar of her heels, boys, and up with you. Don't miss your first holt of her mane, and mind ye get your off stirrup *quick*. Ready!"

There was a leap, a scrambling struggle, a bound, a wild retreat of the crowd, a circle of flying hoofs, two springless leaps that jarred the earth, a rapid play and jingle of spurs, a plunge, and then the voice of Dick somewhere in the darkness. "All right!"

"Don't take the lower road back onless you're hard pushed for time! Don't hold her in downhill! We'll be at the ford at five. G'lang! Hoopa! Mula! GO!"

A splash, a spark struck from the ledge in the road, a clatter in the rocky cut beyond, and Dick was gone.

Sing, O Muse, the ride of Richard Bullen! Sing, O

Muse, of chivalrous men! the sacred quest, the doughty deeds, the battery of low churls, the fearsome ride and gruesome perils of the Flower of Simpson's Bar! Alack! she is dainty, this Muse! She will have none of this bucking brute and swaggering, ragged rider, and I must fain follow him in prose, afoot!

It was one o'clock, and yet he had only gained Rattlesnake Hill. For in that time Jovita had rehearsed to him all her imperfections and practiced all her vices. Thrice had she stumbled. Twice had she thrown up her Roman nose in a straight line with the reins, and resisting bit and spur, struck out madly across country. Twice had she reared, and rearing, fallen backward; and twice had the agile Dick, unharmed, regained his seat before she found her vicious legs again. And a mile beyond them, at the foot of a long hill, was Rattlesnake Creek. Dick knew that here was the crucial test of his ability to perform his enterprise, set his teeth grimly, put his knees well into her flanks, and changed his defensive tactics to brisk aggression. Bullied and maddened, Jovita began the descent of the hill. Here the artful Richard pretended to hold her in with ostentatious objurgation and well-feigned cries of alarm. It is unnecessary to add that Jovita instantly ran away. Nor need I state the time made in the descent; it is written in the chronicles of Simpson's Bar. Enough that in another moment, as it seemed to Dick, she was splashing on the overflowed banks of Rattlesnake Creek. As Dick expected, the momentum she had acquired carried her beyond the point of balking, and holding her well together for a mighty leap, they dashed into the middle of the swiftly flowing current. A few moments of kicking, wading, and swimming, and Dick drew a long breath on the opposite bank.

The road from Rattlesnake Creek to Red Mountain was tolerably level. Either the plunge in Rattlesnake Creek had dampened her baleful fire, or the art which led to it had shown her the superior wickedness of her rider, for Jovita no longer wasted her surplus energy in wanton conceits. Once she bucked, but it was from force of habit; once she shied, but it was from a new, freshly painted meetinghouse at the crossing of the county road. Hollows, ditches, gravelly deposits, patches of freshly springing grasses, flew from beneath her rattling hoofs. She began to smell unpleasantly, once or twice she coughed slightly, but there was no abatement of her strength or speed. By two o'clock he had passed Red Mountain and begun the descent to the plain. Ten minutes later the driver of the fast Pioneer coach was overtaken and passed by a "man on a pinto hoss,"—an event sufficiently notable for remark. At half past two Dick rose in his stirrups with a great shout. Stars were glittering through the rifted clouds, and beyond him, out of the plain, rose two spires, a flagstaff, and a straggling line of black objects. Dick jingled his spurs and swung his *riata,* Jovita bounded forward, and in another moment they swept into Tuttleville, and drew up before the wooden piazza of "The Hotel of All Nations."

What transpired that night at Tuttleville is not strictly a part of this record. Briefly I may state, however, that after Jovita had been handed over to a sleepy ostler, whom she at once kicked into unpleasant consciousness, Dick sallied out with the barkeeper for a tour of the sleeping town. Lights still gleamed from a few saloons and gambling houses; but avoiding these, they stopped before several closed shops, and by persistent tapping and judicious outcry roused the proprietors from their beds, and made them unbar the doors of the magazines and expose their wares. Sometimes they were met by curses, but oftener by interest and some concern in their needs, and the interview was invariably concluded by a drink. It was three o'clock before this pleasantry was given over, and with a small waterproof bag of India rubber strapped on his shoulders, Dick returned to the hotel. But here he was waylaid by Beauty —Beauty opulent in charms, affluent in dress, persuasive in speech, and Spanish in accent! In vain she repeated the invitation in "Excelsior," happily scorned by all Alpine-climbing youth, and rejected by this child of the Sierras—a rejection softened in this instance by a laugh and his last gold coin. And then he sprang to the saddle and dashed down the lonely street and out into the lonelier plain, where presently the lights, the black line of houses, the spires, and the flagstaff sank into the earth behind him again and were lost in the distance.

The storm had cleared away, the air was brisk and cold, the outlines of adjacent landmarks were distinct, but, it was half past four before Dick reached the meetinghouse and the crossing of the county road. To avoid the rising grade he had taken a longer and more circuitous road, in whose viscid mud Jovita sank fetlock deep at every bound. It was a poor preparation for a steady ascent of five miles more; but Jovita, gathering her legs under her, took it with her usual blind, unreasoning fury, and a half-hour later reached the long level that led to Rattlesnake Creek. Another half-hour would bring him to the creek. He threw the reins lightly upon the neck of the mare, chirruped to her, and began to sing.

Suddenly Jovita shied with a bound that would have unseated a less practiced rider. Hanging to her rein was a figure that had leaped from the bank, and at the same time from the road before her arose a shadowy horse and rider.

"Throw up your hands," commanded the second apparition, with an oath.

Dick felt the mare tremble, quiver, and apparently sink under him. He knew what it meant and was prepared.

"Stand aside, Jack Simpson. I know you, you d—d thief! Let me pass, or—"

He did not finish the sentence. Jovita rose straight in the air with a terrific bound, throwing the figure from her bit with a single shake of her vicious head, and charged with deadly malevolence down on the impediment before her. An oath, a pistol shot, horse and highwayman rolled over in the road, and the next moment Jovita was a hundred yards away. But the good right arm of her rider, shattered by a bullet, dropped helplessly at his side.

Without slacking his speed he shifted the reins to his left hand. But a few moments later he was obliged to halt and tighten the saddle girths that had slipped in the onset. This in his crippled condition took some time. He had no fear of pursuit, but looking up he saw that the eastern stars were already paling, and that the distant peaks had lost their ghostly whiteness and now stood out blackly against a lighter sky. Day was upon him. Then completely absorbed in a single idea, he forgot the pain of his wound, and mounting again dashed on toward Rattlesnake Creek. But now Jovita's breath came broken by gasps, Dick reeled in his saddle, and brighter and brighter grew the sky.

Ride, Richard; run, Jovita; linger, O day!

For the last few rods there was a roaring in his ears. Was it exhaustion from loss of blood, or what? He was dazed and giddy as he swept down the hill, and did not recognize his surroundings. Had he taken the wrong road, or was this Rattlesnake Creek?

It was. But the brawling creek he had swam a few hours before had risen, more than doubled its volume, and now rolled a swift and resistless river between him and Rattlesnake Hill. For the first time that night Richard's heart sank within him. The river, the mountain, the quickening east, swam before his eyes. He shut them to recover his self-control. In that brief interval, by some fantastic mental process, the little room at Simpson's Bar and the figures of the sleeping father and son rose upon him. He opened his eyes wildly, cast off his coat, pistol, boots, and saddle, bound his precious pack tightly to his shoulders, grasped the bare flanks of Jovita with his bared knees, and with a shout dashed into the yellow water. A cry rose from the opposite bank as the head

of a man and horse struggled for a few moments
against the battling current, and then were swept
away amidst uprooted trees and whirling driftwood.

The Old Man started and woke. The fire on the
hearth was dead, the candle in the outer room flickering in its socket, and somebody was rapping at the
door. He opened it, but fell back with a cry before
the dripping, half-naked figure that reeled against
the doorpost.

"Dick?"

"Hush! Is he awake yet?"

"No; but, Dick—"

"Dry up, you old fool! Get me some whiskey,
quick!" The Old Man flew and returned with—an
empty bottle! Dick would have sworn, but his strength
was not equal to the occasion. He staggered, caught
at the handle of the door, and motioned to the Old
Man.

"Thar's suthin' in my pack yer for Johnny. Take it
off. I can't."

The Old Man unstrapped the pack, and laid it before the exhausted man.

"Open it, quick."

He did so with trembling fingers. It contained only
a few poor toys—cheap and barbaric enough, goodness knows, but bright with paint and tinsel. One of
them was broken; another, I fear, was irretrievably
ruined by water, and on the third—ah, me! there
was a cruel spot.

"It don't look like much, that's a fact," said Dick
ruefully. . . . "But it's the best we could do. . . .
Take 'em, Old Man, and put 'em in his stocking, and

tell him—tell him, you know—hold me, Old Man—"
The Old Man caught at his sinking figure. "Tell him,"
said Dick, with a weak little laugh—"tell him
Sandy Claus has come."

And even so, bedraggled, ragged, unshaven and
unshorn, with one arm hanging helplessly at his side,
Santa Claus came to Simpson's Bar and fell fainting
on the first threshold. The Christmas dawn came
slowly after, touching the remoter peaks with the
rosy warmth of ineffable love. And it looked so tenderly on Simpson's Bar that the whole mountain, as
if caught in a generous action, blushed to the skies.

MRS. SKAGGS'S HUSBANDS

PART ONE

WEST

The sun was rising in the foothills. But for an hour the black mass of Sierra eastward of Angel's had been outlined with fire, and the conventional morning had come two hours before with the down coach from Placerville. The dry, cold, dewless California night still lingered in the long canyons and folded skirts of Table Mountain. Even on the mountain road the air was still sharp, and that urgent necessity for something to keep out the chill, which sent the barkeeper sleepily among his bottles and wine glasses at the station, obtained all along the road.

Perhaps it might be said that the first stir of life was in the barrooms. A few birds twittered in the sycamores at the roadside, but long before that glasses had clicked and bottles gurgled in the saloon of the Mansion House. This was still lit by a dissipated looking hanging lamp, which was evidently the worse for having been up all night, and bore a singular resemblance to a faded reveler of Angel's, who even then sputtered and flickered in *his* socket in an armchair below it—a resemblance so plain that when the first level sunbeam pierced the windowpane, the barkeeper, moved by a sentiment of consistency and compassion, put them both out together.

Then the sun came up haughtily. When it had passed the eastern ridge it began, after its habit, to lord it over Angel's, sending the thermometer up twenty degrees in as many minutes, driving the mules to the sparse shade of corrals and fences, making the red dust incandescent, and renewing its old imperious aggression on the spiked bosses of the convex shield of pines that defended Table Mountain. Thither by nine o'clock all coolness had retreated, and the "outsides" of the up stage plunged their hot faces in its aromatic shadows as in water.

It was the custom of the Wingdam coach to whip up his horses and enter Angel's at that remarkable pace which the woodcuts in the hotel barroom represented to credulous humanity as the usual rate of speed of that conveyance. At such times the habitual expression of disdainful reticence and lazy official severity which he wore on the box became intensified as the loungers gathered about the vehicle, and only the boldest ventured to address him. It was the Hon. Judge Beeswinger, Member of Assembly, who today presumed, perhaps rashly, on the strength of his official position.

"Any political news from below, Bill?" he asked, as the latter slowly descended from his lofty perch, without, however, any perceptible coming down of mien or manner.

"Not much," said Bill, with deliberate gravity. "The President o' the United States hezn't bin hisself sens you refoosed that seat in the Cabinet. The ginral feelin' in perlitical circles is one o' regret."

Irony, even of this outrageous quality, was too common in Angel's to excite either a smile or a frown. Bill slowly entered the barroom during a dry, dead silence, in which only a faint spirit of emulation survived.

"Ye didn't bring up that agint o' Rothschild's this trip?" asked the barkeeper slowly, by way of vague contribution to the prevailing tone of conversation.

"No," responded Bill, with thoughtful exactitude. "He said he couldn't look inter that claim o' Johnson's without first consultin' the Bank o' England."

The Mr. Johnson here alluded to being present as the faded reveler the barkeeper had lately put out, and as the alleged claim notoriously possessed no attractions whatever to capitalists, expectation naturally looked to him for some response to this evident challenge. He did so by simply stating that he would "take sugar" in his, and by walking unsteadily towards the bar, as if accepting a festive invitation. To the credit of Bill be it recorded that he did not attempt to correct the mistake, but gravely touched glasses with him, and after saying "Here's another nail in your coffin,"—a cheerful sentiment, to which "And the hair all off your head" was playfully added by the others—he threw off his liquor with a single dexterous movement of head and elbow, and stood refreshed.

"Hello, old major!" said Bill, suddenly setting down his glass. "Are *you* there?"

It was a boy, who, becoming bashfully conscious that this epithet was addressed to him, retreated sideways to the doorway, where he stood beating his hat against the doorpost with an assumption of indifference that his downcast but mirthful dark eyes and reddening cheek scarcely bore out. Perhaps it was owing to his size, perhaps it was to a certain cherubic outline of face and figure, perhaps to a peculiar trustfulness of expression, that he did not look half his age, which was really fourteen.

Everybody in Angel's knew the boy. Either under the venerable title bestowed by Bill, or as "Tom Islington," after his adopted father, his was a familiar presence in the settlement, and the theme of much local criticism and comment. His waywardness, indolence, and unaccountable amiability—a quality at once suspicious and gratuitous in a pioneer community like Angel's—had often been the subject of fierce discussion. A large and reputable majority believed him destined for the gallows; a minority not quite so reputable enjoyed his presence without troubling themselves much about his future; to one or two the evil predictions of the majority possessed neither novelty nor terror.

"Anything for me, Bill?" asked the boy half mechanically, with the air of repeating some jocular formulary perfectly understood by Bill.

"Anythin' for you!" echoed Bill, with an overacted severity equally well understood by Tommy—"anythin' for you? No! And it's my opinion there won't be anythin' for you ez long ez you hang around barrooms and spend your valooable time with loafers and bummers. Git!"

The reproof was accompanied by a suitable exaggeration of gesture (Bill had seized a decanter), before which the boy retreated still good-humoredly. Bill followed him to the door. "Dern my skin, if he hezn't gone off with that bummer Johnson," he added, as he looked down the road.

"What's he expectin', Bill?" asked the barkeeper.

"A letter from his aunt. Reckon he'll hev to take it out in expectin'. Likely they're glad to get shut o' him."

"He's leadin' a shiftless, idle life here," interposed the Member of Assembly.

"Well," said Bill, who never allowed anyone but himself to abuse his protégé, "seein' he ain't expectin' no offis from the hands of an enlightened constit-ooency, it *is* rayther a shiftless life." After delivering this Parthian arrow with a gratuitous twanging of the bow to indicate its offensive personality, Bill winked at the barkeeper, slowly resumed a pair of immense, bulgy buckskin gloves, which gave his fingers the appearance of being painfully sore and bandaged, strode to the door without looking at anybody, called out, "All aboard," with a perfunctory air of supreme indifference whether the invitation was heeded, remounted his box, and drove stolidly away.

Perhaps it was well that he did so, for the conversation at once assumed a disrespectful attitude toward Tom and his relatives. It was more than intimated that Tom's alleged aunt was none other than Tom's real mother, while it was also asserted that Tom's alleged uncle did not himself participate in this intimate relationship to the boy to an extent which the fastidious taste of Angel's deemed moral and necessary. Popular opinion also believed that Islington, the adopted father, who received a certain stipend ostensibly for the boy's support, retained it as a reward for his reticence regarding these facts. "He ain't ruinin' hisself by wastin' it on Tom," said the barkeeper, who possibly possessed positive knowledge of much of Islington's disbursements. But at this point exhausted nature languished among some of the debaters, and he turned from the frivolity of conversation to his severer professional duties.

It was also well that Bill's momentary attitude of didactic propriety was not further excited by the subsequent conduct of his protégé. For by this time Tom, half supporting the unstable Johnson, who developed a tendency to occasionally dash across the glaring road, but checked himself midway each time, reached the corral which adjoined the Mansion House. At its farther extremity was a pump and horse trough. Here, without a word being spoken, but evidently in obedience to some habitual custom, Tom led his companion. With the boy's assistance, Johnson removed his coat and neckcloth, turned back the collar of his shirt, and gravely placed his head beneath the pump spout. With equal gravity and deliberation, Tom took his place at the handle. For a few moments only the splashing of water and regular strokes of the pump broke the solemnly ludicrous silence. Then there was a pause in which Johnson put his hands to his dripping head, felt it critically as if it belonged to somebody else, and raised his eyes to his companion. "That ought to fetch *it*," said Tom in answer to the look. "Ef it don't," replied Johnson doggedly, with an air of relieving himself of all further responsibility in the matter, "it's got to, thet's all!"

If "it" referred to some change in the physiognomy of Johnson, "it" had probably been "fetched" by the process just indicated. The head that went under the pump was large, and clothed with bushy, uncertain-colored hair; the face was flushed, puffy, and expressionless, the eyes injected and full. The head that came out from under the pump was of smaller size and different shape, the hair straight, dark, and sleek, the face pale and hollow-cheeked, the eyes bright and restless. In the haggard, nervous ascetic that rose from the horse trough there was very little trace of the Bacchus that had bowed there a moment before. Familiar as Tom must have been with the spectacle, he could not help looking inquiringly at the trough, as if expecting to see some traces of the previous Johnson in its shallow depths.

A narrow strip of willow, alder, and buckeye— a mere dusty, raveled fringe of the green mantle that swept the high shoulders of Table Mountain—lapped the edge of the corral. The silent pair were quick to avail themselves of even its scant shelter from the overpowering sun. They had not proceeded far, before Johnson, who was walking quite rapidly in advance, suddenly brought himself up, and turned to his companion with an interrogative "Eh?"

"I didn't speak," said Tommy quietly.

"Who said you spoke?" said Johnson, with a quick look of cunning. "In course you didn't speak, and I didn't speak neither. Nobody spoke. Wot makes you think you spoke?" he continued, peering curiously into Tommy's eyes.

The smile which habitually shone there quickly vanished as the boy stepped quietly to his companion's side, and took his arm without a word.

"In course you didn't speak, Tommy," said Johnson deprecatingly. "You ain't a boy to go for to play an ole soaker like me. That's wot I like you for. Thet's wot I seed in you from the first. I sez, 'Thet 'ere boy ain't going to play you, Johnson! You can go your whole pile on him, when you can't trust even a bar-keep.' Thet's wot I said. Eh?"

This time Tommy prudently took no notice of the interrogation, and Johnson went on: "Ef I was to ask you another question, you wouldn't go to play me neither—would you, Tommy?"

"No," said the boy.

"Ef I was to ask you," continued Johnson, without heeding the reply, but with a growing anxiety of eye and a nervous twitching of his lips—"ef I was to ask you, fur instance, ef that was a jackass rab-bit that jest passed—eh?—you'd say it was or was not, ez the case may be. You wouldn't play the ole man on thet?"

"No," said Tommy quietly, "it *was* a jackass rab-bit."

"Ef I was to ask you," continued Johnson, "ef it wore, say, fur instance, a green hat with yaller rib-bons, you wouldn't play me, and say it did, on-less"—he added, with intensified cunning—"onless it *did?*"

"No," said Tommy, "of course I wouldn't; but then, you see, *it did.*"

"It did?"

"It did!" repeated Tommy stoutly; "a green hat with yellow ribbons—and—and—a red rosette."

"I didn't get to see the ros-ette," said Johnson, with slow and conscientious deliberation, yet with an evident sense of relief; "but that ain't sayin' it wa'n't there, you know. Eh?"

Tommy glanced quietly at his companion. There were great beads of perspiration on his ashen-gray forehead, and on the ends of his lank hair; the hand which twitched spasmodically in his was cold and clammy, the other, which was free, had a vague, purposeless, jerky activity, as if attached to some deranged mechanism. Without any apparent concern in these phenomena, Tommy halted, and seating himself on a log, motioned his companion to a place beside him. Johnson obeyed without a word. Slight as was the act, perhaps no other incident of their singular companionship indicated as completely the dominance of this careless, half-effeminate, but self-possessed boy over this doggedly self-willed, abnormally excited man.

"It ain't the square thing," said Johnson, after a pause, with a laugh that was neither mirthful nor musical, and frightened away a lizard that had been regarding the pair with breathless suspense—"it ain't the square thing for jackass rabbits to wear hats, Tommy— is it, eh?"

"Well," said Tommy, with unmoved composure, "sometimes they do and sometimes they don't. Animals are mighty queer." And here Tommy went off in an animated, but, I regret to say, utterly untruthful and untrustworthy account of the habits of California fauna, until he was interrupted by Johnson.

"And snakes, eh, Tommy?" said the man, with an abstracted air, gazing intently on the ground before him.

"And snakes," said Tommy, "but they don't bite—at least not that kind you see. There!—don't move, Uncle Ben, don't move; they're gone now. And it's about time you took your dose."

Johnson had hurriedly risen as if to leap upon the log, but Tommy had as quickly caught his arm with

one hand while he drew a bottle from his pocket with
the other. Johnson paused and eyed the bottle. "Ef
you say so, my boy," he faltered, as his fingers closed
nervously around it; "say 'when,' then." He raised
the bottle to his lips and took a long draught,
the boy regarding him critically. "When," said
Tommy suddenly. Johnson started, flushed, and returned the bottle quickly. But the color that had risen
to his cheek stayed there, his eye grew less restless,
and as they moved away again the hand that rested
on Tommy's shoulder was steadier.

Their way lay along the flank of Table Mountain
—a wandering trail through a tangled solitude that
might have seemed virgin and unbroken but for a
few oyster cans, yeast-powder tins, and empty bottles
that had been apparently stranded by the "first low
wash" of pioneer waves. On the ragged trunk of an
enormous pine hung a few tufts of gray hair caught
from a passing grizzly, but in strange juxtaposition
at its foot lay an empty bottle of incomparable bit-
ters—the chef-d'œuvre of a hygienic civilization,
and blazoned with the arms of an all-healing republic. The head of a rattlesnake peered from a case
that had contained tobacco, which was still brightly
placarded with the high-colored effigy of a popular
danseuse. And a little beyond this the soil was
broken and fissured, there was a confused mass of
roughly hewn timber, a straggling line of sluicing,
a heap of gravel and dirt, a rude cabin, and the claim
of Johnson.

Except for the rudest purposes of shelter from rain
and cold, the cabin possessed but little advantage
over the simple savagery of surrounding nature. It

had all the practical directness of the habitation of some animal, without its comfort or picturesque quality; the very birds that haunted it for food must have felt their own superiority as architects. It was inconceivably dirty, even with its scant capacity for accretion; it was singularly stale, even in its newness and freshness of material. Unspeakably dreary as it was in shadow, the sunlight visited it in a blind, aching, purposeless way, as if despairing of mellowing its outlines or of even tanning it into color.

The claim worked by Johnson in his intervals of sobriety was represented by half a dozen rude openings in the mountainside, with the heaped-up debris of rock and gravel before the mouth of each. They gave very little evidence of engineering skill or constructive purpose, or indeed showed anything but the vague, successively abandoned essays of their projector. Today they served another purpose, for as the sun had heated the little cabin almost to the point of combustion, curling up the long dry shingles, and starting aromatic tears from the green pine beams, Tommy led Johnson into one of the larger openings, and with a sense of satisfaction threw himself panting upon its rocky floor. Here and there the grateful dampness was condensed in quiet pools of water, or in a monotonous and soothing drip from the rocks above. Without lay the staring sunlight—colorless, clarified, intense.

For a few moments they lay resting on their elbows in blissful contemplation of the heat they had escaped. "Wot do you say," said Johnson slowly, without looking at his companion, but abstractedly addressing himself to the landscape beyond—"wot do you say to two straight games fur one thousand dollars?"

"Make it five thousand," replied Tommy reflectively also to the landscape, "and I'm in."

"Wot do I owe you now?" said Johnson, after a lengthened silence.

"One hundred and seventy-five thousand, two hundred and fifty dollars," replied Tommy with business-like gravity.

"Well," said Johnson after a deliberation commensurate with the magnitude of the transaction, "ef you win, call it a hundred and eighty thousand, round. War's the keerds?"

They were in an old tin box in a crevice of a rock above his head. They were greasy and worn with service. Johnson dealt, albeit his right hand was still uncertain—hovering, after dropping the cards, aimlessly about Tommy, and being only recalled by a strong nervous effort. Yet, notwithstanding this incapacity for even honest manipulation, Mr. Johnson covertly turned a knave from the bottom of the pack with such shameless inefficiency and gratuitous unskillfulness, that even Tommy was obliged to cough and look elsewhere to hide his embarrassment. Possibly for this reason the young gentleman was himself constrained, by way of correction, to add a valuable card to his own hand, over and above the number he legitimately held.

Nevertheless the game was unexciting and dragged listlessly. Johnson won. He recorded the fact and the amount with a stub of pencil and shaking fingers in wandering hieroglyphics all over a pocket diary. Then there was a long pause, when Johnson slowly drew something from his pocket and held it up before his companion. It was apparently a dull red stone.

"Ef," said Johnson slowly, with his old look of simple cunning—"ef you happened to pick up sich a rock ez that, Tommy, what might you say it was?"

"Don't know," said Tommy.

"Mightn't you say," continued Johnson cautiously, "that it was gold or silver?"

"Neither," said Tommy promptly.

"Mightn't you say it was quicksilver? Mightn't you say that ef thar was a friend o' yourn ez knew war to go and turn out ten ton of it a day, and every ton worth two thousand dollars, that he had a soft thing, a very soft thing—allowin', Tommy, that you used sich language, which you don't?"

"But," said the boy, coming to the point with great directness, "*do* you know where to get it? have you struck it, Uncle Ben?"

Johnson looked carefully round. "I hev, Tommy. Listen. I know whar thar's cartloads of it. But thar's only one other specimen—the mate to this yer—thet's above ground, and thet's in 'Frisco. Thar's an agint comin' up in a day or two to look into it. I sent for him. Eh?"

His bright, restless eyes were concentrated on Tommy's face now, but the boy showed neither surprise nor interest. Least of all did he betray any recollection of Bill's ironical and gratuitous corroboration of this part of the story.

"Nobody knows it," continued Johnson in a nervous whisper—"nobody knows it but you and the agint

in 'Frisco. The boys workin' round yar passes by and
sees the old man grubbin' away, and no signs o' color,
not even rotten quartz; the boys loafin' round the Mansion House sees the old man lyin' round free in barrooms, and they laughs and sez, 'Played out,' and
spects nothin'. Maybe ye think they spects suthin'
now, eh?" queried Johnson suddenly, with a sharp
look of suspicion.

Tommy looked up, shook his head, threw a stone
at a passing rabbit, but did not reply.

"When I fust set eyes on you, Tommy," continued
Johnson, apparently reassured, "the fust day you
kem and pumped for me, an entire stranger, and
hevin' no call to do it, I sez, 'Johnson, Johnson,' sez
I, 'yer's a boy you kin trust. Yer's a boy that won't
play you; yer's a chap that's white and square'—
white and square, Tommy: them's the very words I
used."

He paused for a moment, and then went on in a confidential whisper, " 'You want capital, Johnson,' sez
I, 'to develop your resources, and you want a pardner. Capital you can send for, but your pardner, Johnson—your pardner is right yer. And his name, it is
Tommy Islington.' Them's the very words I used."

He stopped and chafed his clammy hands upon his
knees. "It's six months ago sens I made you my pardner. Thar ain't a lick I've struck sens then, Tommy,
thar ain't a han'ful o' yearth I've washed, thar ain't a
shovelful o' rock I've turned over, but I tho't o' you.
'Share, and share alike,' sez I. When I wrote to my
agint, I wrote ekal for my pardner, Tommy Islington,
he hevin' no call to know ef the same was man or
boy."

He had moved nearer the boy, and would perhaps have laid his hand caressingly upon him, but even in his manifest affection there was a singular element of awed restraint and even fear—a suggestion of something withheld even his fullest confidences, a hopeless perception of some vague barrier that never could be surmounted. He may have been at times dimly conscious that, in the eyes which Tommy raised to his, there was thorough intellectual appreciation, critical good-humor, even feminine softness, but nothing more. His nervousness somewhat heightened by his embarrassment, he went on with an attempt at calmness which his twitching white lips and unsteady fingers made pathetically grotesque. "Thar's a bill o' sale in my bunk, made out accordin' to law, of an ekal ondivided half of the claim, and the consideration is two hundred and fifty thousand dollars—gambling debts—gambling debts from me to you. Tommy, you understand?"—nothing could exceed the intense cunning of his eye at this moment—"and then thar's a will."

"A will?" said Tommy in amused surprise.

Johnson looked frightened.

"Eh?" he said hurriedly, "wot will? Who said anythin' 'bout a will, Tommy?"

"Nobody," replied Tommy with unblushing calm.

Johnson passed his hand over his cold forehead, wrung the damp ends of his hair with his fingers, and went on: "Times when I'm took bad ez I was today, the boys about yer sez—you sez, maybe, Tommy—it's whiskey. It ain't, Tommy. It's pizen—quicksilver pizen. That's what's the matter with me. I'm salivated! Salivated with merkery.

"I've heerd o' it before," continued Johnson, appealing to the boy, "and ez a boy o' permiskus reading, I reckon you hev too. Them men as works in cinnabar sooner or later gets salivated. It's bound to fetch 'em sometime. Salivated by merkery."

"What are you goin' to do for it?" asked Tommy.

"When the agint comes up, and I begins to realize on this yer mine," said Johnson contemplatively, "I goes to New York. I sez to the barkeep' o' the hotel, 'Show me the biggest doctor here.' He shows me. I sez to him, 'Salivated by merkery—a year's standin'—how much?' He sez, 'Five thousand dollars, and take two o' these pills at bedtime, and an ekil number o' powders at meals, and come back in a week.' And I goes back in a week, cured, and signs a certifikit to that effect."

Encouraged by a look of interest in Tommy's eye, he went on.

"So I gets cured. I goes to the barkeep', and I sez, 'Show me the biggest, fashionblest house thet's for sale yer.' And he sez, 'The biggest nat'rally b'longs to John Jacob Astor.' And I sez, 'Show him,' and he shows him. And I sez, 'Wot might you ask for this yer house?' And he looks at me scornful, and sez, 'Go 'way, old man; you must be sick.' And I fetches him one over the left eye and he apologizes, and I gives him his own price for the house. I stocks that house with mahogany furniture and pervisions, and thar we lives—you and me, Tommy, you and me!"

The sun no longer shone upon the hillside. The shadows of the pines were beginning to creep over Johnson's claim, and the air within the cavern was growing chill. In the gathering darkness his eyes shone brightly as he went on: "Then thar comes a day when we gives a big spread. We invites gov'ners, members o' Congress, gentlemen o' fashion, and the like. And among 'em I invites a Man as holds his head very high, a Man I once knew; but he doesn't know I knows him, and he doesn't remember me. And he comes and he sits opposite me, and I watches him. And he's very airy, this Man, and very chipper, and he smiles, and he ketches my eye. And he sez, 'A glass o' wine with you, Mr. Johnson'; and he fills his glass and I fills mine, and we rises. And I heaves that wine, glass and all, right into his damned grinnin' face. And he jumps for me—for he is very game this Man, very game—but some on 'em grabs him, and he sez, 'Who be you?' And I sez, 'Skaggs! Damn you, Skaggs! Look at me! Gimme back my wife and child, gimme back the money you stole, gimme back the good name you took away, gimme back the health you ruined, gimme back the last twelve years! Give 'em to me, damn you, quick, before I cuts your heart out!' And naterally, Tommy, he can't do it. And so I cuts his heart out, my boy; I cuts his heart out."

The purely animal fury of his eye suddenly changed again to cunning. "You think they hangs me for it, Tommy, but they don't. Not much, Tommy. I goes to the biggest lawyer there, and I says to him, 'Salivated by merkery—you hear me——salivated by merkery.' And he winks at me, and he goes to the judge, and he sez, 'This yer unfortnet man isn't responsible—he's been salivated by merkery.' And he brings witnesses; you comes, Tommy, and you sez ez how you've seen me took bad afore; and the doctor, he comes, and he sez as how he's seen me frightful; and the jury, without leavin' their seats, brings in a verdict o' justifiable insanity—salivated by merkery."

In the excitement of his climax he had risen to his feet, but would have fallen had not Tommy caught him and led him into the open air. In this sharper light there was an odd change visible in his yellow-white face—a change which caused Tommy to hurriedly support him, half leading, half dragging him toward the little cabin. When they had reached it, Tommy placed him on a rude "bunk," or shelf, and stood for a moment in anxious contemplation of the tremor-stricken man before him. Then he said rapidly, "Listen, Uncle Ben. I'm goin' to town—to town, you understand—for the doctor. You're not to get up or move on any account until I return. Do you hear?" Johnson nodded violently. "I'll be back in two hours." In another moment he was gone.

For an hour Johnson kept his word. Then he suddenly sat up, and began to gaze fixedly at a corner of the cabin. From gazing at it he began to smile, from smiling at it he began to talk, from talking at it he began to scream, from screaming he passed to cursing and sobbing wildly. Then he lay quiet again.

He was so still that to merely human eyes he might have seemed asleep or dead. But a squirrel, that emboldened by the stillness had entered from the roof, stopped short upon a beam above the bunk, for he saw that the man's foot was slowly and cautiously moving towards the floor, and that the man's eyes were as intent and watchful as his own. Presently, still without a sound, both feet were upon the floor. And then the bunk creaked, and the squirrel whisked into the eaves of the roof. When he peered forth again, everything was quiet, and the man was gone.

An hour later two muleteers on the Placerville Road passed a man with disheveled hair, glaring, bloodshot eyes, and clothes torn with bramble and stained with the red dust of the mountain. They pursued him, when he turned fiercely on the foremost, wrested a pistol from his grasp, and broke away. Later still, when the sun had dropped behind Payne's Ridge, the under-brush on Deadwood Slope crackled with a stealthy but continuous tread. It must have been an animal whose dimly outlined bulk, in the gathering dark-ness, showed here and there in vague but incessant motion; it could be nothing but an animal whose utter-ance was at once so incoherent, monotonous, and un-remitting. Yet, when the sound came nearer, and the chaparral was parted, it seemed to be a man, and that man Johnson.

Above the baying of phantasmal hounds that pressed him hard and drove him on, with never rest or mercy; above the lashing of a spectral whip that curled about his limbs, sang in his ears, and continually stung him forward; above the outcries of the unclean shapes that thronged about him—he could still dis-tinguish one real sound, the rush and sweep of hurry-ing waters. The Stanislaus River! A thousand feet below him drove its yellowing current. Through all the vacillations of his unseated mind he had clung to one idea—to reach the river, to lave in it, to swim in it if need be, but to put it forever between him and the harrying shapes, to drown forever in its turbid depths the thronging specters, to wash away in its yellow flood all stains and color of the past. And now he was leaping from boulder to boulder, from blackened stump to stump, from gnarled bush to bush, caught for a moment and withheld by clinging vines, or plunging downward into dusty hollows, until, rolling, dropping, sliding, and stumbling, he reached the riverbank, whereon he fell, rose, staggered forward and fell again with outstretched arms upon a rock that breasted the swift current. And there he lay as dead.

A few stars came out hesitatingly above Deadwood Slope. A cold wind that had sprung up with the going down of the sun fanned them into momentary brightness, swept the heated flanks of the mountain, and ruffled the river. Where the fallen man lay there was a sharp curve in the stream, so that in the gathering shadows the rushing water seemed to leap out of the darkness and to vanish again. Decayed driftwood, trunks of trees, fragments of broken sluicing—the wash and waste of many a mile—swept into sight a moment, and were gone. All of decay, wreck, and foulness gathered in the long circuit of mining camp and settlement, all the dregs and refuse of a crude and wanton civilization, reappeared for an instant, and then were hurried away in the darkness and lost. No wonder that, as the wind ruffled the yellow waters, the waves seemed to lift their unclean hands toward the rock whereon the fallen man lay, as if eager to snatch him from it, too, and hurry him toward the sea.

It was very still. In the clear air a horn blown a mile away was heard distinctly. The jingling of a spur and a laugh on the highway over Payne's Ridge

sounded clearly across the river. The rattling of harness and hoofs foretold for many minutes the approach of the Wingdam coach, that at last, with
flashing lights, passed within a few feet of the rock.
Then for an hour all again was quiet. Presently the
moon, round and full, lifted herself above the serried
ridge and looked down upon the river. At first the
bared peak of Deadwood Hill gleamed white and
skull-like. Then the shadows of Payne's Ridge cast on
the slope slowly sank away, leaving the unshapely
stumps, the dusty fissures, and clinging outcrop of
Deadwood Slope to stand out in black and silver. Still
stealing softly downward, the moonlight touched the
bank and the rock, and then glittered brightly on the
river. The rock was bare and the man was gone, but
the river still hurried swiftly to the sea.

"Is there anything for me?" asked Tommy Islington, as, a week after, the stage drew up at the Mansion House, and Bill slowly entered the barroom. Bill
did not reply, but turning to a stranger who had entered with him, indicated with a jerk of his finger
the boy. The stranger turned with an air half of business, half of curiosity, and looked critically at Tommy.
"Is there anything for me?" repeated Tommy, a little
confused at the silence and scrutiny. Bill walked deliberately to the bar, and placing his back against it,
faced Tommy with a look of demure enjoyment.

"Ef," he remarked slowly—"ef a hundred thousand
dollars down and half a million in perspektive is ennything, Major, THERE IS!"

PART TWO

EAST

It was characteristic of Angel's that the disappearance of Johnson, and the fact that he had left his entire property to Tommy, thrilled the community but slightly in comparison with the astounding discovery that he had anything to leave. The finding of a cinnabar lode at Angel's absorbed all collateral facts of subsequent details. Prospectors from adjoining camps thronged the settlement; the hillside for a mile on either side of Johnson's claim was staked out and preempted; trade received a sudden stimulus; and, in the excited rhetoric of the *Weekly Record,* "a new era had broken upon Angel's." "On Thursday last," added that paper, "over five hundred dollars were taken in over the bar of the Mansion House."

Of the fate of Johnson there was little doubt. He had been last seen lying on a boulder on the riverbank by outside passengers of the Wingdam night coach, and when Finn of Robinson's Ferry admitted to have fired three shots from a revolver at a dark object struggling in the water near the ferry, which he "suspicioned" to be a bear, the question seemed to be settled. Whatever might have been the fallibility of his judgment, of the accuracy of his aim there could be no doubt. The general belief that Johnson, after possessing himself of the muleteer's pistol, could have run amuck gave a certain retributive justice to this story, which rendered it acceptable to the camp.

It was also characteristic of Angel's that no feeling of envy or opposition to the good fortune of Tommy Islington prevailed there. That he was thoroughly cognizant, from the first, of Johnson's discovery, that his attentions to him were interested, calculating, and speculative, was, however, the general belief of the majority—a belief that, singularly enough, awakened the first feelings of genuine respect for Tommy ever shown by the camp. "He ain't no fool; Yuba Bill seed thet from the first," said the barkeeper. It was Yuba Bill who applied for the guardianship of Tommy after his accession to Johnson's claim, and on whose bonds the richest men of Calaveras were represented. It was Yuba Bill, also, when Tommy was sent East to finish his education, who accompanied him to San Francisco, and before parting with his charge on the steamer's deck, drew him aside, and said, "Ef at enny time you want enny money, Tommy, over and 'bove your 'lowance, you kin write; but ef you'll take my advice," he added, with a sudden huskiness mitigating the severity of his voice, "you'll forget every derned ole spavined, string-halted bummer, as you ever met or knew at Angel's—ev'ry one, Tommy—ev'ry one! And so—boy—take care of yourself—and—and God bless ye, and pertikerly d—n me for a first-class A-1 fool." It was Yuba Bill, also, after this speech, who glared savagely around, walked down the crowded gangplank with a rigid and aggressive shoulder, picked a quarrel with his cabman, and after bundling that functionary into his own vehicle, took the reins himself, and drove furiously to his hotel. "It cost me," said Bill, recounting the occurrence somewhat later at Angel's—"it cost me a matter o' twenty dollars afore the jedge the next mornin'; but you kin bet high thet I taught them 'Frisco chaps suthin' new about drivin'. I didn't make it lively in Montgomery Street for about ten minutes—oh no!"

And so by degrees the two original locators of the great cinnabar lode faded from the memory of Angel's, and Calaveras knew them no more. In five years their very names had been forgotten; in seven the name of the town was changed; in ten the town itself was transported bodily to the hillside, and the chimney of the Union Smelting Works by night flickered like a corpse-light over the site of Johnson's cabin, and by day poisoned the pure spices of the pines. Even the Mansion House was dismantled, and the Wingdam stage deserted the highway for a shorter cut by Quicksilver City. Only the bared crest of Deadwood Hill, as of old, sharply cut the clear blue sky, and at its base, as of old, the Stanislaus River, unwearied and unresting, babbled, whispered, and hurried away to the sea.

A midsummer's day was breaking lazily on the Atlantic. There was not wind enough to move the vapors in the foggy offing, but when the vague distance heaved against a violet sky there were dull red streaks that, growing brighter, presently painted out the stars. Soon the brown rocks of Greyport appeared faintly suffused, and then the whole ashen line of dead coast was kindled, and the lighthouse beacons went out one by one. And then a hundred sail, before invisible, started out of the vapory horizon, and pressed toward the shore. It was morning, indeed, and some of the best society in Greyport, having been up all night, were thinking it was time to go to bed.

For as the sky flashed brighter it fired the clustering red roofs of a picturesque house by the sands that had all that night, from open lattice and illuminated balcony, given light and music to the shore. It glittered on the broad crystal spaces of a great conservatory that looked upon an exquisite lawn, where all night long the blended odors of sea and shore had swooned under the summer moon. But it wrought confusion among the colored lamps on the long veranda, and startled a group of ladies and gentlemen who had stepped from the drawing-room window to gaze upon it. It was so searching and sincere in its way, that as the carriage of the fairest Miss Gillyflower rolled away, that peerless young woman, catching sight of her face in the oval mirror, instantly pulled down the blinds and nestling the whitest shoulders in Greyport against the cushions, went to sleep.

"How haggard everybody is! Rose, dear, you look almost intellectual," said Blanche Masterman.

"I hope not," said Rose simply. "Sunrises are very trying. Look how that pink regularly puts out Mrs. Brown-Robinson, hair and all!"

"The angels," said the Count de Nugat, with a polite gesture toward the sky, "must have found these celestial combinations very bad for the toilette."

"They're safe in white—except when they sit for their pictures in Venice," said Blanche. "How fresh Mr. Islington looks! It's really uncomplimentary to us."

"I suppose the sun recognizes in me no rival," said the young man demurely. "But," he added, "I have

lived much in the open air and require very little sleep."

"How delightful!" said Mrs. Brown-Robinson in a
low, enthusiastic voice, and a manner that held the
glowing sentiment of sixteen and the practical experiences of thirty-two in dangerous combination;
"how perfectly delightful! What sunrises you must
have seen, and in such wild, romantic places! How I
envy you! My nephew was a classmate of yours, and
has often repeated to me those charming stories you
tell of your adventures. Won't you tell some now? Do!
How you must tire of us and this artificial life here, so
frightfully artificial, you know" (in a confidential
whisper); "and then to think of the days when you
roamed the great West with the Indians, and
the bisons, and the grizzly bears! Of course, you have
seen grizzly bears and bisons?"

"Of course he has, dear," said Blanche a little pettishly, throwing a cloak over her shoulders, and seizing her chaperon by the arm; "his earliest infancy was
soothed by bisons, and he proudly points to the grizzly
bear as the playmate of his youth. Come with me, and
I'll tell you all about it. How good it is of you," she
added, *soto voce,* to Islington as he stood by the carriage—"how perfectly good it is of you to be like those
animals you tell us of, and not know your full power.
Think, with your experiences and our credulity, what
stories you *might* tell! And you are going to walk?
Good night, then." A slim, gloved hand was frankly
extended from the window, and the next moment the
carriage rolled away.

"Isn't Islington throwing away a chance there?"
said Captain Merwin on the veranda.

"Perhaps he couldn't stand my lovely aunt's super-added presence. But then, he's the guest of Blanche's father, and I daresay they see enough of each other as it is."

"But isn't it a rather dangerous situation?"

"For him, perhaps; although he's awfully old, and very queer. For her, with an experience that takes in all the available men in both hemispheres, ending with Nugat over there, I should say a man more or less wouldn't affect her much, anyway. Of course," he laughed, "these are the accents of bitterness. But that was last year."

Perhaps Islington did not overhear the speaker; perhaps, if he did, the criticism was not new. He turned carelessly away, and sauntered out on the road to the sea. Thence he strolled along the sands toward the cliffs, where, meeting an impediment in the shape of a garden wall, he leaped it with a certain agile, boyish ease and experience, and struck across an open lawn toward the rocks again. The best society of Greyport were not early risers, and the spectacle of a trespasser in an evening dress excited only the criticism of grooms hanging about the stables, or cleanly housemaids on the broad verandas that in greyport architecture dutifully gave upon the sea. Only once, as he entered the boundaries of Cliffwood Lodge, the famous seat of Renwyck Masterman, was he aware of suspicious scrutiny; but a slouching figure that vanished quickly in the lodge offered no opposition to his progress. Avoiding the pathway to the lodge, Islington kept along the rocks until, reaching a little promontory and rustic pavilion, he sat down and gazed upon the sea.

And presently an infinite peace stole upon him.
Except where the waves lapped lazily the crags below, the vast expanse beyond seemed unbroken by
ripple, heaving only in broad ponderable sheets, and
rhythmically, as if still in sleep. The air was filled
with a luminous haze that caught and held the direct
sunbeams. In the deep calm that lay upon the sea, it
seemed to Islington that all the tenderness of culture,
magic of wealth, and spell of refinement that for years
had wrought upon that favored shore had extended its
gracious influence even here. What a pampered and
caressed old ocean it was; cajoled, flattered, and
feted where it lay! An odd recollection of the turbid
Stanislaus hurrying by the ascetic pines, of the grim
outlines of Deadwood Hill, swam before his eyes, and
made the yellow green of the velvet lawn and graceful
foliage seem almost tropical by contrast. And, looking
up, a few yards distant he beheld a tall slip of a girl
gazing upon the sea—Blanche Masterman.

She had plucked somewhere a large fan-shaped
leaf, which she held parasolwise, shading the blonde
masses of her hair, and hiding her gray eyes. She
had changed her festal dress, with its amplitude of
flounce and train, for a closely fitting, half-antique
habit whose scant outlines would have been trying to
limbs less shapely, but which prettily accented the
graceful curves and sweeping lines of this Greyport
goddess. As Islington rose, she came toward him with
a frankly outstretched hand and unconstrained manner. Had she observed him first? I don't know.

They sat down together on a rustic seat, Miss
Blanche facing the sea and shading her eyes with the
leaf.

"I don't really know how long I have been sitting here," said Islington, "or whether I have not been actually asleep and dreaming. It seemed too lovely a morning to go to bed. But you?"

From behind the leaf, it appeared that Miss Blanche, on retiring, had been pursued by a hideous four-winged insect which defied the efforts of herself and maid to dislodge. Odin, the Spitz dog, had insisted upon scratching at the door. And it made her eyes red to sleep in the morning. And she had an early call to make. And the sea looked lovely.

"I'm glad to find you here, whatever be the cause," said Islington, with his old directness. "Today, as you know, is my last day in Greyport, and it is much pleasanter to say good-by under this blue sky than even beneath your father's wonderful frescoes yonder. I want to remember you, too, as part of this pleasant prospect which belongs to us all, rather than recall you in anybody's particular setting."

"I know," said Blanche, with equal directness, "that houses are one of the defects of our civilization; but I don't think I ever heard the idea as elegantly expressed before. Where do you go?"

"I don't know yet. I have several plans. I may go to South America and become president of one of the republics—I am not particular which. I am rich, but in that part of America which lies outside of Greyport it is necessary for every man to have some work. My friends think I should have some great aim in life, with a capital A. But I was born a vagabond, and a vagabond I shall probably die."

"I don't know anybody in South America," said Blanche languidly. "There were two girls here last season, but they didn't wear stays in the house, and their white frocks never were properly done up. If you go to South America, you must write to me."

"I will. Can you tell me the name of this flower which I found in your greenhouse? It looks much like a California blossom."

"Perhaps it is. Father bought it of a half-crazy old man who came here one day. Do you know him?"

Islington laughed. "I am afraid not. But let me present this in a less businesslike fashion."

"Thank you. Remind me to give you one in return before you go—or will you choose yourself?"

They had both risen as by a common instinct.

"Good-by."

The cool, flowerlike hand lay in his for an instant.

"Will you oblige me by putting aside that leaf a moment before I go?"

"But my eyes are red, and I look like a perfect fright."

Yet, after a long pause, the leaf fluttered down, and a pair of very beautiful but withal very clear and critical eyes met his. Islington was constrained to look away. When he turned again she was gone.

"Mr. Hislington—sir!"

It was Chalker, the English groom, out of breath with running.

"Seein' you alone, sir—beg your pardon, sir—but there's a person—"

"A person! What the devil do you mean? Speak English—no, damn it, I mean don't," said Islington snappishly.

"I said a person, sir. Beg pardon—no offense—but not a gent, sir. In the lib'ry."

A little amused even through the utter dissatisfaction with himself and vague loneliness that had suddenly come upon him, Islington, as he walked toward the lodge, asked, "Why isn't he a gent?"

"No gent—beggin' your pardin, sir—'ud guy a man in sarvis, sir. Takes me 'ands so, sir, as I sits in the rumble at the gate, and puts 'em downd so, sir, and sez, 'Put 'em in your pocket, young man—or is it a road agint you expects to see that you 'olds hup your 'ands, hand crosses 'em like to that?' sez he. ' 'Old 'ard,' sez he, 'on the short curves, or you'll bust your precious crust,' sez he. And hasks for you, sir. This way, sir."

They entered the lodge. Islington hurried down the long Gothic hall and opened the library door.

In an armchair, in the center of the room, a man sat apparently contemplating a large, stiff, yellow hat with an enormous brim that was placed on the floor before him. His hands rested lightly between his knees, but one foot was drawn up at the side of his chair in a peculiar manner. In the first glance that Islington gave, the attitude in some odd, irreconcilable way suggested a brake. In another moment he dashed across the room, and holding out both hands, cried, "Yuba Bill!"

The man rose, caught Islington by the shoulders, wheeled him round, hugged him, felt of his ribs like a good-natured ogre, shook his hands violently, laughed, and then said somewhat ruefully, "And however did you know me?"

Seeing that Yuba Bill evidently regarded himself as in some elaborate disguise, Islington laughed, and suggested that it must have been instinct.

"And you?" said Bill, holding him at arm's length and surveying him critically—"you!—toe think—toe think—a little cuss no higher nor a trace, a boy as I've flicked outer the road with a whip time in agin, a boy ez never hed much clothes to speak of, turned into a sport!"

Islington remembered, with a thrill of ludicrous terror, that he still wore his evening dress.

"Turned," continued Yuba Bill severely—"turned into a restyourant waiter—a garsong! Eh, Alfonse, bring me a patty de foy grass and an omelet, demme!"

"Dear old chap!" said Islington, laughing, and trying to put his hand over Bill's bearded mouth, "but you—*you* don't look exactly like yourself! You're not well, Bill." And indeed, as he turned toward the light, Bill's eyes appeared cavernous, and his hair and beard thickly streaked with gray.

"Maybe it's this yer harness," said Bill a little anxiously. "When I hitches on this yer curb" (he indicated a massive gold watch chain with enormous links), "and mounts this 'morning star' " (he pointed to a very large solitaire pin which had the appearance of blistering his whole shirt front), "it kinder weighs heavy on me, Tommy. Otherwise I'm all right, my boy—all right." But he evaded Islington's keen eye and turned from the light.

"You have something to tell me, Bill," said Islington suddenly and with almost brusque directness; "out with it."

Bill did not speak, but moved uneasily toward his hat.

"You didn't come three thousand miles, without a word of warning, to talk to me of old times," said

Islington more kindly, "glad as I would have been to see you. It isn't your way, Bill, and you know it. We shall not be disturbed here," he added, in reply to an inquiring glance that Bill directed to the door, "and I am ready to hear you."

"Firstly, then," said Bill, drawing his chair nearer Islington, "answer me one question, Tommy, fair and square, and up and down."

"Go on," said Islington with a slight smile.

"Ef I should say to you, Tommy—say to you to-day, right here, you must come with me—you must leave this place for a month, a year, two years, maybe, perhaps forever—is there anything that 'ud keep you—anything, my boy, ez you couldn't leave?"

"No," said Tommy quietly; "I am only visiting here. I thought of leaving Greyport today."

"But if I should say to you, Tommy, come with me on a *pasear* to Chiny, to Japan, to South Ameriky, p'r'aps, could you go?"

"Yes," said Islington after a slight pause.

"Thar isn't ennything," said Bill, drawing a little closer, and lowering his voice confidentially—"ennything in the way of a young woman—you understand, Tommy—ez would keep you? They're mighty sweet about here; and whether a man is young or old, Tommy, there's always some woman as is brake or whip to him!"

In a certain excited bitterness that characterized the delivery of this abstract truth, Bill did not see that the young man's face flushed slightly as he answered "No."

"Then listen. It's seven years ago, Tommy, thet I

was working one o' the Pioneer coaches over from
Gold Hill. Ez I stood in front o' the stage office, the
sheriff o' the county comes to me, and he sez, 'Bill'
sez he, 'I've got a looney chap, as I'm in charge of,
taking 'im down to the 'sylum in Stockton. He'z quiet
and peaceable, but the insides don't like to ride with
him. Hev you enny objection to give him a lift on the
box beside you?' I sez, 'No; put him up.' When I
came to go and get up on that box beside him, that
man, Tommy—that man sittin' there, quiet and peaceable, was—Johnson!

"He didn't know me, my boy," Yuba Bill continued,
rising and putting his hands on Tommy's shoulders—
"he didn't know me. He didn't know nothing about
you, nor Angel's nor the quicksilver lode, nor even his
own name. He said his name was Skaggs, but I
knowed it was Johnson. Thar was times, Tommy, you
might have knocked me off that box with a feather;
thar was times when if the twenty-seven passengers
o' that stage had found theirselves swimming in the
American River five hundred feet below the road, I
never could have explained it satisfactorily to the
company—never.

"The sheriff said," Bill continued hastily, as if to
preclude any interruption from the young man—"the
sheriff said he had been brought into Murphy's Camp
three years before, dripping with water, and sufferin'
from perkussion of the brain, and had been cared for
generally by the boys 'round. When I told the sheriff
I knowed 'im, I got him to leave him in my care;
and I took him to 'Frisco, Tommy, to 'Frisco, and I
put him in charge o' the best doctors there, and paid

his board myself. There was nothin' he didn't have ez he wanted. Don't look that way, my dear boy, for God's sake don't!"

"O Bill!" said Islington, rising and staggering to the window, "why did you keep this from me?"

"Why?" said Bill, turning on him savagely—"why? because I wa'n't a fool. Thar was you winnin' your way in college; thar was *you* risin' in the world, and of some account to it. Yer was an old bummer, ez good ez dead to it—a man ez oughter been dead afore! a man ez never denied it! But you allus liked him better nor me," said Bill bitterly.

"Forgive me, Bill," said the young man, seizing both his hands. "I know you did it for the best; but go on."

"Thar ain't much more to tell, nor much use to tell it, as I can see," said Bill moodily. "He never could be cured, the doctors said, for he had what they called monomania—was always talking about his wife and darter that somebody had stole away years ago, and plannin' revenge on that somebody. And six months ago he was missed. I tracked him to Carson, to Salt Lake City, to Omaha, to Chicago, to New York—and here!"

"Here!" echoed Islington.

"Here! And that's what brings me here today. Whether he's crazy or well, whether he's huntin' you or lookin' up that other man, you must get away from here. You mustn't see him. You and me, Tommy, will go away on a cruise. In three or four years he'll be dead or missing, and then we'll come back. Come." And he rose to his feet.

"Bill," said Islington, rising also, and taking the

hand of his friend with the same quiet obstinacy that in the old days had endeared him to Bill, "wherever he is, here or elsewhere, sane or crazy, I shall seek and find him. Every dollar that I have shall be his, every dollar that I have spent shall be returned to him. I am young yet, thank God, and can work; and if there is a way out of this miserable business, I shall find it."

"I knew," said Bill with a surliness that ill concealed his evident admiration of the calm figure before him —"I knew the partikler style of d—n fool that you was, and expected no better. Good-by, then—God Almighty! who's that?"

He was on his way to the open French window, but had started back, his face quite white and bloodless, and his eyes staring. Islington ran to the window and looked out. A white skirt vanished around the corner of the veranda. When he returned, Bill had dropped into a chair.

"It must have been Miss Masterman, I think; but what's the matter?"

"Nothing," said Bill faintly; "have you got any whiskey handy?"

Islington brought a decanter and, pouring out some spirits, handed the glass to Bill. Bill drained it, and then said, "Who is Miss Masterman?"

"Mr. Masterman's daughter; that is, an adopted daughter, I believe."

"Wot name?"

"I really don't know," said Islington pettishly, more vexed than he cared to own at this questioning.

Yuba Bill rose and walked to the window, closed it, walked back again to the door, glanced at Islington, hesitated, and then returned to his chair.

"I didn't tell you I was married—did I?" he said suddenly, looking up in Islington's face with an unsuccessful attempt at a reckless laugh.

"No," said Islington, more pained at the manner than the words.

"Fact," said Yuba Bill. "Three years ago it was, Tommy—three years ago!"

He looked so hard at Islington that, feelng he was expected to say something, he asked vaguely, "Whom did you marry?"

"Thet's it!" said Yuba Bill; "I can't ezactly say; partikly, though a she-devil! generally, the wife of half a dozen other men."

Accustomed, apparently, to have his conjugal infelicities a theme of mirth among men, and seeing no trace of amusement on Islington's grave face, his dogged, reckless manner softened, and drawing his chair closer to Islington, he went on: "It all began outer this: we was coming down Watson's grade one night pretty free, when the expressman turns to me and says, 'There's a row inside, and you'd better pull up!' I pulls up, and out hops first a woman, and then two or three chaps swearin' and cursin', and tryin' to drag someone arter them. Then it 'peared, Tommy, thet it was this woman's drunken husband they was going to put out for abusin' her and strikin' her in the coach; and if it hadn't been for me, my boy, they'd have left that chap thar in the road. But I fixes matters up by putting her alongside o' me on the box, and we drove on. She was very white, Tommy—for the matter o' that, she was always one o' these very white women, that never got red in the face—but she never cried a whimper. Most women would have cried. It was queer, but she never cried. I thought so at the time.

"She was very tall, with a lot o' light hair meandering down the back of her head, as long as a deerskin whiplash, and about the color. She hed eyes that'd bore ye through at fifty yards, and pooty hands and feet. And when she kinder got out o' that stiff, narvous state she was in, and warmed up a little, and got chipper, by G—d, sir, she was handsome—she was that!"

A little flushed and embarrassed at his own enthusiasm, he stopped, and then said carelessly, "They got off at Murphy's."

"Well," said Islington.

"Well, I used to see her often arter thet, and when she was alone she allus took the box seat. She kinder confided her troubles to me, how her husband got drunk and abused her; and I didn't see much o' him, for he was away in 'Frisco arter thet. But it was all square, Tommy—all square 'twixt me and her.

"I got a-going there a good deal, and then one day I sez to myself, 'Bill, this won't do,' and I got changed to another route. Did you ever know Jackson Filltree, Tommy?" said Bill, breaking off suddenly.

"No."

"Might have heerd of him, p'r'aps?"

"No," said Islington impatiently.

"Jackson Filltree ran the express from White's out to Summit, 'cross the North Fork of the Yuba. One day he sez to me, 'Bill, that's a mighty bad ford at the North Fork.' I sez, 'I believe you, Jackson.' 'It'll git me some day, Bill, sure,' sez he. I sez, 'Why don't you take the lower ford?' 'I don't know,' sez he, 'but I can't.' So ever after, when I met him, he sez, 'That North Fork ain't got me yet.' One day I was in Sacramento, and up comes Filltree. He sez, 'I've sold out the express business on account of the North Fork, but it's bound to get me yet, Bill, sure;' and he laughs. Two weeks after they finds his body below the ford, whar he tried to cross, comin' down from the summit way. Folks said it was foolishness; Tommy, I sez it was Fate! The second day arter I was changed to the Placerville route thet woman comes outer the hotel above the stage office. Her husband, she said, was lying sick in Placerville; that's what she said; but it was Fate, Tommy, Fate. Three months afterward her husband takes an overdose of morphine for delirium tremens, and dies. There's folks ez sez she gave it to him, but it's Fate. A year after that I married her— Fate, Tommy, Fate!

"I lived with her jest three months," he went on, after a long breath—"three months! It ain't much time for a happy man. I've seen a good deal o' hard life in my day, but there was days in that three months longer than any day in my life—days, Tommy, when it was a tossup whether I should kill her or she me. But thar, I'm done. You are a young man, Tommy, and I ain't goin' to tell things thet, old as I am, three years ago I couldn't have believed."

When at last, with his grim face turned toward the window, he sat silently with his clenched hands on his knees before him, Islington asked where his wife was now.

"Ask me no more, my boy—no more. I've said my say." With a gesture as of throwing down a pair of reins before him, he rose, and walked to the window.

"You kin understand, Tommy, why a little trip around the world 'ud do me good. Ef you can't go with me, well and good. But go I must."

"Not before luncheon, I hope," said a very sweet voice, as Blanche Masterman suddenly stood before them. "Father would never forgive me if in his absence I permitted one of Mr. Islington's friends to go in this way. You will stay, won't you? Do! And you will give me your arm now; and when Mr. Islington has done staring, he will follow us into the dining room and introduce you."

"I have quite fallen in love with your friend," said Miss Blanche, as they stood in the drawing room looking at the figure of Bill, strolling with his short pipe in his mouth through the distant shrubbery. "He asks very queer questions, though. He wanted to know my mother's maiden name."

"He is an honest fellow," said Islington gravely.

"You are very much subdued. You don't thank me, I daresay, for keeping you and your friend here; but you couldn't go, you know, until father returned."

Islington smiled, but not very gaily.

"And then I think it much better for us to part here under these frescoes, don't you? Good-by."

She extended her long, slim hand.

"Out in the sunlight there, when my eyes were red, you were very anxious to look at me," she added in a dangerous voice.

Islington raised his sad eyes to hers. Something glittering upon her own sweet lashes trembled and fell.

"Blanche!"

She was rosy enough now, and would have withdrawn her hand, but Islington detained it. She was not quite certain but that her waist was also in jeopardy. Yet she could not help saying, "Are you sure that there isn't anything in the way of a young woman that would keep you?"

"Blanche!" said Islington in reproachful horror.

"If gentlemen will roar out their secrets before an open window, with a young woman lying on a sofa on the veranda reading a stupid French novel, they must not be surprised if she gives more attention to them than to her book."

"Then you know all, Blanche?"

"I know," said Blanche, "let's see—I know the partikler style of—ahem!—fool you was, and expected no better. Good-by." And, gliding like a lovely and innocent milk snake out of his grasp, she slipped away.

To the pleasant ripple of waves, the sound of music and light voices, the yellow midsummer moon again rose over Greyport. It looked upon formless masses of rock and shrubbery, wide spaces of lawn and beach, and a shimmering expanse of water. It singled out particular objects—a white sail in shore, a crystal globe upon the lawn, and flashed upon something held between the teeth of a crouching figure scaling the low wall of Cliffwood Lodge. Then, as a man and woman passed out from under the shadows of the foliage into the open moonlight of the garden path, the figure leaped from the wall, and stood erect and waiting in the shadow.

It was the figure of an old man, with rolling eyes, his trembling hand grasping a long, keen knife—a figure more pitiable than pitiless, more pathetic than terrible. But the next moment the knife was stricken from his hand, and he struggled in the firm grasp of another figure that apparently sprang from the wall beside him.

"D—n you, Masterman!" cried the old man hoarsely; "give me fair play, and I'll kill you yet!"

"Which my name is Yuba Bill," said Bill quietly, "and it's time this d—n fooling was stopped."

The old man glared in Bill's face savagely. "I know you. You're one of Masterman's friends—d—n you,— let me go till I cut his heart out—let me go! Where is my Mary?—where is my wife?—there she is! there!— there!—there! Mary!" He would have screamed, but Bill placed his powerful hand upon his mouth as he turned in the direction of the old man's glance. Distinct in the moonlight the figures of Islington and Blanche, arm in arm, stood out upon the garden path.

"Give me my wife!" muttered the old man hoarsely between Bill's fingers. "Where is she?"

As sudden fury passed over Yuba Bill's face. "Where is your wife?" he echoed, pressing the old man back against the garden wall, and holding him there as in a vise. "Where is your wife?" he repeated, thrusting his grim sardonic jaw and savage eyes into the old man's frightened face. "Where is Jack Adam's wife? Where is *my* wife? Where is the she-devil that drove one man mad, that sent another to hell by his own hand, that eternally broke and ruined me? Where! Where! Do you ask where? In jail in Sacramento— in jail, do you hear—in jail for murder, Johnson— murder!"

The old man gasped, stiffened, and then, relaxing,

suddenly slipped, a mere inanimate mass at Yuba Bill's feet. With a sudden revulsion of feeling, Yuba Bill dropped at his side, and lifting him tenderly in his arms, whispered, "Look up, old man, Johnson! look up, for God's sake!—it's me—Yuba Bill! and yonder is your daughter, and—Tommy—don't you know—Tommy, little Tommy Islington?"

Johnson's eyes slowly opened. He whispered, "Tommy! yes, Tommy! Sit by me, Tommy. But don't sit so near the bank. Don't you see how the river is rising and beckoning to me—hissing, and boilin' over the rocks? It's gittin' higher!—hold me, Tommy— hold me, and don't let me go yet. We'll live to cut his heart out, Tommy—we'll live—we'll—"

His head sank, and the rushing river, invisible to all eyes save his, leaped toward him out of the darkness, and bore him away, no longer to the darkness, but through it to the distant, peaceful, shining sea.

THE FOUR GUARDIANS
OF LAGRANGE

PART ONE

THE TRUST

It certainly was a matter of serious import that so gravely interested the four most experienced and self-contained citizens of Lagrange. For nearly half an hour they had been sitting in the private room of Riker's grocery without exchanging a word. Even the silent communion of libation was wanting; their liquor stood untasted before them, a fact that aroused the serious concern of the barkeeper and the free comment of the outside bar. "Mebbe it's some new 'skin' game imported from 'Frisco, and they want to keep their heads level," was suggested by a cautious gossiper.

The barkeeper shook his head. "Nary deck o' keerds thar—onless they plays 'm under the table, and that ain't their style."

"Ye didn't notice no lumps o' sugar, sorter lyin' round, keerless like, before each man," insinuated another, "and them chaps lyin' low and quiet, waitin' for some d——d fly to light and rake down the pile. I've heerd," the speaker continued cautiously, "that heaps o' good money hez been lost in thet onchristian-like way."

"Yes," interpolated a third, "and *trained* flies, ez

knew jest when to light, hez been rung in on green-horns. Thar was a man down at French Camp, et they say picked up about seven thousand dollars outer ther camp with an innocent lookin' hoss fly, and et wuzent ontil one o' the boys accidently sot his glass down on thet harmless inseck thet the boys smelt a mice."

" 'Tain't no game, I tell ye," reiterated the barkeeper stoutly. "That's suthin' more'n flies and sugar on their minds. My belief is they're reck'nin' to revive the old vigilants of '52. Thar's a lot o' dead beats in this yer camp," he continued darkly, with an aggressive rec-ollection of certain unsettled scores, "ez mebbe will find out soon enough wot's up."

Unfortunately, none of these surmises, however in-genious or reasonable, were correct. The simple fact was that a lately deceased miner had on his death-bed called to his side the above-mentioned four citi-zens of Lagrange, and solemnly confided to them the care of his only child in the "States," with the little property he possessed in trust for her maintenance. This trust was further burdened with the fact that the dying man had withheld from the child the news of the death of her mother, a year previous, and it now devolved upon the guardians to inform the orphan of her double bereavement. This was the first meeting of the guardians since they had last looked upon the face of their dead comrade. Hence their grave silence and perplexity.

At last the spell was broken. One of the party, a tall, thin, rickety man, who had been softly pacing the room with a certain deprecatory manner and a smile of imbecile acquiescence in everything and anything that shone out at the slightest expression, even of vexation or anxiety on the part of his companions, gradually neared the door, and laid a large, bony, good-humored hand on the lock. The act was instantly detected by one of the party, who coolly locked the door and put the key on the table. "Ye can't slip outer this, Rats," he said; "ye must sit down here with the rest of us, and see what's to be done."

Captain Rats weakly succumbed, and began to apologize. "I warn't goin' back on ye, Horton," he began. "I only reckoned as ye all seemed to be gitting along famous a-thinking, I'd jest slip out and 'tend to some business, and allow ye to make up yer mind without me—countin' me out, and yourselves as my proxies. Fer wot's agreeable to you is agreeable to me. I'm no sharp at this game."

"You're a guardian," responded Horton decisively.

"In course. Thet's so. But I allow it ain't no valid app'intment. The very fact thet the old man app'inted a d——d fool like me shows he warn't in his right mind."

"That's so, boys," ejaculated the eldest of the four, with a sudden gleam of hopefulness. "The old man was sorter flighty just afore he went off, and we can slip our heads outer this lasso he flung over us by allowin' insanity, you know."

"We can't slouch out of *this* kind of a trust though, Colonel," said Joe Feet, the youngest of the party, yet with a leader's peremptoriness. "It ain't white to do it!"

The gleam faded from the Colonel's face.

"That's so, it wouldn't be the squar' thing," he said dejectedly; "kick me, boys."

"Couldn't we sorter club together and app'int a kind of subguardian to take care o' the whole thing on a high salary. I'll come down heavy," suggested Horton.

"If you could get a chap to do your feelin' for you at the same figure I don't know but it might suit," said Fleet with decided sarcasm. "As for me I ain't rich enough to buy up any chap's conscience."

"Ye may as well quit this foolin'," broke in the Colonel, with a groan. "The game's made, and we're goin' to wade in like men. Mebbe suthin' may turn up. Afore long some one of us may get shot or buried in a tunnel, and so get excused on the squar'. But just now we must wade in."

"Oh, yes, 'wade in'!" said Horton derisively. "Do you know the first thing we've got to do? Why, write to that gal, and tell her thet her father was a d——d old liar, and thet her mother's been dead a year, and thet now he's dead too, and thet the d——d old fool's property won't bring five hundred dollars, and that we're goin' to give her five thousand dollars for charity, and adopt her, and if she's a loving sort of gal, and a high-spirited gal, she'll like it, and like us all the better. Oh, yes!" he continued with sardonic shrillness, "it's easy enough to do that, of course. Wade in! Yes! Wade in—drop right out o' the ford into deep water over yer head the first thing."

The men looked aghast at each other, and there was another ominous silence. "Couldn't ye let it on easy?" suggested the Colonel despairingly, "sorter begin to-day with the mother, and next month, when she's feelin' better and more able to bear it, kinder light gently down on her with the decease of her father, and so on ontil, in the course of a year or so, she'll take the charity business quite peaceful?"

But Joe Fleet dismissed the idea fiercely. "Ef she's got any pluck she'll take it in a lump. You go to work driftin' into her feelin's like that instead of sinking your shaft straight down, and you'll hev her crazy here on your hands in a week!"

The latter idea was so awful as to compel another gloomy silence for its stern contemplation. "Couldn't ye drop it on her all in a lump,—money, deceased parients, et cettery," suggested Captain Rats, with vague and imbecile good humor, "kinder brisk and business like."

"It's a gal," said the Colonel, shaking his head, "over fourteen."

"Hold on, and give Cap'n Rats a show," interrupted Fleet. "Ef there's a man ez can do it, it's him. Didn't he edit the 'Record' up at Murphy's? Wade in and give us a specimen."

The suggestion met with unanimous favor. Captain Rats was shamelessly pleased with this compliment to his literary abilities, and at once began: " 'Honored Miss,—Not knowin' what a day may bring forth, we beg to inform you'— No," reflected the Captain slowly, feeling some unfavorable criticism in the air, "no, that won't do. Let's see! Ah! 'The death of your mother, followed by the illness of your father, resulting in his decease, and the entire loss'—"

"Ain't them bricks follerin' each other rather close?" suggested the Colonel faintly. The Captain stopped, rubbed his long chin thoughtfully, and looked at the others. It was evident that this was the prevailing impression.

"Well, yes; I was rather thinkin' so myself," he assented vaguely.

"And it's bein' a gal, don't you want to heave in here and thar a little sentiment," said Horton, "and sorter touch her up gently? They say when you make 'em cry easy, they kinder like it, and get over it quicker."

"Jess so," returned Captain Rats cheerfully. "I was thinkin' that very thing, only jist now I was sorter samplin' it; showin' ye what *could* be done. A good way," he added, now completely lost in the fascinations of condoling composition,—"a very good, takin' sort of way is to tell it, and yet seem not to tell it; to kinder ring in a cold deck of information, and never let her see ye shuffle the keerds. Suthin' like this, ye know: 'Honored Miss,—Enclosed please fine draft for five thousand dollars; same would have been sent before but for Wells-Fargo's office being closed the day of your father's funeral. The weather here is fine, but we suppose is fur different with you in the East, as your deceased mother often remarked to the writer. Business is dull, and ores are running light, most o' the claims on the North Fork sharing the fate of your late father's property.' Ye see," continued Captain Rats, with the glow of successful authorship mantling his cheek, "that kind of letter mout be written so that by the time she got through with it, it would seem as if she'd knew it all before, and she couldn't get nary soul to sympathize with her, and help her take on." The feeling of the majority was so strongly in favor of the last composition that they all turned impatiently to the only dissenter, Joe Fleet. But at this moment a knock on the door checked further discussion.

It was Jack Foster, expressman,—alert, vigilant, familiar, and fateful,—holding a letter.

"For John Meritoe," said the Sierran Mercury crisply. "As we don't have no office nor agent at his present address, we deliver at his last residence." He tossed the letter on the table, winked, and was gone.

It was for the dead man, the great first cause of their perplexity. For a few moments it lay there undisturbed, while the men looked at each other in silence. Then Captain Rats, with a decision and independence new to him, took it up. "Ther's no one, boys, hez a better right to it than we has," he said. "I propose that we open it here afore each other and read it."

"As to opening it, I second the motion," said Joe Fleet's voice, "but we'll see who it's from before we read it," added that honorable man.

The letter was opened. It was signed "Fanny Meritoe."

"The girl herself," said Fleet promptly. "Read it."

With a hesitating voice, that at last seemed to almost simulate what might have been the hesitating youthful accents of the writer, Captain Rats began.

How shall I describe it? It was simple, it was girlish, it was affectionate, it was real. Against its candid frankness and simplicity poor Rats's previous rhetoric assumed the appearance of the most monstrous duplicity and deceitful sophistry. It was evident that the writer had seen but little of her real father, and that the rather commonplace, homely, often somewhat despicable figure known to the men who now listened to her yearnings was not the ideal parent of her dreams. At last Captain Rats finished. There was a slight huskiness in the Captain's voice, a slight dimness in his eyesight as he ended, and a blur upon the fair page that was not there when he began.

The Colonel had dropped his head between his hands. Horton had never taken his eyes from the paper. Fleet, who had walked to the window and had been apparently absorbed in staring at the staring sunlight without, suddenly turned, advanced to the table, and held out both his hands. In another moment they were locked in his companions', and the four men, holding hands, closed round the table and the letter that lay in its centre.

"We don't want no letter of condolence, Captain Rats," said Joe Fleet sturdily, "for there ain't anythin' to condole for. I don't see just how it is, or how we can fix it, but I *know* that girl's parents *ain't* dead, ez long, please God, as we are living!"

The men pressed each other's hands in silence, until Captain Rats, with a burst of revelation, disengaged his, and suddenly brought it against his right leg with resounding emphasis.

"That's it—and it makes the whole thing clar. We don't write no letters of condolence—for why? We goes straight on and writes ez if we was the old man. He's let on enough to me about hisself and his affairs to make it easy as fallin' off a log. We'll just chip in whar he let off. We'll take his hand as it is, play out his little game, win or lose; and if four sharps like us can't make it easy for that child and rake in the pot every time, we'll leave the board. Yes, gentlemen," continued Rats, taking up the letter, "I'll answer this to-night myself, I, Captain Rats, late Meritoe, deceased."

PART TWO

HOW THE TRUST WAS FULFILLED

When the combined guardians of Lagrange first
practiced to deceive, they did not forecast the tangled
web whose pleasant intricacies and sinuosities they were
presently to weave. And when Captain Rats calmly
announced to his gentle confederates his intention of
writing his first letter—*in loco parentis*—to the or-
phaned girl with his left hand, explaining to her the
thereby changed chirography through the ingenious
fiction of an accident that had happened to his right,
it was accepted with acclamation. "You see," said the
Captain sententiously, "every man slings ink with his
left hand at about the same gait. The style ain't pretty
nor plain, but she'll never find out it ain't the old
man's."

The possibility of detection thus obviated,—and,
indeed, it afterwards appeared that the simple-minded
girl dwelt more anxiously upon the discomforts of the
accident to her father than on his changed and almost
illegible hand,—various other gentle frauds and de-
ceits were introduced in the correspondence. A certain emulation of the Captain's skill and importance
as a correspondent grew up among the other guardians. They began to make suggestions of their own,
until at last steamer day brought them generally together, in conclave, in the back room of the saloon,
where the fortnightly epistle was dictated finally by

all. Captain Rats's pride, which at first resented this interference, was finally placated by the compromise that the composition or "wording" of the letter should be his own, although the subject matter might be a various contribution.

The result of this unhallowed collaboration was a series of the most extraordinary letters ever inflicted on a single correspondent. It was not long before their fame reached beyond the horizon of their fair recipient. "Do you know, papa dear," wrote the simple girl from the seclusion of Madame Brimborion's academy, "do you know, your letters are so very, *very* interesting, I could not help showing them to some of the girls here! Your account [the Colonel's] of the fight with the bear was so *real* that I almost saw it. I laughed till I cried over the funny story of the Chinaman mending your clothes [a characteristic contribution from Horton], but then I did cry, really, too, papa, over what you [Fleet] said about your feeling that Sunday you saw the sunset from the poor little forlorn cemetery on the hill. Oh, papa! it was just lovely—and so sad—so very sad! Mary Ricketts said it was just like Shakespeare, and she knows, oh, so much, and is considered very, very smart! They all think I ought to be so fond of my dear papa, as if I wanted anything to make me love him! She, Mary, asked me if you were very old, and I said you couldn't be very—are you? Then that was very good about the mines that you [the Colonel] wrote. Mme. Brimborion asked permission to copy that part where you [the Colonel] describe the manner of reducing ores; she said it was so instructive and valuable. Dear papa, how much you do know! But I think I like you better when you're a little, just a little—sad, and say such sweet things about the landscape and your longings. I'm sure you're a real poet, papa, ain't you?"

It is scarcely necessary to say that when this letter was read Fleet coughed slightly, colored perceptibly, muttered something vaguely about "really having forgotten it all," but remembered only that he had dictated to Captain Rats some suggestions that he "thought might please the young thing," etc.; nor that a slight feeling of jealousy crept into the breasts of all but the complacent Captain. Indeed, the Colonel is said to have afterward remarked aside to Horton that he was of the opinion that Fleet's "flapdoodle" and "purp stuff" wasn't exactly the thing "to ladle out" to a young girl that was already "overdosed with chewing gum and licorice"; and Fleet is reported to have cautioned Captain Rats against the freedom of some of the Colonel's stories. "Ez fur as the wordin' goes," explained Captain Rats, "I plays my own cards; so don't you get skeert. On'y the other day, tellin' that story about the coon hunt, the Kernel allowed the dogs was 'hell bent' on gettin' the coon. Lord love ye! do ye think I set that down for that little gal's eye? Not much! I jist sat down sorter keerless and quiet like, and sling her this: 'Meanwhile, the noble hounds, justly emulating the feverish impatience and ambitious spirit of their master!' Lord, it's easy enough to turn the Kernel into decent English—ef you've got the *sabe!* Why, it's just wonderful how keerless men is in their composition. Why, even *you*, Fleet, I hed to take you down last letter. Don't ye mind ye was lettin' on about Night walkin' in her scant robes on the hill? Did ye think I was goin' to hand that over to that child? No, sir. I stopped it! How? Why, I jest said, 'suitably appareled.' That's all. It's easy when you know how."

Another unlooked-for result naturally followed the baleful excellence of this correspondence. Miss Fanny grew more and more anxious to behold again the author of her being and of these extraordinary letters. One or two vague hints to that effect, thrown out in her correspondence, were received with alarm by her guardians, and it was finally resolved that the next letter should be composed in such a manner as to effectually check this wanton desire. For this purpose all the guardians assembled. Considerable excitement was manifested. I grieve to record the fact that much liquor was drunk, and that Captain Rats was somewhat exalted and discursive. But your true gentleman is never more fastidious and refined than in his cups; and the gentle Captain Rats, during the whole letter (save an occasional slip), held his rhetorical hat deferentially in his hand. A copy of this epistle has been preserved, and runs as follows:—

MY OWN DARLING CHILD,—Your esteemed and precious favor came promptly to hand, and contents noted. We—that is, your sainted mother and myself— are glad to hear that the draft for two hundred and fifty dollars came promptly to hand, and trust that the balance of one hundred and fifty dollars, which you retained after paying Mme. Brimborion's bill, will be sufficient for you to purchase laces, furbelows, bonnets, shoe-ties, and hosiery suitable to the season and the fashions. We (that is, your mother—who is still unable to write by reason of a sore finger—and myself) hope you will not spare any expense to clothe yourself equal to your schoolmates. We note what you say about Mary Rickett's new silk dress, that cost seventy-five dollars. You are to see that seventy-five, and go her fifty or one hundred better, drawing on us for the balance, if short. Raise the Rickett girl or bust. We trust you are careful of your health, and do not partake too frequently of confectionery, and that your French and music lessons are the same. We trust that you wrap up warmly when you go out, and are careful about your flannels in that dreadful Eastern climate, and always wear your rubbers. The wheat crop this year will average nearly forty bushels to the acre, or supply each inhabitant of the State with forty-four barrels of flour, and still leave one hundred thousand bushels for exportation. With the Pacific Railroad finished, and the effete nations of Europe and Asia knocking at the Golden Gate for breadstuffs, the time is not far distant when the State will be entirely self-producing. We often picture you, dear child, sitting at your tasks, your bright eyes occasionally dropping in reverie as you think of your parents so far away. Do you ever wander with us through these dim woods— God's first temples—and breathe with us the infinite peace of solitude, or reflect that long before we had our being or existence these grand old monarchs looked down on others as they do on us? Do you? We hope—that is, your mother and myself trust you do, although we earnestly beg and implore you not to dream of visiting us here. For the society is quite unfitted for a person of your age and sex. Murder not unfrequently stalks abroad, and sluice robbing is as common as the red hand of the assassin. Scarcely a day passes that we do not consign some victim to the silent tomb. Consumption is epidemic, and smallpox, too, often has marked the loveliest of your sex for his prey. The face of beauty fades quickly through a pestilential fever now quite common, and the exquisite daughter of one of the first families has been taken for an Indian squaw by reason of the same. Freckles are paramount. The hair withers and falls out,—the teeth likewise the same. Much as we hope to once more behold that darling face, we could not expose you to such certain ruin. Your mother fainted on reading your request to visit her. I fear, in her present state of health, a visit from you would be fatal! If you value your parents' love, banish this idea from your mind. In a few years, probably, we will be able to once more clasp you in our arms by the Atlantic shores.

YOUR AFFECTIONATE PARENTS.

Six weeks had elapsed, and the dutiful answer to the above, confidently looked for by the guardians, was due. Nevertheless, as the time approached, some nervousness on the part of Fleet was manifested by that gentleman's unrest, and his frequent visits to Captain Rats, to whom all letters addressed to their deceased friend were delivered. "Nothing from the young lady yet, I suppose?" Fleet would say indifferently. "No," the Captain would respond quietly. "I reckon it'll take her about two weeks to get over her disappointment. Then she'll write sassy—like as not—or mebbe not at all." Fleet turned pale, then red, and then bit his mustache. "You don't think, Captain," he asked with an affected laugh, "that we were a little— just a little too hard?" "Not too much for peace and quietness," replied the Captain gravely. "Women don't take a halfway 'no'; they can't believe a man means it," he added, "any more than *they* do." Nevertheless, the Captain himself grew a little anxious, and having to visit Sacramento, left strict orders with his comrades that he was to be recalled promptly on the arrival of Miss Fanny's reply.

But his visit was not interrupted, and it was nearly three weeks later that he mounted the box seat of the Pioneer stagecoach to return to Lagrange. As he settled himself beside the driver, after the interchange of a few complimentary epithets, his eye glanced down toward the wheels, and was attracted by an open letter and part of a female head obtruded from the coach. The fair reader had evidently thus sought to evade the gloom of the coach's interior and possibly the prying eyes of her fellow passengers, while she perused it. But why did the Captain's withered cheeks instantly change color, and why did he convulsively clasp the railing by his side? The letter was in his own handwriting, and had been mailed to Miss Fanny nine weeks before!

It was impossible, even by the utmost craning, and at the risk of his life, to see anything more than a bit of lace, some artificial flowers, a front of blonde hair, and the fatal letter. Yet his guilty conscience instantly recognized in these scant facts the formidable presentment of the deceived orphan. Had she discovered their trick, and was she now on their trail, with this terrible indictment in her hand? Or was she still in ignorance—an ignorance which a single chance question and answer now might dispel, amid faintings, shrieks, tears, and wailing? Captain Rats grew apopletic with bewilderment; he dared not even ask a question of the driver, who was already beginning to survey him with a sardonic leer, and had audibly sought information if he, the Captain, called this kind of conduct proper at "his time o' life." "Let the gal alone, Rats! Don't you see it ain't a love letter from you she's porin' over?" he added, a statement that again covered the Captain with guilty blushes. But a sudden jolt of the vehicle, a little shriek, and the fluttering of the letter to the road, jarred from the reader's fingers, gave the Captain a providential opportunity. To jump from the box to the road and seize the truant epistle was the work of a moment. When he approached the coach to restore it to its fair owner, another passenger had appropriated his own seat on the box, and thus gave color and reason for his exchange to the "inside." The young lady thanked him, the coach again started forward, and Captain Rats fell into the seat beside her. Here was the supreme moment! With a profuse apology, the Captain drew his knees together, slipped into a respectfully diagonal position, so as to oppose the narrowest point of contact with her, and carefully dusted his knees and her dress softly with his handkerchief. The shyest nymph would scarcely have been startled, the coldest and most antiquated of duennas would not have been discomposed by the submissive respect of the Captain. The young lady, who evidently was neither, turned a pair of calm large gray eyes on her neighbor, and sat expectant. But how the Captain improved his chances I must refer the reader to his own account of the interview, delivered gravely the same evening to his brother guardians.

"When I saw we was in for it, boys," he said, rubbing his knees upward softly, "I kinder measured the gal afore I commenced, to see what sort of a hand she might hold. But you couldn't hev told anything by her looks. And short of axing her a downright saucy question, you couldn't get a word out of her about her own business, nor what she war up to. And then— well," continued the Captain, with a languid smile of conscious success, "I calkilated that this was one o' them peculiar cases that wanted skill and science, and I jist applied 'em, and in course I won. Thet's all. Yes," said the Captain, with a yawn of stifled indifference, "it's all right now, boys. Everything's explained."

"But how?" queried the others eagerly.

"Well," said the Captain lazily, "I sorter slipped into a gineral conversation about the opery, the fashions, and po'try, and sich. Speakin' o' literatoor, I told her of a yarn I'd read t' other day in a magazine, and then, kinder keerless and easy, I jist up and told her the whole story about her father and us and herself, giving her the name o' Seraphina, calling you and Horton 'Oscar' and 'Roderigo,' and Fleet 'Gustavus,' and myself 'Rodentio,' which is Latin for 'Rats.' Well, if I do say it myself, it wasn't no slouch of a story, fur I was kinder clipper and fresh, and the other passengers was jist about as much interested as she was. Then I sorter looked in her eye, you know, this way," and Captain Rats here achieved a peculiar leer, "and said that I allowed it wasn't true, and asked her what she thought about it as a story. And she said it might be true and it might not, but it was quite interesting. Them's her very words, gentlemen."

"Well, go on," said the Colonel eagerly.

"That's all!"

"All! All!" shrieked the guardians together. "Didn't she say anything else? Didn't you"—

"Nary," said the Captain coolly. "But it's all right, boys! You'll see."

Horton seized Captain Rats by one shoulder, and the Colonel grappled the other. For a few seconds they shook him furiously.

"Where is she now, you blank, blank mule? Answer us!"

"Why, I reckon she's over at the Union Hotel with Fleet. I forgot to say that he happened accidental to be there when the stage kem in. She seemed to be kinder easy and nat'ral with him, and I"—

But before Captain Rats had finished his speech the two men rose furiously and dashed out of the room bareheaded. And even as the Captain sat there, mute and astonished, yet with his usual vague smile of acquiescence lingering around his mouth, Horton returned, shook his fist fiercely at the Captain, seized his hat, and vanished. In another moment the Colonel also reentered hastily, grasped his hat, kicked Captain Rats, and dashed out again.

As the door slammed on the last of his fellow guardians, Captain Rats slowly emptied his glass, thoughtfully placed one knee on a chair, and rubbed it in silence. Presently a more decided smile came into his eye, and crept to his mouth as his lips slowly fashioned this astounding reflection:—

"That's so—that's *it!* Fleet was allers kinder soft on the gal! Like as not—like as not—he's up and writ to her on the sly."

About the author of

THE LUCK OF
ROARING CAMP

Although Bret Harte is known for his stories of the west, he was, in fact, an easterner who spent some of his life in Europe. He was born in Albany, New York, on August 25, 1836, moving to California when he was 16 to join his widowed mother who had remarried and settled there. He was to remain in the west for just two decades.

In 1857, after a variety of jobs, Harte became a typesetter on the *Golden Era* in San Francisco, writing poems and local-color stories on the side. He then edited two magazines, *Outcroppings* and the *Overland Monthly*. The second issue of the latter printed his "The Luck of Roaring Camp," the January 1869 issue his "The Outcasts of Poker Flat." Both stories achieved wide success, and when a later poem, "Plain Language from Truthful James," was also acclaimed, Harte accepted a $10,000 offer to write for the *Atlantic Monthly* for one year. In 1871, he left San Francisco for the east.

Harte soon ran into debt, however, as his popularity waned. He took political appointments to Germany and Scotland but lost his post in 1885 and retired to London. Though his stories are still read today, he died, on May 5, 1902, in relative obscurity.

If your dealer does not have any of the MAGNUM EASY EYE CLASSICS, send price of book plus 10 cents to cover postage to MAGNUM CLASSICS, 18 East 41st Street, Room 1501, New York, N.Y. 10017.